Death Defiant

Candice Beebe

CONTENTS

This is for my sixth-grade teacher, Ms. Swanson.
Thank you for encouraging and teaching me to believe in myself.

Chapter One

Y ou don't cozy up to death and not have it affect your soul.

Lula made her way down the busy Portland, Oregon street. The beautiful midday sun reflected off the tall buildings surrounding her as she walked through downtown. The city was in full swing. People passed her in a blur on their way to live their lives. Lula wandered through the world, always surrounded, but forever alone. The sun, such a mid-September gift in the Pacific Northwest, warmed her skin but not her heart. As she followed the pull, that knot in the center of her chest became tighter as she closed in on the Marked, and her stomach turned. Every step brought her a little closer to the next soul she would be forced to take. The next soul Marked for death. Being a Death God's Pet was not what she'd signed up for when she made her deal almost three hundred years ago. That didn't stop Doyle—the Death God in question—from forcing her to do his bidding—also known as *his* job.

Rounding the corner, Lula paused in front of a tiny café hidden in a line of retail shops. The knot in her chest pulled tight, telling her the soul she had been ordered to take hung out somewhere inside.

Slipping through the front door, Lula scanned the crowd. Smiling faces ringed the tiny tables as people sipped their beverages and nibbled their artisanal meals. Sunlight filled the café, setting everything aglow, leaving Lula even further in the dark while she struggled to remember why she had abandoned her old life. The face of her former love and current curse, Max, flashed in her mind. Stuck in this strange purgatory as a ghost, he remained invisible to everyone, and tied to her by the deal she struck with Doyle. Now he walked this earth as her companion, only able to talk with her and Doyle before sulking off to Lula had no idea where. She'd once attempted to ask him where he disappeared to, only to be told a "glorious place" he could finally be alone before sticking out his tongue. Good or bad, that was what her relationship with him had matured to, and she couldn't help but giggle.

Lula caught the eye of more than a couple of patrons as she made her way through the café. Most simply gawked at her. It didn't help that her long, black Victorian-style dress blended so well with her long black hair. You'd think a girl like her would fit in better in a city praised for being weird.

In the sea of faces, one man in particular caught her eye. He sat alone at a small two-top table surrounded by a couple and two small groups of lunchgoers. With his long arms resting in front of him, he cradled a book, his fingers wrapped around an oversized mug he lifted to occasionally sip at. Black hair framed his pale face, and a pair of dark eyes glanced her way as she weaved past him. The group of friends talking loudly suddenly sounded a million miles away when their gazes collided. Her eyes widened along with his as they stared at one another, locked in place for a heartbeat.

Lula's step faltered under the full force of his presence. Her breath hitched when an overwhelming sense of familiarity washed over her. Did she know this man? The thought struck her like a hammer, impossible as it was. Anyone she knew before her deal with Doyle was long since dead. Still, the feeling she knew him refused to be ignored.

The impulse to join him at his table—or, even worse, throw herself at him—nearly brought her to a halt. The way he looked up at her made it hard to dismiss. The mixture of surprise and what she could only see as wanting did nothing to help her desire to stay with him instead of completing her job.

Someone at a table nearby burst into laughter, bringing her back to reality. Lula forced herself to break eye contact. She blinked a few times to refocus and quickly soldiered on, weaving past a server carrying a large tray, never daring to look back.

Lula followed the pull of the soul and found herself all the way back in the doorway to the kitchen. There, in front of a large sink, stood a young girl with a glow surrounding her entire body—the Mark of a soul ready to be taken. The color identified the goodness of the soul, while the brightness displayed how close to death the body was. This girl's was a bright blue—pure. She had clearly lived a good life, and her body wouldn't support her much longer.

Lula stood in the doorway, watching for a moment, getting a read on her. Knowing details about the soul before her was one of the "gifts" Doyle had bestowed upon her when he gave her part of his powers as a Death God, along with an ever-growing guilt complex.

Clair wasn't much taller than Lula. She had reached the same age of eighteen, or at least as old as Lula was a few centuries ago. Lula smiled at the girl's long, auburn hair with a streak of purple that sat in a high ponytail. She wished she could have fun with her hair like that, only there was no way Doyle would allow such a thing. Clair scrubbed at the pots and pans, stopping often to give in to coughing fits that rolled out of her like a storm. Lula's heart clenched, knowing how hard Clair worked to take care of herself.

A pang of jealousy hit Lula. Clair lived in a small apartment but had surrounded herself with so many friends in her life, roommates, and people she could trust and talk to. They were there for Clair. She could even confide in them about all her medical expenses and health issues. Doyle always kept Lula so isolated from everyone but Max, her bitter ghost of an ex-not-even-boyfriend. She rubbed her chest as she thought back to her days when she was alive, before the deal she made with Death.

Despite all the hospital trips, Clair loved the life she had. Today, though, Lula would take it all away from her.

Today, Clair was going to die.

Lula took in a ragged breath. There was no way she could take Clair's soul from where she stood, and there were far too many other staff members around to do it in the kitchen. Lula would have to wait until they were alone. Mortal eyes were not meant to see the brutality that went into ripping a soul from its body. Waiting out back would be her best option.

Only three people worked in the kitchen. Aside from Clair, one man stood hunched over a grill, flipping patties. The other man raced around the small area, gathering ingredients before ducking into the walk-in fridge. Seeing that they were distracted with their work, Lula slipped by without being noticed. She made her way through the kitchen and out the back door to the narrow alley. The potent smell of garbage wafted from the line of dumpsters. Lula leaned against the rough brick wall by the door. She only had to wait a few minutes before Clair came out with two large bags of trash.

Tossing them into the dumpster, Clair stopped short as Lula blocked her path back inside.

"Hey." Clair wiped her hands on her long, white apron. "Can I help you with something?"

"Yes, Clair, you can." Lula took a step closer and extended her hand. "I'm afraid your time here is up. You're to come with me now."

Clair's eyebrows pinched as she studied Lula, giving her a skeptical appraisal. "Yeah, I don't think so. I'm working."

"Not anymore," Lula said.

She took a step toward Clair in order to do the one thing Death Gods didn't care about. Lula was going to try to prepare Clair, to get her to accept her fate.

Keeping her voice low and steady, Lula tried again. "Your body is sick, Clair. It is time for your soul to be free. I will take you to your next life, where you will never suffer again."

Clair's whole body stiffened, her face completely scrunching up. A harsh laugh burst out of her. "What the hell are you talking about?"

Lula kept her hand extended. "Let me show you."

Clair's dark eyes, so much like Lula's, narrowed as she took a step back. "You need to stay away from me."

Lula took a deep breath and braced herself for the part of her job she hated the most. "I'm sorry."

Lula reached for Clair, and the second they touched, Clair jerked like she'd been hit by a bolt of lightning. Her spine stiffened and knees locked while Lula pulled her deeper into the alley, away from the door. Gathering her reaper energy, Lula focused on the soul glowing at the center of the girl's heart. Clair's mouth flew open in a silent scream as Lula reached with her free hand into Clair's chest and pulled out the innocent soul.

Clair collapsed to the ground. Lula worked to lay her on a pile of clean, broken-down boxes, making sure she didn't end up in a puddle of greasy water and food wrappers. She knelt beside Clair's body, cradling the bright blue soul to her chest. She reached out and tucked the few stray purple hairs that had come loose behind Clair's ear.

"I'm so sorry," Lula whispered again.

She stood and started down the alley, further away from the kitchen entrance. The blue soul danced like a flame in her hand. She stepped lightly, making her way over to open the Gate leading from the Realm of the Living to the Realm of the Dead.

A powerful presence hit Lula, almost knocking her off her feet. She frantically looked around to see where it had come from. A wave of terror shot down her spine at the sight of a dark figure standing at the end of the alley. Their aura pulsed with dark energy and power. Before she could determine who it could be, they disappeared.

Lula stayed frozen for a moment, collecting herself. Very few things in this world held such a level of power in their aura. She could sense the aura of another Pet with ease or the aura put off by souls. With a power level that large, she knew she had just crossed paths with another Death God—and an incredibly powerful one at that. Lucky for her, the figure hadn't stuck around. The consequences of her getting caught passing through the Gate were high. Only Death Gods held the power to open the Gate to the Realm of the Dead, and the Gate was the only way for a soul to get through.

As powerful as they were, Death Gods were notoriously power-hungry and, for whatever reason, lazy when it came to the main purpose of their existence. They were constantly on the lookout for scared people or loved ones, like Lula had been, not ready to let the soul cross over. They would trap them into servitude with promises of immortality or saving their loved ones. It worked like a charm. After all, why not trick a soul into giving up paradise so you can have someone to boss around? The only thing easier than deceiving a soul was to steal a Pet already bound to a Death God.

Sometimes, deals would be struck, but battles for Pets weren't unheard of. Other times, they would violently attack the Pet, forcibly transferring the bond to them before the original Death God found out. They also weren't opposed to having more than one Pet either. To Death Gods, Pets were objects to be collected and used. Since Pets got their power from Death Gods, the more power a Pet held, the more desirable they became since it meant the new Death God would have to give less of their own power over.

If another Death God found out the level of power Doyle had given her, they could make a push to capture her for sure since she had received so much power, including being able to operate the Gate. Doyle was bad, but she knew for a fact that there were Death Gods out there that would make him look like a cuddly teddy bear. Lula needed to hurry in case whoever they were decided to come back.

She touched the side of the building before stepping back. A massive doorway made of sparkling gold opened on the side of the building, revealing an archway filled with pure light. Lula slipped through to the Realm of the Dead.

Around her, the air remained still and smelled of fresh flowers. Above her, a kaleidoscope of colors spread out in an endless sky. Lula took a moment to kick off her shoes so she could feel the velvet-soft grass under her feet. A smile spread across her face as she dug in her toes, and peace settled into her heart as Lula filled her lungs with sweet, warm air. The same sense of belonging enveloped her as when she lived in her beautiful home, in her small English village, among her loving family. Her real family.

Tears blurred her vision as the need to stay overwhelmed her. So many years had passed since she had been in the presence of someone who loved her, cared for her, and made sure she was happy and safe. Lula would almost sell her soul again just to be here, so she could feel this way again. But she couldn't stay. She had a job to do.

Lula peered down at the soul she cradled, watching it dance, growing taller, reaching for the sky. "Be at peace, Clair," she said, lifting the bright blue flame higher. "I know you'll be happy here, free of your broken body."

The vibrant soul rose and hovered above her head before shooting like a star across the heavens and disappearing. At least Lula knew that here, Clair would never feel the pain that a mortal life could bring again. That helped ease the guilt that came with taking away the life they had, and in such a violent way. Whispered rumors told of a time when souls were gently taken from their bodies before being led through the Gate rather than ripped out like they were now by most of the Death Gods. Lula longed for a way to bring back such a practice, and was always as tender and humane as possible. If she could ever get a soul to come with her willingly, maybe then she could be more at ease with what she had to do.

Lula soaked in the peace and light for just a little longer before stepping back into the alley and closing the Gate behind her. She searched for any sign of the Death God she had sensed earlier, but found only the hum of everyday life around her. With one last deep breath, Lula dusted herself off and marched down the alley, back to her car.

Chapter Two

Lula made her way back down the street, her only goal to get home as fast as she could. Glancing over her shoulder, she looked for the Death God she had sensed earlier. All she saw was the café fading with every step, becoming lost in the rush of pedestrians. Lula closed her eyes for a moment, letting out a sigh of relief.

"Who are we looking for?"

Lula jumped at the sound of Max's voice. She turned to see his ghostly form walking beside her. A solid form that interacted with the world with ease, he existed invisible to everyone around them but her and the Death Gods.

"What are you doing here?" Lula breathed through unmoving lips, so she didn't look like she was talking to herself.

"I tapped into our handy-dandy connection and could tell you were done, so I thought I would check on you. Honestly, I was getting pretty bored waiting around." He shrugged his shoulders unrepentantly.

She sneered at the reminder of the unbreakable link the three of them shared due to the deal she had made.

She answered him, keeping her voice low, "I thought I felt a Death God."

Lula slowed her pace as Max stopped short.

"Another Death God? Where?" he asked, looking wildly around them.

"Don't worry, he's gone," she said a little too loudly, earning her a concerned look from a woman who passed Lula by.

Max shook his head slowly, his blond hair falling into his blue eyes as they started walking once again. "That's dangerous, Lula. You could have gotten hurt, or worse. You remember what happened to Alice?"

Lula hugged herself tight, knowing all too well what Max was talking about. Poor Alice. Having a terminal illness at a young age had made her a prime target for any Death God. Doyle's friend Roger had gotten to her first. He wasted no time manipulating her into the life of a Pet. Ever the friend, Doyle convinced Roger that Alice needed to be able to take souls like Lula did, instead of just running errands, so they could hang out and drink wine.

However, unlike Doyle, Roger hadn't given her the ability to sense when other Death Gods were around—an extra important trait to have, as Lula knew all too well. Especially since the more power a Pet was given, the more their aura lit up with a unique glow. Sensing when Death Gods were close had saved Lula more than once, unlike Alice. Two Death Gods found her at the same time and tracked her down one night while she was out. She had no idea she was being stalked from the shadows until the two clashed and fought over her. They were so distracted by the fight Alice had been able to get away.

Unfortunately, her miracle was short-lived. When she told Roger what had happened, he became irate and accused her of being "careless and stupid." Lashing out, he ended up destroying her in a fit of rage. Alice's Death God reduced her to nothing more than a pile of ash and shattered her soul. Without her soul, she couldn't pass through the Gate and therefore denied eternity in the Realm of the Dead.

A shiver walked up Lula's spine at the memory. She looked over her shoulder again to find only normal people enjoying their lives behind her. She half expected to see the dark figure pop up and try to grab her.

"I know," she said. "But whoever it was disappeared before I opened the Gate, so I think I'm good."

Max raised an eyebrow. "Any chance it was Doyle showing up to do his job?"

Lula rolled her eyes at the notion. "Why would he do that when he has his little Pet?" She pointed a finger at herself.

They turned the corner. Max scrunched his brows in thought. After a beat of silence, Max nudged her arm. "So, how did it go?"

Lula clenched her jaw. She didn't know why Max kept asking for details after she collected a soul. Part of her couldn't even stand thinking about it. Another part of her used Max as a therapist, helping her work through all her feelings. Over the centuries, his resentment toward her for making the deal had melted and morphed. They had developed a deep friendship, reliving memories of their lives before and remembering why they liked each other in the first place. They had also bonded over their mutual hatred of Doyle. Seeing how Doyle treated her, Max had become incredibly supportive. Even if he continued to be super annoying most of the time, he made her laugh and made the unbearable bearable.

Lula shrugged. "Fine, I guess. As well as any time I've done it before."

"Did you try to talk them through it again?"

"Yes." Lula let out a long sigh. "I think I need to work on my speech because talking to her made no difference. I still had to..." Lula stopped to pull the keys out of her tiny vintage purse and fiddled with them.

Max bit back a smile. "It could also be your archaic choice of outfits."

Lula glared daggers at Max, ignoring all the side glances that whizzed past her. "This is serious."

"I'm sorry, my belle."

Lula let out a laugh, void of humor, and shrugged. Max's sweet sentiment did nothing to ease the guilt squeezing in her chest. Doyle should be doing this, taking souls to the next Realm. He never would, though. The big reason he kept having her do his job was so he could be lazy. Her only consolation was her ever-vigilant attempt to make the crossover as smooth as possible for the soul.

Worthless Death God.

Lula licked her lips and focused on the keys in her hand. "I just hate ripping the souls out, you know? They're always so scared. That fear kills me every time, I swear."

Max put an arm around her shoulders and squeezed. His firm but cold embrace did wonders for helping her find her center again.

"I know you hate it, and I'm sorry you have to go through it. I wish there was something I could do to help you. You know, besides being your gorgeous, ghostly ex-ish boyfriend and counselor."

"My counselor, huh?"

"Yeah, and I'm sorry to inform you I'm going to be raising my rates. Inflation is a bitch."

Lula had to laugh. Leave it to Max to be so ridiculous that he managed to cheer her up.

They made it to her red sports car parked on the street. Doyle may have deceived her into signing away her soul, but at least he made up for it in gifts. She got whatever material possessions she wanted in exchange for doing the job of a Death God. He showered her with all the clothes and jewelry she could ever hope for in the interest of keeping her happy, or at the very least, not fighting him about what he asked her to do. Last year, it was this cherry-red baby that went so fast she could have sworn she was flying.

"Besides," she said as she unlocked the car, "like you've got room to talk with your super fancy dress code."

Max scoffed and shoved his hands into the pockets of his slacks. His fine attire was a far cry from the shepherd's clothes he had worn when still alive in their tiny English village, but Max thought if he was cursed to this existence, he should at least have some of the finer clothes available.

"I can't help it if I look good."

"I look good too." Lula smoothed the fabric of her slim skirt and stuck out her tongue.

"You and your fancy dresses. You're not happy unless the skirt takes up two seats."

It may be true that her entire closet was a physical timeline of women's fashion over the past century or two, but Lula didn't care. It made her happy to be covered in silk and lace. It also reminded her of her mother and the advice she had given Lula growing up—about how to always present herself as a lady. Holding onto that was holding onto her mother. So that meant she had a closet full of history and high fashion.

Lula opened the door and climbed in. Max, being the ghostly apparition that he was, appeared beside her in the passenger seat and rolled the window down. She eased out of traffic as he turned on some music, a catchy little number that had them dancing a jig in their seats. As she drove down the city streets, wind rushed in without stirring a single blond hair on his head.

Knowing she needed a pick-me-up after the reaping she had just completed, she stopped at Burgerville, the local fast-food restaurant, to grab a shake. Marionberries were in season, and she loved indulging in the delicious treat. They never cured her of the guilt she carried, but the shakes did make her life a little sweeter. Lula gave Max a wicked grin as she took a big drink through the straw. He stuck his ghostly tongue out at her, making her laugh. A small moment of happiness while weaving through traffic. She sped onto the freeway, aiming for North Portland.

Max broke the silence. "Are you done for the day?"

"God, I hope so."

Clair was the second soul she had taken that day, right after some poor man who should have looked both ways before crossing the street. Lula prayed Clair would be the last, at least for today. She wanted to go home and listen to music. Music was the only true love that gave her any sense of peace. It reminded her of home—that small village in England where she had helped her father tend to their flock of sheep. She ached for her family and friends, the people she could trust.

"You need a vacation." Lula glanced over at Max, who wore a wicked grin on his face. His blue eyes danced as he waited for her to say something. He always did this, worked to push her buttons. "Or a friend, you know, other than me."

"You have been really boring to hang out with recently." Lula nodded sagely. "I also had better friends in England."

"True." Max scrunched his face up, pondering. "Too bad they're all dead."

"Wow."

"Do you remember Riccardo? He worked with his dad at the little tavern in town," Max asked, turning towards her in his seat. "He always wanted to kiss everyone on the cheek."

"Ew." Lula smacked her hand at him. "He smelled awful, and that is saying a lot coming from someone who hung out with sheep all day."

"Do you remember the blacksmith's son with the buckteeth? He had such a crush on you."

"Do you remember the butcher's daughter?" Lula glared at him.

Max winced, but didn't respond. He couldn't say much since the butcher's daughter had been the love of his life, not Lula like he'd made her believe. Of course, Lula hadn't found that out until after she'd made the deal with Doyle. She thought back to that night with a curse. Maxwell had lain in his house, dying after injuring himself. Come to find out, he'd never returned her feelings at all. They'd spent much of the first years bound together, hating each other. She lashing out, out of anger at being heartbroken. Max didn't hold back his own anger at being thrown into a deal he had no say over. He now faced eternity stuck not alive, but not really dead. Solitude from the world and a proximity to each other had made them now amicable companions.

"Yeah, I remember her." He bit his lip and picked at the invisible lint on his pants.

Lula white knuckled the steering wheel and adjusted in her seat. Nausea rode on a wave of guilt as the shake curdled in her stomach. "I'm sorry, Max. That was uncalled for. It's in the past."

Max shot her a sad smile before turning to take in the city skyline.

Lula sighed. "I wish we could both get out and meet new people. I wish we weren't *trapped* by Doyle and the dumb deal I made. I wish...a lot."

The two sat in a strained silence, speeding down the highway. Lula distracted herself by turning up the music. A musician played the guitar, and she lost herself as the artist's fingers danced across the strings. Her mind wandered further, somehow finding its way back to the café. A sudden desire took root—she wanted to find the dark-haired man who'd been sitting alone, reading. Lula bit into her lip as she rolled the idea over in her mind. Those dark eyes had called to her. He had felt so familiar. What would she have done if she'd approached him? Sit down at his table? Say hi? What would he have done? Lula scoffed and rolled her eyes at the scene that played out in her head. He would have no doubt told her to scram. She was just a stranger, after all.

Another scene flashed through her mind. She was back in England, tending to her family's sheep. A boy sat with her. Dark hair. A guitar. A warm smile. He was so familiar, and yet...

Lula adjusted herself in her seat, frustrated that her heart seemed to remember what her mind couldn't.

Lula steadied herself as the vision faded away. Her heart pounded in her chest, and she had to take another drink of her shake to calm herself down. Who was that man who had provoked such feelings in her?

It didn't matter, anyway. First, there was no way she would ever see him again. Second, if Doyle ever found out she'd tried to socialize with other people, he would be furious. The Death God had a temper that only rarely appeared in full force.

Lula shivered as she thought back to the early days of the deal, when provoking Doyle had landed her in a locked room, unable to see Max even. Endless days spent away from the sun or company until she agreed to do as she was told. Years had passed since the last time Doyle had made her tremble with that kind of fear. They may have settled into a toxic banter with each other, but the ever-present threat of the power he wielded always hung thick around him. It would be better for everyone if she went home and forgot all about the man at the café.

CHAPTER THREE

Lula drove through the neighborhood, eyeing the new builds dotting the street between the old houses. The sounds of children playing and dogs barking wafted through her window as she passed the giant park known as Pier Park. Turning down a narrow street, she pulled into the driveway of the two-story home she shared with Doyle, the bane of her existence. She pulled into the garage next to an old green Plymouth Fury. Max had already vanished to wherever he went when she turned on her favorite band, so she sat in the car by herself until she mustered the courage to go inside.

Slamming the door behind her, she reached out with her powers, checking to see if Doyle was home. Thanking all the gods for a moment of peace, she heaved a breath. He seemed to be gone. She practically ran through the living room, past the library and kitchen, bolting up the stairs, and straight to her room. A classical four-poster bed sat in the middle of the room, against the wall. A mix of antique knickknacks and modern amenities dotted the top of the old-world dressers and tables. It was comforting being immersed in a sea of old and gone, a bit of an oddity considering how much she despised Death—the king of old and definitely gone—but the objects reminded her of a simpler life and time. Her antique furniture left the air bathed in a musty aroma that reminded her so much of home. Her old home. Her real home.

She grabbed her wireless headphones off her dresser and slid them around her neck. As she turned towards her bed, her eyes snagged on a small wooden box that sat at the center of her dresser. She let her fingers trace the engraved designs carved into the lid. Lifting it open, she pulled out the necklace she kept hidden inside. The delicate silver chain was long enough to sit at the base of her throat. In the center, nestled between two oval rubies, was a square black opal. The dark black mixed with the deep red made it look like the stone was on fire. Lula ran a finger over the precious relic, the only thing she had left from her life in England before the deal with Doyle.

The necklace had been a gift, only for the love of her, she couldn't remember who it was from. Every time she attempted to remember, she came up with a blank. The only thing she knew for certain was that whenever she wore it, unfettered joy would settle over her, enveloping her in love. She may not remember who gave it to her, but she knew they were special. The feel of the chain against her skin sent pleasure dancing across her nerve endings. The weight of the jewels were a warm embrace. Lula had worn it every day until, one day, in a rage, Doyle had broken it.

He had found her sitting, looking out the window, stroking the necklace with her fingers, and feeling homesick. He had roared about how she belonged to him and how she insulted him by pining for what was long gone and never coming back. Doyle had proceeded to rip the necklace from her neck, breaking the clasp on the chain. He had left her cowering on the floor, confused and petrified. It was only with Max's help that she was able to retrieve and fix it without Doyle finding out. Scared that he would destroy her beloved keepsake, even more than he already had, she now only wore it in the privacy of her room.

Lula dropped onto her bed, snuggling into the thick, down comforter. She made herself comfortable before putting the shake down and laid the necklace over her throat. Adjusting her headphones over her ears, she cranked on heavy metal music from the stereo on her bedside table. She closed her eyes, trying to ease the strain weighing on her heart while reaching for her shake and taking a giant drink.

One would think gathering Marked souls for the Realm of the Dead would get easier. Instead, each soul she ripped from its body seemed harder than the last. She knew people had to die, a natural part of life. However, even when they glowed like a beacon in the night, showing that their body wouldn't last even another day, the fact that she had to *rip* them out wore on her, leaving her broken. How nice it would be if she could numb herself to the process?

At least she had Max. He always met her after every soul she collected. She talked. He talked. They teased and annoyed each other. They got through it together.

Lula touched the volume knob, turning up the music. She soaked up the strong beats that filled her ears, erasing the afternoon's events. Lula was as close to heaven as her broken soul could get. She bit her lip and squeezed her eyes shut while the vocalist screamed his heart out. His lyrics spoke to her, even calling out her name.

Lula's eyes cracked open, and she brushed the hair out of her face. Her name filled her ears again, or at least she thought it did. Sitting up, she gathered her necklace in her hand and scanned the room until her gaze landed on the door.

"Lula…" wafted through the music, becoming louder and more demanding with every call.

Max materialized on the opposite side of the bed. Her phantasm of a companion looked prim and proper in his new slacks and dress shirt, different from what he wore in the car. He loved changing clothes. In his words, if he couldn't take part in the world, he would at least reflect it in his style. Lula had to admit, he looked good in the now forest-green shirt.

Prima donna.

A smirk played at the edge of Max's mouth, making her wonder if he could read her mind as he reclined on the bed. "Incoming."

She turned off her music just in time to hear her name called out once more. This time, the deep, booming voice came rushing in with a hurricane force, smashing her bedroom door open against the wall. Lula jumped as her heart skipped a beat.

Lula glared at the open door, and she jerked off her headphones, with her hand still gripping the necklace, as black fog seeped into the room from the hall and the smell of rotten eggs became overpowering. A dark shadow filled the doorway. In stepped a tall, thin man with short, red hair and a full, fiery beard. He wore a gray pinstripe suit and black shoes with a mirror shine. Stopping at the foot of the bed, he crossed his arms and met Lula's glare head-on.

Death had come calling.

"Lula, my Pet, I have been calling for you," Doyle said.

Lula winced at the use of the derogatory nickname given to the poor fools who had made a deal with a Death God. She hated how demeaning it was, emphasizing her station in life.

"I do not appreciate it when you ignore me." His dark green eyes narrowed as he spoke.

"I wasn't ignoring you, Doyle. I was trying to listen to my music and relax for five minutes after getting back from taking *another* soul through the Gate today," she snapped back, refusing to break eye contact while she slid the hand holding her necklace under the comforter.

"Listening to music seems to be all you want to do anymore, and I am tiring of it," Doyle drawled as more smoke filled the room. "Especially when your plate is so full."

"Hey." Lula waved her hand in front of her face as her nose burned. "This is a non-smoking room. Do you want me to get lung cancer and die?"

Doyle smirked. "Do not worry, Lula, I will save you."

"Or you could just let me have some alone time."

"Ha." He rolled his eyes. "Like that is going to happen."

"Harsh," Max huffed, sending chills down her spine.

"Shut up, Max. I just want some time alone, but neither of you will cut me some slack."

"Not my fault," Max sang.

It wasn't his fault, not entirely. Lula had struck the bargain with Doyle that fateful day, linking their souls together forever. She would have thought twice if she knew things would turn out this way.

"Watch your tone. I just wanted to know how it went," Doyle said, crossing his arms.

Lula shrugged, stroking the chain of her necklace. "Fine."

Overall, it had gone fine. Lula had found the Marked soul, taken it, and escorted it through the Gate. She didn't feel a need to mention the Death God that had *almost* caught her doing all of those things. Partly because nothing had happened and partly because she didn't want to deal with Doyle's inevitable reaction. He'd filled her room with enough smoke as it was.

Doyle's eyes narrowed. "Just fine? No trouble getting it whatsoever?"

"Yes, Doyle, it went just fine. I found her, I escorted her, I got a marionberry shake on the way home." She wiggled her shake at him before taking a drink and putting it on the table.

Doyle took a deep breath as his stance became more rigid, clearly annoyed by her for some reason she could only guess. "Fine, I believe you."

Lula rolled her eyes. "Thank you so much for your trust in me."

Doyle's entire frame sagged. "Lula, my dear, it is not that I do not trust you. I do. I simply need you to reassure me that your task was completed without incident. You have one job: get the souls from those Marked for death and then take the soul through the Gate to the Realm of the Dead. It really is that simple. Anyone could do it."

"If anyone could do it, why don't you give it a try?"

Doyle's lips lifted, looking rather smug. As much as he complained, he seemed to love their verbal duels. He waved his hand in a grand gesture towards Max. "Because, my Pet, it is your job. *You* made the deal with me that in exchange for staying with the soul that you loved oh-so much, you would do what I say, without complaint."

Lula ground her teeth as she glanced over at Max. The whole time she and Doyle had been talking, he had been lying there, watching Doyle.

"You already knew she did her job. You always know, you know, since we are all connected in your very short-leash kind of way."

Doyle pointed a stern finger Max's way. "You stay out of this."

"Don't provoke him," Lula warned.

She reached for her headphones, then paused. Doyle fidgeted at the end of the bed but stayed where he stood.

"Is there anything else?" she asked.

"I need you."

Lula's eyes popped wider. "*Again*?"

"Yes, again. The Ledger has revealed a new name."

Of course, the Great Ledger would have revealed another name already. The mystic book all Death Gods possessed let them know which souls they were to collect and transport next. The large, leather-bound book was connected to their Death God. Most kept their copies on them at all times. Doyle kept his on a pompous stand in the library when he was home. The book was normally no bigger than a pocket guide, but Doyle was all about showing off his power in any way he could.

Lula gaped at him. "I just got back from the last soul."

"Tough." Doyle drawled. "A reaper's work is never done."

Lula plopped back again, squeezing her eyes shut. "Who is it this time?"

A dark chuckle filled the room. "Some little punk who should have listened to his mother."

She cracked an eye open, seeing a sinister grin slide across Death's face.

"His name is Melvin, but he goes by Rage. Can you believe it?" Doyle mocked.

Lula's whole body locked up against the need to punch something...or someone. These were people Doyle was talking about, and to hear him mock them lit a fire in her chest.

"Rage? Are you serious?" Max coughed out a laugh.

Lula covered her eyes again, praying she would just disappear. "Where do I find him?" she finally asked.

She had a good idea of where she would have to go, considering all the seedy places he had forced her to go collect souls. At least Clair had worked at a nice place. Lula could only imagine where someone calling himself Rage would be. A shudder rolled through her. She was immortal—but not immune from getting the crap kicked out of her.

"Some underground club called Pit—or was it Hole? I do not remember. It will be easy enough to find him. Just follow the pull of the Marked." He turned and sauntered toward her bedroom door. "And be quick about it."

"Worried the other Death Gods will catch you slacking?" she taunted.

"Watch your mouth, little girl, or you just might find yourself in real trouble," he snapped back at her, never breaking his stride.

"Hey," Lula called out after him. "Are you ever going to get one of these souls yourself?"

Doyle paused, glancing over his shoulder at her. That sinister grin turned devious. "Why would I go when I have you?" He closed the door behind him.

Lula threw a pillow at the door and screamed. Why couldn't he just give her a break, just one break, so she could try to heal? Doyle had to be the laziest Death God out there. First, he put a target on her and gave her—a *Pet*—enough power to collect a soul. Then he decided she needed even more so she could pass through the Gate. All so he could do...what? Did he hang out with his Death God friends and collect more junk? Definitely could not be bothered to do what his entire purpose was.

"God, I hate him!" she screamed. "Doesn't he know what collecting souls for him does to me?"

"I don't think he cares." Max shrugged, lacing his fingers behind his head.

Lula's eyes burned as she let out a long sigh. "You're right, he doesn't."

Because if he did care, he wouldn't keep putting her in danger by breaking all the rules so he could indulge himself. At least she had Max, she thought for the thousandth time. Any fondness that Max and Lula had held for each other had evaporated the day he died. She remembered the look of abject horror on his face when he learned of the sentence that had been given to him. But from the ashes of their old relationship rose a new one. One of love, even if it was only platonic. Together they teased and annoyed and laughed and even cried. They were bonded in a way that went beyond the magic that tied their souls together because of the deal.

"If it's any consolation, I'm sorry he does this to you," Max said in a rare moment of sincerity. Before she could reply, he disappeared himself.

"Not as sorry as I am."

Lula shoved her headphones into place, cranking the music back up. Very carefully, she opened her hand to reveal the necklace. Straightening it out with extreme care, she laid the necklace across her once more. Lula covered the necklace with her whole hand, her fingers wrapping around her throat.

No one was as sorry as she was.

Chapter Four

The soft fabric of Lula's spaghetti-strap dress brushed her legs as she marched down the dark alley. Her heels clicking against the asphalt echoed off the big industrial buildings towering overhead. Fire escapes clung to the sides. All it would take was one fat pigeon landing in the wrong place, and they would all crash down like dominoes. The smell of stale garbage and oil mixed, permeating the air, finally diluting at the end of the alley.

One lone light shone above a side entrance, casting deep shadows in the corners of the building. A steep set of concrete stairs led down to where the sound of music rumbled into the night. There was no mistaking the pull of the soon-to-be-departed Melvin coming from somewhere down those steps. The dying soul's call tightened deep in her chest.

Lula rolled her eyes as she saw the name of the club—Descent.

Thank you, Doyle, for being oh-so-helpful.

Guarding the stairwell leading down into the club stood a large bald man with ink covering both arms from his wrists up to the edge of his cutoff T-shirt. His round face sprouted a fire-red goatee and squished itself into a glare capable of sending a lesser man running. Lucky for Lula, she wasn't a man.

Strutting up to tall, pale, and scary, she batted her eyes while running her hands down the dress that ended too high up with a neckline that swooped too low for her own liking. The skimpy thing was a far cry from the vintage-inspired dresses she normally loved wearing.

"Hey there, handsome." She struggled to keep her voice sultry. "How are you doing tonight?"

"Beat it."

Okay. Seemed her choice of attire didn't have the usual effect on Mr. Grumpy. Lula rolled her eyes. They didn't need to be friends. She just needed to get past him.

"Charmed, truly." Snarky, yes, but this guy had brought out Lula's natural charm. "Well, nice talking to you. I have a friend I'm supposed to be meeting, so I'll just see myself inside."

He stepped over and blocked her path down the stairs. "Take a hike."

Lula's cheeks ached as she held a stiff smile in place. "Trying to."

"Not past me, you're not."

Lula gaped. "You can't keep me from going in."

His eyes narrowed, and he crossed his arms before leaning down to meet her eyes. "Naïve little girls have a habit of getting themselves into trouble. Especially in there."

Lula had a good idea of what "trouble" could be, not that she cared. After all, he could only do so much to her.

She shifted forward so their faces were only a few inches apart. The smell of his foul breath washed over her, kicking up her pounding heart. "Listen here, kid." She had the pleasure of watching his nostrils flare. "I eat *trouble* for breakfast. There is nothing you, or anyone in this club, can dish out that I can't handle. Let me by so I can find Rage and go home. Cause I'm telling you now, I'm not leaving without him."

"That's it." Big man's lip pulled up in a snarl and he reached for her arm.

Lula side-stepped out of the way, ready to go for the stairs.

"Hey, Gunner, what's going on?" A deep, masculine voice behind her stopped them both in their tracks.

Lula turned to see who had interrupted her escape into the club and froze when her eyes met two dark pools set in a pale face. That tall drink of water with short hair, black as coal, smirked down at Lula. His long arms were crossed over his chest, pulling his T-shirt tight. Baggy jeans hugged low enough on his hips to send the most chaste of imaginations racing. A sense of *déjà vu* struck her hard, and it took a moment to realize this was the same man she had seen at the café where Clair had worked.

Gunner let his hand drop. "Little girl here is looking for trouble, Shea. What's a guy supposed to do?"

"For starters, find out what kind of trouble she's in the market for." Shea looked Lula up and down. As their eyes finally met, his widened for a moment before the side of his mouth twitched up like he wanted to smile. "How about it …?" He drew out his sentence like he wanted her to fill in the blank.

"Lulabelle," she obliged.

"Lulabelle." Her name slid through his lips like he was savoring the sound. "Are you looking for trouble, Lulabelle?" he asked again, closing the distance between them.

Since she only came up to his shoulders, even with her heels on, Lula strained her neck to meet his eyes. Her heart kicked into a new gear. A warmth she hadn't experienced in at least a century washed over her as she lost herself in those beautiful, dark eyes. Lula worked to control her breathing and maintain her cool. She wasn't here for this. She was here to collect Melvin's soul. The thought helped to calm her fiery nerves as she looked at this stranger.

"Maybe." Lula bit her bottom lip. Shea's eyes drifted at the movement, and a surge of pleasure followed, nearly causing Lula to groan. "My trouble has a name though," she somehow continued. "Rage."

Shea's eyes snapped back to hers. "What do you want with him?"

"He has something I need." She shifted away from Shea, giving herself some much-needed space before she did something stupid. Or more stupid, considering she was an open book at the moment.

Shea closed the distance, refusing to let her get far. "What in the world does Rage have that you need?"

"Why do you want to know?" She grinned at him. "Are you his friend or something?"

Shea let out a harsh laugh. "Not even close."

"Then what makes you think you have the right to know?" Lula challenged, fighting the urge to run her fingers up his arms.

Shea shifted a little closer, leaning in so only a sliver of space separated them. Lula took in a deep breath, trying to steady herself. Big mistake. The smell of cinnamon and something purely masculine filled her nose. Her eyes landed on his mouth as he spoke. She wondered for a moment how he would taste.

"Because I'm making it my business. Tell me, what do you need from him?"

Lula swallowed hard. "It doesn't matter."

"Then why do you want it?"

Everything good she had up to that moment drained away, leaving her empty and cold. She blinked away the burn that flashed in her eyes and concentrated on the ground. "Who said I want it?"

Shea's brow furrowed, looking as confused as she was. Why had she let that piece of truth slip? It didn't make it any less true. She didn't *want* Melvin's soul. She didn't even want her own soul anymore. There wasn't enough of it left to even count as a whole soul. Years of servitude had eaten away at it.

Taking advantage of the stalemate, Lula turned and shoved past both Shea and Gunner. She raced down the stairs and into the club before either of the men could react. Leaving Shea behind was the smartest thing she could do. Lula needed to remember herself and why she was here.

Eye on the prize, then get yourself home.

People danced to the industrial music pounding off the walls. Darkness shrouded the entire place, except for the neon and strobe lights flashing from the ceiling. A long bar hugged the wall, along with the DJ's stand at the head of the club. On top of each table sat a small lamp casting shadows on the faces gathered around them. A foul mix of smoke, sweat, and other bodily fluids Lula didn't want to think about hung in the air.

Lula sauntered up to the bar, scanning the crowd for Melvin. Using the power Doyle had been kind enough to bestow upon her to do his dirty work, she searched for the distinctive aura showing Melvin's time was up.

In the back corner of the club sat a scrawny, long-haired man in tight jeans and a ratty T-shirt. He leaned into a plastic blonde with big boobs, skin that was too pale, and the beginnings of her own end seeping from her. The man, however, glowed, and not in the sappy way they write about in love stories.

Found him.

Lula cut through the mass of dancers, her eyes pinned on Melvin the whole time. She was shoving her way through the crowd when long fingers slid around her arm. She spun to find Shea staring down at her.

"You gave me the slip!" he yelled over the pounding music.

Lula crossed her arms, trying to put space between them. "The conversation wasn't very enthralling."

"Next time, I'll have to do better," he said, stepping back just enough to offer his hand. "First, allow me to introduce myself properly. I'm Shea."

"Shea." She shook his hand. "I have to go." She turned to leave, but he hooked an arm around her waist, pulling her back flush against his front.

"Where are you going?" he asked, lips grazing her ear.

"I told you," she answered, more breathless than she should have been.

"He can wait."

Lula turned in Shea's arms to look into his eyes. Those deep pools pulled her in and refused to let her go.

"Who are you?"

Shea lifted a shoulder in a shrug. "I told you. I'm Shea?"

Lula huffed out a laugh. "I got that, it's just..."

His eyes closed, and his lip twitched with the hint of a smile. "I remember you from this afternoon. You were at the coffee shop. I haven't been able to stop thinking about you all day."

"I remember you too. I just..." Lula bit her lip, not sure how to articulate the whirl of thoughts and emotions churning through her mind.

"Then don't go."

"What do you want?"

Even if he did remember her, what could he possibly want from her, of all people?

Shea's smile widened as he offered her a hand. "Dance with me."

Lula took his hand, unable to resist.

Shea led the dance with skilled moves. His searing touch found its way up and down her body. Lula swayed and dipped with him to the rhythm of the music. Ripples of pleasure flowed like the tide from the pit of her stomach out to her fingertips and toes. She traced her own fingers up his arms and neck, not stopping until she buried her fingers in his thick hair, soft as silk.

Shea nestled his face in the crook of her neck. "What have you done to me?" he all but moaned.

Lula opened her mouth to ask the same question but lost herself in the sensation and raw pleasure of having his arms around her. Her skin blazed, and she loved it. She was home in his arms. Her life was so cold, and he was the warmth and comfort she had been searching for.

Could he be feeling the same thing?

In a slow, sultry move, he dipped her back until her long, loose hair brushed the floor. His hooded eyes were full of desire as he drank her in. She let her head fall back, giving into things she had not even thought about in her entire existence.

When he pulled her back up, she watched his eyes harden as he locked onto something behind her. Shea released Lula, and a rush of cold returned instantly. As much as she longed to feel that heat again, the absence brought her back to her senses.

While Shea kept his eyes trained on whatever had captured his attention, Lula used the distraction to slip away. Glancing over her shoulder to see if Shea had followed, she caught sight of a dark figure standing against a far wall, cloaked in shadow and hidden behind a mass of dancers. The same power that had struck her earlier in the day slammed into her once more. A wave of fear shot down Lula's spine as soon as her eyes found him. She had no idea who this was, but every instinct told her to get away. Lula needed to find Melvin, and now.

She emerged from the crowd in time to see Melvin get up from his table and make his way toward the bathrooms. He held a small baggie in his hand, making Lula's heart break a little. She followed him down the little hall and right into the men's room that reeked of urine and vomit.

Melvin startled as the door slammed behind her, almost dropping the needle in his hand. He relaxed, taking Lula in. "Well, hello there, beautiful. What are you doing in here?" he slurred.

"Rage?"

"That's me," he said as his chapped lips spread into a smile. "You come to join me for a good time?" He lifted the full syringe he held.

Lula stepped forward, drawn in by the pull of his soul.

Melvin's glazed eyes danced as he used the sink to hold himself up. His cigarette breath reached her nose, and she had to fight to keep from pulling away. *Just get this over with, then you can go home and hide again.*

"I have come to join you, but not for a good time."

Melvin's brow pulled together as Lula brought her hand to his chest.

"I'm so sorry, Melvin," she whispered. "Your time is up."

His eyes widened, and his face paled as the blood slowly drained away. His heart beat harder and faster against her hand on his chest as she concentrated, gathering the soul inside him. He started struggling, trying desperately to move away as she pulled, but there wasn't enough fight in him. He'd destroyed himself. Now it fell to Lula to bring this failed life to an end.

Melvin's lifeless body slumped against the dirty wall, his skin now gray and eyes dull. The orb of energy, his soul, sat balanced in Lula's hand. She watched the brilliant blue flame dance in her hand. He was a good soul that had been led down a destructive path. He would do anything to make a friend, always aiming to please. The only people willing to give this awkward kid the time of day were the same ones who were such a bad influence on him. Was there no one in his life who could have saved him? Not that any of it mattered now. His life had ended, and Lula's job was done. For now.

"It is about time."

Lula nearly jumped out of her skin as she came face to face with Doyle. He stood rigid behind her, arms crossed as he stroked his beard.

"What are you doing here?"

"What do you think? I am here to collect Rage." He scrunched his face like the name left an unpleasant taste in his mouth.

"I thought that was my job?"

"Well, I decided I needed to make sure your job got done."

Her eyes narrowed as she took in his nervous movements. "You didn't think I would take him, or is it something else?"

"Do not question me, Pet. Just hand over the soul and be gone with you."

Goosebumps rose on her skin as she recalled the dark figure she had encountered earlier with Clair and now in this club. "What's going on? Is someone snooping?" she asked, handing over Melvin's soul.

Though Doyle wasn't the first deity to take on a Pet, he had to be the most brazen, giving Lula as much power as he had. Sometimes she wondered if he was that arrogant to think he could get away with such a display or that dumb.

"Poe, the nosy bastard. Apparently, he lacks enough to do. He dropped in on me right after you left. Now I actually have to go deliver this to the Realm of the Dead so he does not become even more suspicious," Doyle grumbled, lifting the soul to inspect it. "I do not want him to get any ideas about you."

"You think he might try to take me?"

Doyle's voice dropped as he answered. "He can try."

Lula shifted from one foot to the other, wringing her hands together. The last thing she wanted was to end up under some other Death

God's control. Especially Poe's. He was horrible to Pets, and with the amount of power Doyle had given Lula, Poe would be a tyrant.

Doyle eyed her for a moment and apparently saw the panic written across her face.

"Do not concern yourself with thoughts like those." He scoffed and glared once more at the soul dancing in his hand. "I will just have to be more careful, troublesome as these souls are."

Lula narrowed her eyes. "What do you mean? He's a good soul. He deserves to go through the Gate."

"Of course he does," Doyle said, having the decency to look surprised.

Lula knew not every soul got to cross over to the Realm of the Dead. Some were so evil, so corrupt, they were black when pulled from their bodies. The best thing to do was to destroy those so they couldn't torment the other souls. Souls like Melvin, who shone a bright, clean blue, deserved to live on in the Realm of the Dead.

"Go home, Lula. I shall meet you there."

Doyle opened the door leading to the Realm of the Dead and stepped through without a backward glance.

Lula stood alone in the men's room, hating herself a little more. How black was *her* soul by now? How much darker would it get before her sentence was up?

Chapter Five

Lula shoved her way through the mass of bodies, desperate to get out of the club. A vision of Melvin's dead, dull eyes staring up at her haunted her every thought. She had tried to make him as comfortable as possible, futile as it was. Guilt sat heavy in her chest, making it hard to breathe.

Shoving past the wall of drunks, she finally caught sight of the exit. A pair of meaty paws clamped down on her shoulders. Lula's whole body locked up for only a moment until fury washed away the fear in an instant.

"Let me go." Lula pushed the words through her lip.

"Come on now, baby," the man slurred, snaking an arm around her waist. "I want to dance with you."

"Not gonna happen."

Before she could fight him off, Shea appeared in front of them.

Dark eyes sliced into her unwanted Romeo. Shea reached out and took Lula's hand. "You're going to let her go, aren't you?" His smooth voice was laced with a barely contained threat.

The guy pulled his arm back until Lula could step away. The pasty dude had a mohawk and enough piercings to make him sparkle. "I just wanted to dance with her. How was I supposed to know she came with someone?" He backed up another step with his arms raised in surrender.

Shea pulled Lula close to his side, and she eagerly went without a fight. "Well, now you do." He clenched his jaw so hard she was afraid he'd break his teeth.

Lula watched the guy turn tail and disappear into the crowd. Looking up at Shea, she wondered again who he could be. The draw toward this stranger left her spinning and her heart pounding.

Shea visibly relaxed when the man vanished from sight. Without glancing her way, Shea seized her hand so he could tow her up the stairs and out into the night.

People now littered the alley, hanging in the shadows and on the fire escapes, drinking and doing who-knows-what-else. Lula couldn't help but wonder which of these souls she would come to collect next. A shiver ran down her spine at the thought.

She kept her head bent as they raced past, refusing to look at anyone for too long. They didn't stop walking until they were down the street from the alley and next to a black Jeep.

Shea opened the passenger door before finally facing her. "Get in," he ordered, motioning toward the empty seat.

Lula took a step back instead. "I don't ride with strangers."

"You have to. Now get in." When she still didn't move, he asked, "What are you afraid of?"

Lula lifted a delicate brow. "Gee, I wonder."

"I'm not going to hurt you, Lulabelle. I'm going to help you. Now get in."

"No, thank you."

She spun on her heels and started marching to where she'd parked her car. There were so many reasons to decline his offer. This guy, who seemed to cause so much emotional turmoil within her, wanted to get her alone? No, she didn't think he would hurt her physically, but mentally, emotionally? Lula had too many fond memories of the last guy who made her heart beat faster—Max's cocky grin flashed in her mind—to just trust Shea and hop in. Not to mention, if Doyle caught her with this guy, who knew what he would do? For reasons beyond Lula's comprehension, she couldn't stand the idea of seeing Shea in Death's path.

"You need to come with me," Shea called out, catching up to her.

"No, Shea, I don't."

"Yes, you do." Grabbing her arm, he brought her to an abrupt halt.

"Look…" She rubbed her forehead, trying to find the best way to tell him to back off.

"No, you don't understand." Shea's voice dropped, "You're in danger."

"No, *you* don't understand—" Lula stopped short. She peered up at Shea for a moment. He stood still as stone, frowning. His eyebrows were pulled so closely together that they practically touched. "Wait, why do you think I'm in danger?"

"Did you find Rage tonight?" he asked instead.

"Yeah, I did," she confessed. "What's that got to do with anything?"

"He's dead now. Did you know that too?"

Lula locked eyes with him and found herself unable to lie. Nodding, she watched an array of emotions play on his face.

"The person responsible is after you."

"I appreciate your concern," she tried again, placing her hand on his chest, "but I promise you, I am in no trouble, or danger, or anything else."

Shea placed his hand over hers, as their eyes locked, and squeezed. "There's more here than meets the eye. You *are* in danger, Lulabelle, trust me. Now please, come with me. I'm going to take you somewhere that you'll be safe. I don't want to see anything happen to you."

"W-why do you care?" The question wavered as she could only guess his motive.

It had been so long since anyone had cared about what happened to Lula that the thought of this stranger threatened to break down her carefully constructed walls.

"Because I do. I can't tell you exactly why, but I know I do." Shea reached up and tucked her hair behind her ear. Letting out a long sigh, he dropped his head and squeezed his eyes shut. "Please, at least let me take you home."

"What about my car?" she asked, pointing to where she'd parked her little red sports car on the street.

Shea looked over his shoulder and narrowed his eyes. "What car?"

"That car right—" She gaped at the now-empty spot. "What happened to my car?"

Walking over to where she'd parked under a streetlamp, only broken glass now littered the street where it once sat.

"Looks like someone stole it." Shea kicked at a shard.

"Thank you, Captain Obvious!" She shuffled in a small circle where her beautiful car once sat. How could this have happened? To her? Doyle was going to give her so much grief when he found out someone had stolen her car. She would never hear the end of it.

"Now you *have* to let me give you a ride home," Shea said, sounding confident.

"No, I don't," she insisted, refusing to put him in danger of meeting Doyle. She didn't want to think how Doyle would react to Mr. White Knight bringing her home.

Shea took her hand, looking at her through his lashes, fluttering them at her as his dark eyes warmed. "Please, Lulabelle?"

How was a girl supposed to say no to that? But if she liked this guy, she could not let him anywhere near her house.

"My dad is kind of overprotective. If he sees me with you, he'll kill you."

And that is no joke.

Shea gave her a cocky grin. "I bet I could take him."

A laugh burst out of her, the first genuine laugh in a century of sorrow. She had to give him credit; he had guts. With a reluctant sigh, she gave in. "It's your funeral."

Shea opened the passenger door to his Jeep. She took his hand, allowing him to help her in, and warm tingles walked their way up her arm. She adjusted in her seat and forced herself to relax into the soft leather. She pulled in a calming breath and almost choked. The whole car smelled of his cinnamon spice. He jumped in and shot her a smile as he turned on the engine.

"Where to?"

She ended up giving him the address of a house a couple of blocks from hers. Lula crossed her fingers they would be far enough away that Doyle wouldn't notice her coming yet. If not, the stolen car might distract him from the fact that she was with a guy. Lula could handle Doyle's wrath...Shea, not so much.

Streetlights and neon signs streaked by as Shea flew down the Portland roads toward her bogus home. Rolling down her window, Lula closed her eyes, and the night air caressed her face. At that moment, she couldn't help but feel a little bit free.

A rush of wind from beside her caught Lula's attention. She turned to see Shea had rolled down his window as well. One arm propped on the door, one hand on the wheel, he was a picture of ease. The longer she watched him, the more something pulled in the back of her mind. This wasn't just a familiarity she shared with him. There was more. Lula just couldn't put her finger on it. Lula contemplated the mystery all the way into North Portland.

Shea parked in front of the quiet house, the low rumble of the engine filling the silence. Lula opened her door to get out but stopped, remaining in her seat. The cool night air filled the Jeep. The night's events brought a flood of goosebumps, bringing a question to the forefront of her mind.

She looked over to see Shea watching her. "How did you know about Rage?" she asked, biting her lip as her stomach turned.

"I found him. Just like..." He clenched his jaw. "Someone killed him. That's all you need to know."

"But how do you know someone killed him? I mean, the guy had a serious drug problem."

"You're right, he did." Shea's eyes narrowed, looking out the window and into the night.

Lula could only guess what he searched for. He was definitely hiding something from her.

"What aren't you telling me?" Lula demanded.

"Nothing." He shook his head but continued to gaze out the window.

"Bullshit."

"Fine." He tapped his finger against the steering wheel, twisting to face her. "Nothing you need to know about. Yet."

"Yet?"

"Yes, yet," Shea insisted.

"Is this connected to the whole 'things are not what they seem' bit?" she said, making air quotes.

Shea tapped the steering wheel harder until the rhythm was the only sounds that filled the car. "Look..." He let out a long breath. "I have connections to certain...people. They have information about things mere mortals shouldn't know about."

"Mere mortals?" Lula laughed. "You make it sound so epic. Should I be keeping my eye out for the Avengers?"

Shea's soft chuckle didn't last long. "No, but things are out of balance, and it's going to be a fight to put it back."

Lula swallowed hard, the words making her stomach sour. "Maybe I could help."

Shea watched her for a long, quiet moment before realization dawned on his face, pulling his lips into a small smile. "I know what it is," Shea's low timber voice tickled Lula's ears. "I know what it is about you that keeps pulling me back. You remind me of someone. Someone I used to know."

Lula's breath caught. His words rang and woke something in her heart. Could that be what this was? This connection to a complete stranger?

The moment of silence settled over Lula like a heavy wool blanket. She shook it off since it didn't matter. After tonight, she wouldn't see him again.

Lula played with the hem of her dress, trying to fight the sudden emptiness. "Thanks for the ride."

Her words seemed to pull him out of his trance. "It was nice meeting you, Lulabelle."

"Lula," she informs him.

"Lula?"

"Everyone calls me Lula." she dared to tell him that intimate detail.

Shea leaned in, closing the distance between them. His voice dropped to a purr as he spoke. "It was nice meeting you, Lula."

"It was nice meeting you, too, Shea."

Getting out, Lula closed the door quietly, trying not to wake the neighborhood.

"Hey," he called through the open passenger window. "No more looking for trouble."

"No promises." She shot him a wink.

"I'll see you soon."

Lula gaped at his declaration as he drove off into the night.

Chapter Six

L ula watched the taillights retreat down the street. It wasn't until Shea's Jeep turned the corner that she breathed out a sigh of relief. This night could not get any weirder if it tried.

Strolling down the street, she dared to let her thoughts wander. Almost three hundred years had passed since Doyle found her weeping in that field and struck a bargain in bad faith. Just shy of three hundred years since she found out Max had been leading her on, making her think he cared for her when he really only cared about using her to win over someone else. Doyle had lied to her about the deal, just as Max had lied to her about his feelings, and now she and Max were paying for their lies.

Even though Shea hadn't lied to her, he was keeping something hidden. As much as his secrets irritated her, his statement had taken Lula aback. She reminded him of someone, someone he knew? As soon as the words were out of his mouth, a floodgate had opened in her heart. She knew him too, or at least there was an overpowering familiarity at the source of this connection. Her heart somehow thought it knew Shea. One big question remained: who did he remind her of? She wracked her brain, trying to remember someone, anyone that could be Shea. Every time she came close to forming a memory, her mind would cloud over, and it would be gone.

Shaking her head, she banished Shea from her thoughts. At the end of the day, it didn't matter. None of it mattered because Shea was gone.

Pain gripped her chest at the thought, stealing her breath. The crazy feeling made her stumble on the sidewalk. Lula took a deep breath and refocused. More important things needed to be commanding her attention. The dark figure that kept showing up today, for one. Never had she felt power so strong. Lula didn't know who it could be, but thinking about them made her skin cold. The fact that another Death God had been snooping around didn't sit well, even if it was only Poe. She didn't trust the way Doyle had been acting tonight, either. The conversation in that bathroom nagged at her, leaving the knots in her stomach tighter than usual.

As she made her way down the dark street, the tree branches rustled in the cool breeze. The only sound echoing off the sleeping houses was her heels clicking against the pavement. Lula shivered, wrapping her arms tightly around herself as icy fingers walked up her spine. Why couldn't Doyle have given her the power to teleport?

Max materialized in front of her. "Lula."

She jumped before clutching her hand to her chest. "Holy shit, Max. You scared the crap out of me."

"Man, you need to relax." He gave her shoulder a playful shove. "How did it go?"

Lula shrugged as they began walking down the street once more. She wasn't up for spilling the details of her night or telling her ex-boyfriend about the handsome stranger she'd met.

"Fine, I guess."

"Did everything go, you know, all right? Nothing out of the ordinary happened?" Max persisted, keeping his eyes forward.

Lula shot him a sideways glance and narrowed her eyes. He seemed unusually nervous, asking how things went. "Out of the ordinary?"

"Answer."

"Can we have this discussion when I'm not walking down a public street?" She strained to keep her voice down.

"Who's going to hear? It's two in the morning." He swept his hand in a grand gesture at the quiet line of homes. "The neighborhood is sound asleep, and you talk to me with people around all the time. Now tell me what happened."

"Okay." Lula let out a huff and hugged herself tighter. "It went fine, like I said. Doyle showed up, though, spouting about Poe being nosy and how he needed to take the soul. That felt super weird, especially with the way he acted. He seemed nervous, like someone was out to get him or me. Other than that...fine."

"Not Poe," Max corrected, shaking his head, his blond hair flying side to side. He went on before Lula could even open her mouth. "Doyle actually made the kill this time?"

"Nice way of putting it, but no, *I* still made the kill. Doyle just took the soul through the Gate." A fact that still sat like a rock in the pit of her stomach. "And what do you mean, 'not Poe'?"

Max's eyes were the size of saucers as he recounted his story. "A visitor showed up at the house not long after you left tonight to talk to

Doyle. They were definitely another Death God, but this guy looked even scarier than Doyle and Poe combined. And the vibes he gave off?" Max shuddered.

"Doyle looked me straight in the eyes and told me Poe had visited. Why in the hell would he lie about who it was? I mean, he doesn't need to. He doesn't answer to me."

"Right? After all, you are Doyle's Pet."

Lula glared daggers at Max. Did he really need to use the P-word?

"Doyle has a pretty small group of Death friends," Max continued, "and I've seen them all. I swear, I've never seen this Death God before."

Lula slowed her pace, trying to process what she was hearing. "What did Doyle and this new Death God talk about?"

Max dramatically looked around, making sure no one was around to listen, never mind he was invisible to any mortal out there. "The guy shows up not long after you left, like I said." He stepped closer to Lula. "The Death God rants and raves about how Doyle needed to do his job and do it right, like he's supposed to. He said Doyle needed to be more careful with his 'little Pet.'" Max added air quotes. Lula winced, hating the nickname even more. Max didn't seem to notice because he continued without missing a beat. "Doyle kept saying everything was under control, and a book about Enid was safe. Then the visitor said something that scared the crap out of Doyle because he raced out of the house like it was on fire."

Lula froze. "What did he say?"

"The Death God said, 'The Death Gods are under attack,' then something about balance and finding some S-person. Apparently, they're running out of time, or it was almost time for something?"

Max shrugged. "I don't know what they were talking about. I don't think I want to know."

"Under attack?"

How could that be? Who would risk their life to take on a deity? Shea's face flashed in her mind. Lula stood, frozen on the cracked sidewalk, as his words came back to her in a rush. *Things are out of balance, and it will be a fight to put things back.* As quickly as the thought raced through her mind, she dismissed it. Whatever Shea was involved with had nothing to do with Death Gods.

"I wanted to tell you sooner, but I couldn't find you," Max said.

"What?"

Ever since they entered this life, Max and Lula had been bound. Because of the sealed bond, he could find her anywhere, anytime, something he used frequently to bug the hell out of her. Between Max and Doyle, she never got a moment to herself.

"I couldn't find you," Max repeated. "Well, that's not entirely true. I knew broadly where you were. I just couldn't pinpoint where you were to get to you. It wasn't until just a moment ago I got a lock on you. Weird, huh?"

"Maybe Doyle's visitor messed with us?" She could see a Death God having enough power to be able to do that.

"Could be. That guy was terrifying." He shivered. "Clearly had anger issues."

Lula started walking again. "Come on, let's get home."

"Hey, Lula, why are you walking? Didn't you take your car?" Max asked after they passed a couple of houses.

She groaned, not really wanting to talk about it, but knowing it was useless to keep quiet. "Someone stole it."

Max's eyes nearly popped out of his head. "Someone stole it? Oh, man." he laughed.

"Yes, Max, and it isn't funny."

"How did you get here then? You didn't walk the entire way from that club, did you? Did you sink to catching a bus?"

"A cab."

"Why didn't you just take it to the house?"

"It's not that far." She shot him a dirty look before picking up the pace.

"It's far enough."

"Max, we have bigger things to worry about than why I chose to be dropped off back there."

"True."

They walked the rest of the way home in silent peace, at odds with the storm of thoughts swirling in Lula's mind. They walked through the door to find Doyle poised in the foyer.

He crossed his arms and narrowed his fiery eyes on Lula. "Where did you go?" he demanded before she could even get all the way through the front door.

"Sorry, Doyle, someone stole my car." Lula pushed to get past, but he blocked her path.

"Do not lie to me, Pet," he seethed. "What did you do?"

Lula shrank under his menacing scrutiny. He slid closer, towering over her as smoke filled the entryway.

"I...I swear I'm not lying to you, Doyle," Lula stammered, trying to find her voice. "Why would I do that? I came straight home. It just took longer because of my car being stolen. I swear!"

Every step that Doyle took forward, she shrank back until he pressed her against the front door.

Max worked to wedge himself between them. "Doyle, she's telling the truth. I met her on the street and watched her get out of the cab."

"Why could I not find you then?" Doyle's deep voice rumbled as he leaned forward, his face an inch away from Lula's. His eyes shone like fire under his red hair, making him look like the devil himself.

"What do you mean?" Lula's wide eyes locked on Doyle like a deer in headlights.

"When I came back through the Gate, I could not find you through our link. It appeared as though it had been cut. How did you hide from me?" His voice hissed like a snake as more smoke filled the room.

Lula's eyes were round as saucers as she gaped up at Doyle. Her thoughts raced in a tailspin as tiny sparks of hope and freedom followed close behind. First Max said he couldn't find her. Now Doyle was saying the same thing? She didn't know how she'd vanished from view, but if she ever learned how, a new world could open up for her.

A boldness she never knew before came over her. "Maybe it was your new friend who came to visit you this evening. He could have jammed your signal somehow. Maybe he wanted you to lose me."

Doyle let out a deafening roar, slamming his fist into the wall inches from Lula's head. Pieces of drywall sprinkled onto the floor. "My guest is a subject best left alone. He has nothing to do with you, and you are nothing to him. You are mine, and nothing will change that, my Pet." Doyle scowled at her until her entire body quivered.

All hope melted away as he inspired a genuine fear like she hadn't felt in a long time filled her. He would never let her go. If she attempted anything, she knew what Doyle would do to her.

"Doyle, I don't understand how you couldn't find me. I did exactly what you said. I promise." Her voice quivered as a tear slipped down her cheek.

Doyle backed away as he kept his narrow eyes pinned on her. A low rumble emanated from him as he straightened and stroked his beard, watching her with a critical stare. "Mark my words. If you are lying to me, you will pay dearly. I am freeing you of your duties for now. Be grateful."

Without another word, he turned and marched out of the room. Lula dropped to the floor, burying her face in her hands. Her head swam in a mess of thoughts and questions. She would need hours of death metal to calm down after everything that had happened tonight.

Max sat next to her and bumped her shoulder. "At least you're off the hook for a while."

"Oh, yeah." Lula let out a strained laugh. "I've been gifted a real vacation."

Chapter Seven

The next morning, Lula peeled her eyes open and blinked several times before she could focus. Light streamed past the dark curtains that barely covered the window. She breathed in the aroma of coffee, wafting past her nose. Sitting up, Lula saw Max sitting on the end of her bed, holding a cup.

"How did you sleep last night?" he asked, offering her the mug.

Shooting him a grateful smile, she reached out and took it, cradling it. She took a sip, then sighed as her eyes fell closed. *Heaven,* she thought. Clearing her throat, she shifted in bed so she could sit up before answering. All her attention remained focused on the beverage in hand. "Fine, I guess."

"Just fine?"

"Fine enough." She raised her eyes to the bedroom door. "Is it safe to leave my room?"

Max glanced at the bedroom door before shrugging a shoulder. "I think so." He turned his gaze back to Lula and cocked his head to the side. Blond locks fell into his eyes. "Do you think he was serious last night?"

Lula let out a harsh laugh. "About what, in particular? That I will pay dearly if I lie to him or that I've been given a reprieve from my duties?"

Max's eyes widened. "I don't want to think about what would happen if he found out you were lying. Anyway, I was talking more about the reprieve."

"I don't know. It's hard to think he would give me a break from everything. That means he'll have to be the one to collect souls."

"Perish the thought."

Lula took another sip of her coffee. The perfect blend of sweet and bitter danced on her tongue and slid down her throat. "Thank you for the coffee." She raised the cup to Max.

"Figured it was the best way to start your time off."

"If I really do have time off."

Max puckered his lips in thought. "You did just take a vacation like fifty years ago."

"Yeah, but it was only for a weekend. So does it really count?"

Lula slid out of bed and made her way to the kitchen. Max's ghostly chuckle chased her out of the room. It would be wonderful to have time to recuperate. The thought seemed too good to be true, but she dared to consider it as she popped two pieces of bread into the toaster.

"Good morning, my Pet," Doyle's deep voice pulled her from her fantasy.

Lula swallowed hard as she watched him saunter into the kitchen. He wore a green pinstripe suit with black dress shoes that glinted in the kitchen's bright light. He stroked his fire-red beard as he made his way over to stand next to her, watching her through wickedly perceptive eyes.

"Morning," Lula mumbled, focusing on the toaster. "How are you this morning?" She fiddled with her cup of coffee.

"I am well. Still confused about how you hid yourself from me last night."

"Doyle, I—"

Doyle held up a hand, silencing her. "I know what you said. The fact is, I still could not find where you were."

Lula's heart pounded in her chest. She desperately wanted to know how she'd pulled off last night's disappearing act. Nothing like that had happened before, and it terrified her that it could happen again. There was no limit to what Doyle could do to make her existence worse.

"I promise you, I do *not* know how I disappeared." Her voice trembled.

Doyle moved closer, looming over her. The smile he gave her radiated anything but warmth. "I can guarantee you it had nothing to do with my guest. And if you are wise, you will forget all about my social call. Understand?"

"Yes," she whispered as a shiver raced down her spine.

"Good." Doyle backed up and poured himself a cup of coffee. "Now, what do you plan to do today? I hope you do not waste your time off here at home in your room. Though, with your car gone, it might be harder. I suppose you could use the Plymouth to get around. I have heard no one enjoys the bus."

Lula almost snapped her neck when she looked at him. Her mouth fell open, and any response she had became lodged in her throat.

Doyle let out a low chuckle and raised the cup to take a sip. "What is that look for? Sorry, Lula, but I will not cave and get you another red sports car. Not if you allow my precious gifts to be stolen."

"No. I mean, I didn't think—I didn't know if you were serious?" Lula stuttered.

"Of course I meant what I said last night. I meant all of it." *Including the barely contained threat.*

"So I really have time off from my duties? I can relax and unwind?"

"I realized perhaps some time off would do you good." Doyle pursed his lips and furrowed his brow. One could almost believe he held genuine concern for Lula.

"Yes—I mean, you're right. I need some time to reset. You know what I mean?"

"I think I do."

"How much time will you let me have?"

Doyle stroked his beard, pondering. "Let us start with a week."

"Only a week?" It was more than she had ever hoped for, but it still didn't feel near enough.

"To start with." He sipped from his mug once more. "If you manage to behave yourself and keep out of trouble, perhaps I shall gift you with more."

A tentative smile graced Lula, and her heart raced. *Freedom.* He was giving her the freedom to enjoy herself. She didn't take the gift for granted. Max would flip when he found out. There were movies they could watch, books she wanted to read. Lula was dizzy with all the things she wanted to pack into this respite.

"Thank you, Doyle. This means so much to me."

"Anything for you, my Pet. Go out, enjoy the day." He reached out and stroked her hair. "Just remember, I have my eye on you."

Lula's blood ran cold, draining all the joy away. Message received, loud and clear. He may have loosened the leash, but he still held it tight around her neck.

The toaster popped, making her heart skip a beat. She turned her attention to finishing her breakfast.

"So, you never told me. What are you going to do with your day?" Doyle asked.

Lula focused on buttering her toast, trying to come up with something to do that wouldn't offend Doyle. "It's supposed to be in the eighties and clear today. Maybe I could go to the park?" She dared a glance at Doyle, who smiled in her direction.

"Lovely." He clapped, as his eyes danced. "It warms my heart to know you shall be out taking advantage of the beautiful Oregon day."

"Will you also get to spend some time outside?" She bit her lip.

"Oh, I have things that need to be taken care of. No rest for the weary."

Lula managed to keep from rolling her eyes. "Well, don't work too hard."

"Please." His green eyes twinkled. "You know me better than that."

Boy, did she.

Doyle placed his cup in the sink and turned to leave the kitchen. "I will see you tonight."

Lula stood in the kitchen with her stomach in a knot, too afraid to make an actual move. Despite what he'd said, her gut warned that, somehow, this was still a test. Still, she would be a fool not to take advantage of this time gifted to her, and she knew just where to go first.

Chapter Eight

L ula giggled, watching Max's jaw hit the floor as she told him about the conversation she had had with Doyle in the kitchen.

He covered his gaping mouth. "Doyle is really letting you have time off? For real?" Max asked. "This has got to be a sign of the apocalypse."

Doyle never brought up how much time she had left in her sentence, and to be honest, Lula was too afraid to ask. The way he worded the bargain all those years ago alluded to an end after her debt was "paid." Deep in her heart, she knew Doyle would never let her go. Instead of dwelling on the melancholy, today Lula would focus on the joy. She danced in her room as she dressed in her favorite fifties-style blue dress with giant daisies on the skirt and short sleeves that folded over to a large, white cuff. The skirt billowed out as she spun in front of the mirror with a big smile on her face. Even if only for one day, she was going to savor every moment of her freedom.

Freedom.

Lula couldn't wipe the smile from her face. Racing through the house, she threw herself into the old Plymouth Fury that sat next to the empty spot her beloved sports car had once occupied. She gave her cherry-red beauty a moment of silence before tearing off down the street.

Max appeared in the passenger seat wearing oversized sunglasses.

Lula choked out a laugh. "You look like a bad Tom Cruise in *Top Gun*."

Max shot her a thousand-watt smile. "All I'm missing is the jacket."

"And didn't he ride a motorcycle?"

"You'll never catch me on one of those things. They can kill you." Max shot her a wink.

Lula burst out laughing so hard tears streamed down her cheeks. Grabbing a marionberry shake, she rolled down the windows and drove like a woman on a mission. Being with a Death God meant moving frequently after Doyle would squabble with other Death Gods and ending up all over the world. Of all the places they had lived over the hundreds of years she had been bound to Doyle, Portland was her favorite American City. The only other place she loved more, with the exception of her home village in England, was Paris. The beauty and culture were like no other.

Lula drove aimlessly up and down the streets until they reached a park nestled deep in one of Portland's nicer neighborhoods. The grounds had a playground off to one side, but the main attraction was the rose bushes. They lined all the various paths woven through the extensive park, leading to a large fountain that cascaded down cement bowls in the middle into a shallow pool. Something deep inside pulled at her, begging her to come and enjoy the day here. Just barely fitting the large car into a spot, Lula turned off the engine and took a deep breath as her heart fluttered in her chest. Nothing would spoil her day.

The afternoon sun shone brightly, warming Lula's skin. She found a park bench to sit down and sip her marionberry shake. Throngs of people glided past her, going about their day, indulging in the sun. Using the powers Doyle gave her, she blinked until the rainbow of auras before her came into focus. A couple walked hand in hand, covered in the energy of their love, a soft shade of pink mixed with their dark green. Children played on swings and chased each other down slides and across the monkey bars, their youthful yellow energy streaking across the playground. An old man sat on the bench, his nose buried in a book. Lula's breath caught as she saw the slight tint of blue peeking through his light green. Looking deeper, she saw the battle with his illness approaching its end.

Most days, scenes like this would invoke dark feelings. She sat back, nothing more than an outsider, unable to interact with the world around her. Not today. Today, she focused on simply just being. She closed her eyes and drank in the sun.

"What are we doing?" Max's whining cut through the tranquility.

She gestured to the crowd of people before them. "People watching."

"Shouldn't we be trying to figure out who came to visit Doyle last night?"

"Maybe, but not today. Today, I just want to enjoy."

Max rolled his eyes and slumped against the bench, letting out a groan. He stuck his legs out far enough that an unsuspecting woman walked right through his feet. Lula giggled, and Max cursed under his breath.

"This is boring," he complained, sitting back up again.

"Nobody says you have to stay with me," Lula said around her straw.

Max glared daggers at her. "Fine." He jumped up and waved a dramatic hand at her. "I'm out of here. Call me when you decide to do something fun."

"Hey, Max!" she called out, earning her curious glances. He frowned over his shoulder. "I *am* doing something fun."

Max flipped her off before disappearing.

Lula knew she looked like a crazy person doubled over laughing, but she didn't care. Today was her day, and she would enjoy it how she wanted to, dammit.

Against her better judgment, her mind made its way to Doyle's guest. If he found out about her and what she was capable of, Lula was as good as dead, or whatever her version of it would be. The idea should be a relief. No one should be forced to exist as long as she had. No one should be forced to do what Doyle did. Nothing good had come out of the past two hundred and some-odd years. Nothing except...maybe Shea.

Why was she still thinking about Shea? They had met one time for five minutes. Still, he was handsome and captivating and somehow familiar. He cared about what happened to her. For the first time since she was a small girl in that little English village, someone cared about what happened to Lula. She held onto it with everything she had. Even if it was a lie. Even if it had only lasted for five minutes.

Lula was watching the people around her without seeing when a melody caught her ear. Her eyes scanned the park, searching for the source, finally landing on a man sitting on another park bench playing his guitar. The most beautiful music she'd ever heard drifted past her on the breeze, calling to her. Commanding her attention. The sun shone off his dark hair as he bobbed in time to the music while his fingers danced across the strings. As Lula got closer, she could see he sat curled around the instrument. She caught a glimpse of his face that revealed his eyes squeezed shut. At that moment, passion clearly lit his face as every note radiated down to his soul. She followed the call of the music until she sat down beside him. Strumming the last chord of the song, he lifted his head, and his mouth dropped open as their wide eyes locked.

"Lula," Shea almost choked on his words.

"Shea," she breathed, hardly able to believe her own eyes.

"What are you doing here? Still looking for trouble?" He put the guitar in its case.

"Not today." Lula brushed her long hair behind her ear. "What are *you* doing here?"

"Enjoying the nice weather. I needed to get out of the house and felt like a day in the city would be fun. Saw this park and just had to stop for a while."

"The city?"

"I'm more of a country guy."

"Wait, you don't live in Portland?"

"You sound surprised." He chuckled, sliding closer to her.

"I am…a little. You just seem like someone who is at home in the big city."

Shea chuckled, causing his nose to scrunch a bit. The two remained locked in a staring contest.

"You're staring," Lula accused.

"You're staring, too," Shea pointed out.

"I figured you were a once-in-a-lifetime kind of guy." She smiled, leaning back on the bench so she could take him in.

He looked just as handsome in broad daylight as he had last night in the club. His dark eyes sparkled in the sun. She could make out the hard lines of his jaw. Dimples appeared as he smiled back at her.

"Sorry to disappoint you," he said.

"You didn't disappoint me. I'm actually really glad we ran into each other again."

"Need me to get you into another club?"

Lula snorted a laugh. "No, I'm good."

He leaned slightly forward while his eyes searched her face. "I'm happy about it, too. Running into you, I mean, after leaving you alone last night. I hoped you were okay."

Taken aback by Shea's intensity, she let her eyes take their fill. "Was there ever any doubt?"

"For a minute there, yeah."

Lula struggled to keep her smile in place. "I told you I would be fine."

Shea rubbed his knees, looking around the park. "You doing anything right now?"

Lula shook her head, "Just people watching."

"Let's go for a walk then."

Shea slung his guitar case over his shoulder, and they began strolling down the paved path. For a while, neither spoke as they wandered. They ended up next to the fountain in the center of the park. It sprayed water straight up into the air before gravity brought it down in an arch, causing the deeper water around it to dance. Light reflected off the surface like diamonds. Lula's mind drifted to memories of home.

"My grandpa once told me that secrets could be kept in water. It holds them tight, keeping them from getting away." Lula blinked back the tears that burned her eyes.

"We all have secrets," Shea said in a haunting whisper. "Maybe someday we can learn each other's?"

"Maybe," Lula lied, knowing she could never reveal her life to Shea. "Though I don't know why you would want to know me at all, let alone my secrets."

Shea turned, facing her. He held her eyes, slowly bringing a hand up to her cheek. His touch seared, blazing all the way to her toes, lighting her on fire. However, this fire burned differently, filling her with a sense of comfort. Protection. Somehow, Lula stood there, more connected to this stranger than anyone else in the world. She never wanted to let this moment go.

His thumb made lazy circles on her cheek. "Because there's something about you. I feel drawn to you, and I don't want to let you go."

Lula let out a soft laugh and leaned into his touch. "Are you always this forward?"

"Never, actually." His brow furrowed. "Which is why this is all so strange to me."

They stared at each other for the longest time. Lula kept trying to figure Shea out, and she could imagine him doing the same to her.

"Stay with me," he said so quietly she wasn't sure she heard him right.

"What?" Lula blinked, like she was coming out of a dream.

"For lunch." His hand dropped, and he took a step back. "We can talk and get to know each other more."

She looked up at him through her lashes. "Are you trying to find out my secrets?"

A Cheshire grin spread. "Not yet."

She raised a questioning brow.

"I've got to save something for the second date," he continued.

"Well." Lula reached out and took his hand. "As long as you leave something."

A phone rang. Shea cursed under his breath and dug the offending device out of his pocket.

"Yeah," he answered, glaring holes into the ground. "Are you sure?" His eyes flashed to Lula before dropping. He squeezed her hand. "I'm at a park in the city. Yeah. Okay. I said okay." Hanging up the phone, he cursed again.

"Is everything good?"

"Yeah, I just... I'm sorry, Lula, but I have to go. It's a..." He ran a frustrated hand through his hair.

"It's okay, Shea. That just means we get to meet again for our first date." She smiled encouragingly at him.

"Absolutely. Tomorrow." He grabbed her hand.

"Where should we meet?"

He tapped the screen on his phone. "Why don't we exchange numbers?"

Lula looked away and bit her lip. This would be hard to explain. Not like she could admit her overly controlling Death God wouldn't let her have a cell phone. "I don't have one."

Shea stopped tapping and looked up at her like she'd grown a second head. "You don't have a phone?"

"No, I—" She would need to come up with a good excuse and fast. "My old one broke, and I haven't been able to replace it yet."

That sounded like a good reason. Right? Lula held her breath as Shea let out a sigh and looked around. Indecision pinched his face. "How about I meet you here this time tomorrow?"

"It's a date then."

Shea's smile lit up Lula's world, and for a moment, it almost looked like he wanted to kiss her. She knew she wanted to kiss him. Probably not the smartest thought she'd ever had, but she didn't care.

"It's a date. I'm sorry I have to go."

"Just don't stand me up tomorrow, and I'll forgive you."

"Wouldn't dream of it."

Lula watched Shea disappear, wondering what had just happened. He had his secrets, but with her own skeletons, how much could she judge?

Chapter Nine

Butterflies warred with the nerves in Lula's stomach. Her feet hardly touched the floor as she raced around the house the next morning. There was no one to greet or question her. As relieved as it left her, caution had her checking over her shoulder. Were they actually going to let her be? She had just grabbed her keys and was making her way to the garage when Max appeared in front of her, causing her to stumble a step.

"Max!" She brushed her hair behind her ear.

"So, where are we off to this morning?" Max asked.

"I was going back to the park. It's supposed to be another beautiful day."

"Again?" he grumbled. "Can't we do something else today? Something fun?"

"The park *is* fun. I spent hours there yesterday watching the clouds." Pink kissed her cheeks as memories bombarded her.

Max's whole frame sagged, and he stomped his feet. "You are so boring. We should go check out the zoo. Or a theme park! Let's go ride the rollercoaster at Oaks Park."

"Max, I want to go to the park."

"Can we at least go to a new one?"

"No." Lula bit her lip. "And I would actually like to go by myself."

"By yourself?"

"Please?" She looked up at him with big eyes, trying to say what she wasn't allowed to say out loud.

Max stood quiet and unmoving, never taking his eyes off her. Finally, with a sigh, he took a deliberate step out of her way. "Sure, Lula. Have a good one."

"Thank you, Max," she called just before he disappeared.

Lula refused to feel guilty as she slammed the car door, at the same time turning the key and starting the engine. Not today. Today, she was meeting Shea for a date. A first date. Laughter burst out of her as she pulled out of the driveway before racing down the street, all because she was on her way to meet a guy. Not just any guy, a guy that made her heart so light she could fly. Weaving through the Portland streets, a tiny voice in the back of her mind told her to slow down, be careful. Giving it the attention it deserved proved harder than Lula thought until she found herself making the final turn toward the park.

When she parked, she stayed glued to her seat, suddenly arguing with herself. Half past ten stared up at her from her rose wristwatch, almost mockingly. The countdown had begun until her respite ended, and her sentence started again. Only Lula didn't know how long she had. She fussed with her skirt, straightening it, as she surveyed the park. Doyle and Max could show up at any moment. What would they do if they saw Shea? Was she willing to put him in danger?

Lula looked out over the park again, and her breath caught. Shea wandered down a path, his guitar case slung over his shoulder. A tremor rolled down her spine, the pull to see him overwhelming her. She should turn on the car and leave. That was the only sure way to keep him safe from her world. Even as the thought repeated itself like a broken record, Lula got out of the car and smoothed the skirt of her pink, babydoll dress one more time. She shoved down the impending heart break and made her way to where he stood.

The moment his eyes found hers, a bright smile lit his face. Lula knew her answering smile had to be just as bright.

"Hi." Shea cleared his throat. "You look beautiful."

Lula's face flushed as she averted her gaze. "Flatterer."

"I just call it like I see it. Though I have to ask, do you own any pants?"

She took a step back and looked down at herself again. "Why?"

"Don't get me wrong, I'm not complaining. I just only see you in dresses."

Lula shrugged. "I love dresses, always have. My mom told me that's what ladies wear."

"That thinking is a bit old-fashioned."

It was a fair point. However, considering her mom was born in the early 1700s, who could blame her? Lula smiled at the memory of her mother sitting in their tiny home, teaching her all she needed to know about being a lady and catching a husband. *You know his feelings are true, and he's worth your time if he gives you gifts. That's how your father got me.*

She made quote signs with her fingers. "Well, my mom was admittedly a bit 'old fashioned' by today's standards, and that's fine with me. Besides, I think they suit me." Lula twirled in place.

"That they do." His smile remained as he reached out and took her hand. He huffed a laugh and squeezed her fingers. "You actually came."

"You dared to doubt me?"

"Well, I wouldn't say I doubted you. I just wasn't sure you'd be willing to meet up with the strange dude who drove you home or not."

"That fact did give me pause. In the end, I decided to go for it, against my better judgment," she half-teased him.

"I see." Shea became somber.

She averted her gaze to the small crowd around them. "My dad would be angry if he knew what I was doing, is all."

Shea pulled her closer to him and purred in her ear, "I won't tell if you don't."

Lula smiled, placing a hand against her warming cheek. "Deal."

Despite the unease still stirring in her stomach, she followed Shea without a second thought. They made their way over to an open grassy area and settled in. The cool grass threw Lula back to a time she loved—a time before her world fell apart—and she relaxed.

"I used to do this all the time when I was a kid," she said, watching the clouds roll by.

"Stare at the clouds?" She could hear a smile in his voice.

She grinned. "Yeah."

Shea lay beside her, so close she could feel the heat coming off his side. Daring a glance his way, she admired his soft profile, the way his long lashes curled at the ends, and how a small dimple formed in his cheek when he smiled at the sky.

Lula nudged him. "Relaxing, isn't it?"

"It is. Sort of surreal, the way the clouds are moving."

Lula sighed and focused on the view above. The fragrance of flowers mixed with grass tickled her nose. Dogs barked in the distance, transporting her back to England...to a simpler time.

"Do you do this a lot?" Shea asked.

Lula might have thought he was teasing her, but the look on his face made her think he genuinely wanted to know. Nodding, she mused, "Doing this all the time is probably why my dad didn't trust me alone with the herd."

"The herd?"

"I, too, am a country girl," she quipped, referring to yesterday's conversation. "At least I used to be. I *used* to live on a farm. We herded sheep."

Lula looked over to see Shea staring at her, his face scrunched up.

"What?" she asked.

"I'm trying to picture you as a sheep herder and honestly having a hard time."

"Wow, thanks!"

They laughed together, especially when she shoved him.

"Fine, tell me more," he relented.

Lula was as open as she could but kept it to her time before Doyle. Before she lost herself to a life she never wanted. They might be superficial, but they were the only stories she wanted to share.

"My sisters always wanted to help Mom with the house. I always wanted to run off with my dad and brother to tend to the herd. I loved being out in the open with the animals."

"A brother, huh? Do I need to watch my back?" Shea looked dramatically around them.

"Ha! You probably should. My sisters could definitely take you. My brother, on the other hand, would beg you to take me off his hands."

"Brutal."

Lula shrugged. "You know how siblings are."

"Not really." He pointed to himself. "Only child."

"I think I might envy you."

Easy conversation led to easy laughs. She held his hand as she recalled the summer she nearly lost her way home from a friend's house one late night. He brushed her hair behind her ear as he told her about playing his guitar at a coffee house during an open mike night. Each story brought smiles to their faces. When Shea pulled the guitar out of his case, Lula sat up and watched him play. His fingers danced across the strings, creating a soothing melody that filled the air.

"What song is this?" Lula asked, her eyes drifting closed.

"Nothing special. Just something I made up a long time ago."

"It's beautiful."

"This is how I relax."

Lula hummed along without missing a beat, like she'd heard the song a thousand times before. The song ended, and Lula opened her eyes to find Shea looking at her. Her breath caught in her throat. The way he drank her in, stirred those butterflies into a frenzy. The beginnings of a smile appeared, and he slowly leaned in, closing the distance between them. Lula held her breath. Everything in her begged for him to kiss her. With only an inch between their lips, he suddenly pulled away with a curse.

Pulling the phone out of his pocket, he glared at the tiny device. "Lula, I'm so sorry. I have to go."

Lula sat back and glanced at her watch, seeing it was just after three in the afternoon. She shrugged casually. "You're fine. I should probably head back home myself. You know, before Dad wonders where I disappeared to."

"He keeps that close of an eye on you?"

"Unfortunately."

"Can we meet tomorrow?"

Lula bit her lip. She thought of every reason she should stay away. Still, the idea of not seeing Shea, even one more time, sent her heart crashing into her stomach.

"Same time?" she asked with a smile.

"Same place."

Chapter Ten

Lula sprang out of bed early the next morning. She dressed in one of her favorite sundresses from the seventies with loose sleeves and an empire waist. Checking herself several times in the mirror, then her watch, seeing it was just before ten. She bolted out of her room and straight into Max.

"Hi, Max." She fidgeted nervously. "How are you this morning?"

"Fine. Just wondering what we are doing today?"

"I'm going to the park. It's supposed to be another beautiful day."

"I don't suppose you want company?"

"Max." She looked anywhere but at him as she searched to find the words to tell him. "It's not that I don't want to hang out with you..."

He held up a hand, silencing her. "It's okay, Lula. I understand."

"Max," she started to say, but he disappeared.

Lula cursed at the ceiling before she rushed out the door. She had spent the better part of two, almost three, centuries with him. One week of her going out on her own wasn't going to kill him. Sitting in the drive-thru of Burgerville, Lula refused to feel guilt over leaving him behind again.

Fifteen minutes later, she pulled into a parking spot and then took a moment to check herself in the mirror. Her cheeks were flushed, and her windblown hair looked like a rat's nest. Laughing as she ran her fingers through the long, dark strands, Lula felt light as air. She grabbed the two marionberry shakes she had bought on her way and got out of the car. Using her powers to reach out, she made sure there was no sign of Doyle or Max before picking up speed. She practically ran, nearly tripping over her own feet when she saw Shea seated at a bench.

Lula stopped for a moment and drank him in. She watched him looking everywhere but where she stood. His button-up shirt with khaki pants made him look much dressier than the graphic T-shirt he wore yesterday. The shirt stretched as he twisted in his seat. She looked down at the dress she'd chosen and frowned, wondering if she should have chosen something dressier.

Her insecurities rooted Lula in place when Shea's gaze locked on her. His eyes went wide as he slowly rose from his seat, and he swallowed hard as he took her in. With no chance of a getaway, Lula managed to get her feet to carry her the rest of the way.

"Good morning," Lula greeted him.

"Good morning." Shea cleared his throat. "You look fantastic in your dress."

She took a step back and looked down at herself again. "Thank you, I think?"

"Sorry, it's just..." Shea kicked at a pebble on the walkway. "You have such eclectic taste."

"I can't tell if you are teasing me or not."

Shea's eyes widened in horror. "I didn't mean it like an insult. It's just every time I see you, you look like you just stepped out of another time."

"If you like my dresses, you should see my room."

"You like antiques or something?"

Lula shrugged. "It's called vintage, and I love it. My dresses are like a timeline, maybe even a memory."

"A memory, I like that." Shea seemed to drift off, there in body alone, before refocusing on Lula. "For the record, I love your dresses, too. You look beautiful."

Lula sealed her mouth shut to keep from giggling like some love-sick teenager. Bitting the inside of her cheek, she offered Shea the shake. "I got this for you. It's marionberry, my favorite."

"Thank you. Marionberry is my favorite, too."

"Really?"

Shea raised the cup in a toast before he took a long drink. The two stood in a comfortable silence while enjoying the cold treats.

"So, what do you want to do today?" Lula asked.

"I thought I could take you to lunch. There's a great Mexican food truck just down the street. If you're hungry, we could get some tacos. Then we could bring them back to the park and watch the clouds some more."

"I'd love that."

They began walking through the park, Shea leading the way. Lula kept her eyes down until a hand slip into her own. Looking up, she found Shea smiling warmly down at her. Those ever-persistent nerves eased away as they walked hand in hand toward the opposite end of the park.

At the very southern end, they crossed the street and entered a small neighborhood. Old houses lined up side by side with large trees in every yard. Cars sped past, and pedestrians hustled around them. Everyone seemed in a hurry. Everyone except Lula and Shea. They found a leisurely pace walking down the sidewalk, taking in the sunny day. If anything, Lula wanted time to slow down so she could enjoy this more. Instead, time marched on at the same steady beat as they made their way.

Just past the Portland Community College campus, Killingsworth Street came into view.

Shea pointed at a small taqueria truck parked off to the side. "That's the truck I was talking about. They have the best tacos in town."

Lula raised an eyebrow. "I'm excited to try them."

They walked up to the brightly colored food truck. A wave of mouth-watering aromas immediately hit Lula. It was an exercise in self-control, not ordering one of everything off the menu. After placing their orders, they found a place to wait off to the side.

"This is one of my dad's favorite food trucks," Shea said.

"How about your mom? She a big taco fan?"

Shea frowned at his shoes before answering. "My mom died when I was born. Dad doesn't talk about her. I think it hurts too much."

"I'm sorry, Shea."

Shea gave a small smile. "I worry more about Dad. I mourn what could have been. He still mourns what he lost."

"So it's just the two of you?"

"I have an uncle, but we never see him. I honestly don't remember the last time he came to visit, and we sure don't go see him."

"Where does he live?"

"I'm not sure exactly. Somewhere in California, last I heard. I get so frustrated with him, with Dad. It's just us living on ten acres of land. Even our neighbors are far away. It just gets lonely."

Lula knew all too well about feeling isolated and alone. She placed a hand on his arm, drawing his attention. Refusing to think about what she was doing, she stepped forward and wrapped her arms around him, pulling him into a tight hug. Shea's arms enveloped her in return. They stood together in the warm sun, holding each other.

"Please tell me you use the ten acres for more than dirt biking," she said, trying to chase the sadness out of Shea's eyes.

"Of course." A "no duh" rang in his voice. "We also drive ATVs and have bonfires. There is also a huge pond you can fish in, as long as the neighbor doesn't catch you. It's technically on his property, but only technically."

Lula laughed into his chest. "You are playing with fire, young man."

"What can I say? I like to live dangerously." He waggled his eyebrows.

"Shea!" a deep voice called, announcing their order was ready.

Shea dropped his hold so he could retrieve their order. "Shall we go back to the park?" he asked.

Lula watched as he reached out a hand to her. Whatever this was turning into between them was crazy, but she was learning to love crazy. Taking his hand and walking back to the park, something bright and warm settled in her chest. Something she never wanted to let go of again.

***

Lula savored the last bite of her taco and moaned. Beside her, Shea smirked as he gathered all the trash into the bag on their picnic table.

"I guess the tacos are a hit," he said, throwing the bag into the trash can.

"Best tacos I've had in a long time, and I mean in a long time. Not since I was in Mexico."

"When were you in Mexico?" Shea turned around, facing away from the table, and pulled out his guitar.

Lula opened her mouth but caught the truth on the tips of her tongue. No way could she tell him she lived in Mexico City for thirty years in the mid-1800s.

She opened her mouth again and, this time, pushed out a vague half-truth. "When I was younger."

"Family vacation?"

She focused on anything but Shea. "Something like that."

Strumming a few chords, Shea peeked at her, trying to catch her eyes. "I'm jealous. I've never been outside the country."

"You should go. It's tons of fun."

"Maybe someday." Shea continued to strum and focused on the guitar.

The way he concentrated on the way he played the instrument, like maybe he wasn't seeing it at all, made Lula wonder what he could be thinking. She bumped his shoulder with hers. "Not anytime soon?"

Shea shrugged. "As much as I would love to, I can't. At least, not for a while. The family business is...busy."

Irritation prickled her skin. He seemed to be tethered to his phone, and any time his dad said jump, he had to ask how high. No one should be controlled like that. He was an adult and should be free to live however he wanted.

He shouldn't be trapped.

Lula froze, staring at Shea. Shea was just some guy she met at a club. Right? He couldn't be a Pet, right? He just had an overbearing parent. Lots of mortals had that. Leaning back, she tapped into her powers and took a closer look at Shea. His young and healthy aura flared around him in a brilliant emerald green. On the edges, sparks of another color burst up, never high enough to tell what it was. Not gold like a Pet, but something else? Lula was trying to focus harder, to see what second color lay hidden, when a power brushed over her before it quickly disappeared. Lula stiffened and searched for where it came from. All she found were people enjoying the afternoon.

"Are you okay?" Shea asked.

"I'm fine." Lula worked to keep the tremor out of her voice. After all, she *was* fine. There was nothing out there. "I just hate that you can't do what you want. No one should feel trapped," she answered him honestly.

He set down his guitar and cupped her face, forcing her to look at him. Lula took in his wide eyes as he searched her face.

"For now, anyway." He sounded so confident. She didn't know what to say. Leaning forward, he touched his forehead to hers and sighed. "I promise you this right now. One of these days, we will both be free to go wherever we desire."

The weight and conviction of his words settled over her like a warm blanket. Everything in her believed him, even if she shouldn't.

"I'll hold you to that."

Chapter Eleven

Lula woke up the next morning early enough to watch the sunrise through her window. Low light peeked around the edges of her curtains, growing brighter as the moments ticked by. Moments she spent reliving the past days with Shea. The consequences of her afternoon escapes with him were now in the far reaches of her mind. Her only thoughts now revolved around the joy of having met Shea. Two days in a row now, she had left without seeing Doyle. She'd returned yesterday to find him tucked away in his study. He'd given no sign that he knew what she was up to and showed no interest in finding out. The only thing he'd asked was if she'd enjoyed herself. His question still held the edge of a warning.

Lula saw very little of Max, which surprised her. He'd drifted into her room last night only to say he was glad Doyle hadn't put her back to work. He'd never asked about her day. This morning, he hadn't even shown up to ask if he could join her. The forlorn look on his face clenched at her heart, but she refused to feel guilty about her outings with Shea. She had spent almost three whole centuries hanging out with Max. It was high time she spent her days with someone new.

Lula wasted no time racing to the park to find Shea right where she'd left him the day before.

Lula crossed her arms. "Please tell me you actually went home."

Shea frowned. "Yeah. Why?"

"It doesn't look like it. In fact, it doesn't look like you've moved an inch from where I left you yesterday."

"What can I say? I couldn't bear the thought of missing you, so I camped out here, waiting oh-so patiently for your return."

She rolled her eyes. "Now you're laying it on a little too thick."

"Really? I thought I was being romantic."

"Well, you were definitely being sweet."

"What if I gave you a present?"

"A present?"

"Yes, I found something at the waterfront market." He pulled a tiny pouch out of his pocket and handed it to her.

Lula bit her lip. "You really got me a present?"

"It made me think of you. Something to wear with all your dresses."

She took the pouch with shaking fingers. Lula's heart pounded in her chest as a storm of thoughts barreled through her mind. Lula didn't know how to take it. Every gift over the past two hundred-plus years had been given as a way to appease or manipulate her. Every gift except for the one that she had no memory of who gave it to her. She studied the innocent-looking velvet pouch and struggled to reconcile her past with this moment. Glancing up at Shea, all those sour thoughts melted away. This wasn't Max trying to manipulate her favor. This wasn't Doyle trying to buy her obedience. This was Shea, with nothing but affection shining in his dark eyes.

Lula's mind raced with wonder. She pulled on the strings and reached into the bag, her long fingers touching the cool metal. Her brow furrowed as she revealed the piece of jewelry. She felt a little dizzy as she took in the delicate necklace. The long silver chain pooled in her palm, and at its center, nestled between two square-cut rubies, was an oval-cut moonstone. Flecks of blue, nestled in the creamy stone, shone in the sun. She was speechless, gaping at the lovely gift.

"Do you like it?" he asked.

"Yes." She couldn't take her eyes off of it.

Shea took it and placed it around her neck, the stones landing at the base of her throat. "It's a moonstone. Apparently, it has some supernatural protection powers. At least, that's what the lady who sold it to me said."

"It's beautiful. It actually reminds me of a necklace I got long ago." Lula touched the stone with her fingertips.

"I'm glad that you like it."

Lula threw her arms around Shea and gripped him. "I love it," she murmured in his chest.

He returned her embrace, enveloping her in warmth. They held each other in a perfect moment she tucked away close to her heart. She wanted to keep Shea and this memory forever. Running her fingers over her new necklace, warmth and comfort washed over her. He took her hand, and they found a spot to spread out a blanket and sit next to each other. The day lazed by under the warm sun. The two shared stories and laughed together. Every so often, she would run a finger over the stones and smile. Lula had never been this content in her life.

Eventually, the sun had sunk low enough in the sky that she knew their time together was coming to an end.

Lula picked at the corner of the blanket. "I still say that sunsets on the coast are better than sunrises."

Shea rolled his eyes. "That's only because of your morbid fascination with endings. I still can't believe you read the end of a book first."

"Sue me. I like to know where stories are heading."

"Does that mean you want to know where we're heading?"

His innocent question caught Lula off guard. She already knew where they were heading, and she hated it. Despite knowing that, her heart wouldn't let up on the idea of a happy ending. Lula blamed all the romance movies she had seen over the years.

"Maybe." She bit her lip.

"Maybe? I figured you'd want a step-by-step dating guide."

"Do you have one?"

Shea laughed. "Not on me, but I'll bring it tomorrow."

"I—"

Lula's eyes widened as one of her worst fears stood at the edge of the path. Max's glare made her squirm as she guessed how long he had been standing there, watching. She swallowed hard before turning her attention back to Shea, who seemed blissfully ignorant of the fact that they were being watched.

"You..." Shea egged on.

"I have to go."

Shea jumped up with her and grabbed her hand before she could bolt away. "What's wrong?"

"Nothing," she lied. "I just forgot that I'm supposed to meet someone. I think I'm running late."

Shea's face paled. "Someone?"

"He's a friend. This dude is like family."

"Okay."

Lula paused and cradled Shea's face. A smile warmed her cheeks as she leaned in close. "Please don't get any wrong ideas, okay? There's only one guy I dream about at night."

"You dream about me?" The question made her pulse race.

"Every night."

Shea closed the distance between them. The kiss they shared was soft and slow, and it warmed her down to her toes.

Reluctantly, she forced herself to take a step back. "I'll see you soon."

"Tomorrow," he emphasized.

"Tomorrow," she promised.

Lula marched right past Max on the way to her car, never looking back. She couldn't bring herself to acknowledge either of the men she could feel watching her every step.

"Nice necklace," Max said right beside her.

She covered her necklace but didn't reply.

Max let out a sigh. "He will only hurt you. You know that, right?"

"I've survived worse than him." She glared over at the ghost of her former lover. He had the decency to look guilty. "What do you care who I talk to, anyway?"

"I don't care."

"Is that why you were stalking me?"

Max narrowed his eyes. "But Doyle might," he continued, ignoring her question.

A shiver danced across Lula's skin. Max was right. She hated it, but he was.

"And I'm keeping an eye on you, not stalking you."

Lula rolled her eyes. "Right. For how long?"

His silence was answer enough. He'd been watching her the whole time she'd been meeting with Shea. All four days. His melancholy now made sense.

At that moment, Lula could hear her heart pounding in her ears. Her cheeks were on fire, along with her chest. Lula had reached her breaking point. For almost three hundred years, she had done everything that Doyle had asked of her in the name of a deal she'd made in a moment clouded by despair over a man who didn't even love her.

"Lula," Max pleaded as she climbed into her car.

She slammed the door shut on him, but he appeared right beside her in the passenger seat.

"Lula, I won't tell Doyle. I wouldn't do that."

"You know what, Maxwell? I don't even care anymore." She peered over at him as she sped out of the parking lot.

"Wait a minute." Max's eyes bugged. "Remember, it's not just your ass on the line here. We are irrevocably connected."

"I remember." Lula gripped the steering wheel tighter.

How could she forget her end meant Max's end, and his end meant an end to the deal she'd made with Doyle? A lifetime of being with the one she loved in exchange for a lifetime of servitude. Lula swallowed hard against the implacable facts of her existence.

"I'm sorry if you get caught in the crossfire, but I am done."

Max spoke with the same desperation that gripped Lula. "Please, just think about this, my belle."

Hearing his old nickname for her nearly caused her to crash the car. Slamming on the brakes, the car slid to a stop on this side of the road, the front tire coming up on the curb. A car blared its horn as it swerved by.

"Max, I am tired of living—no, *existing*—under Doyle's thumb because of something he tricked me into when I was vulnerable and distraught. I mean, what is he going to do? What are any of them going to do? Kill me? Destroy my soul? All because I found one spark of happiness in this joyless existence? I have walked this earth longer than anyone should be allowed to. If he decides he doesn't want to deal with me because I'm too defiant, then fine. I welcome the sweet relief of oblivion."

"You're right, Lula." Max's translucent hand came to rest upon hers.

When she brought herself to look him in the eyes, she saw not the man who had betrayed her and broken her heart but the man that she had fallen in love with so long ago. She also saw her friend.

"I know you don't believe me, and I-I understand why—" his voice broke "—but I do care for you, and I don't want anything to happen to you."

Lula shot him a scathing look.

"Okay, maybe I'm a little worried about what will happen to me, too, but that isn't my biggest concern."

Tears spilled down her cheeks. She squeezed her eyes shut, and Shea appeared in her mind. "I care about him, Max. I don't know why, but I do. He feels like a fresh start."

"Look, if you like this guy, good. Great. I'm happy for you. I want you to run off with him and live happily ever after. God knows you deserve it. But let's get rid of Doyle in a way that releases you for good. Don't give him a reason to destroy you."

She sniffled. "*Us.*"

"Yes, us. We won't give him a reason to destroy *us.*" Max held her gaze, promise shining in his eyes.

"Deal." Lula pulled back onto the road, ready to try but prepared to fight.

Chapter Twelve

Lula woke to a loud banging on her bedroom door in time to the beat of the banging in her head. She had spent most of the night tossing and turning. Sleep had been elusive as thoughts over the events of yesterday in the park screamed at her late into the night. Between the feelings growing in her heart for Shea and the excitement and uncertainty over Max's vow to help her, she was an emotional wreck.

"Lula," Doyle's voice vibrated the door. "Get up, I need you."

She dragged herself out of bed and trudged to the door. Opening it just a crack, she peered up at the imposing deity. "I thought you said I was on break right now?"

Granted, Doyle had given her five glorious days of peace, but Lula's stomach dropped as she realized she had naively hoped she would get more. Especially since he'd promised her a week, which equaled seven days in her opinion.

"What I have for you has nothing to do with collecting souls. I need you to run a simple errand for me, nothing more."

Lula opened her door wider and leaned against the frame. Her stomach twisted into knots as she worked to look relaxed. "Just an errand?" She eyed him skeptically. "That's all?"

"Why must you always question me, Pet? You will do what you are told. Now get dressed. You are going to Poe's house to retrieve a very important item, so be quick about it."

Lula watched his stiff figure stomp down the hall and into his room. A trail of smoke followed behind him.

"Are you coming with me?" Lula asked Max, who was lurking at the end of the hall.

"I'll catch up with you later." He waggled his eyebrows before disappearing.

Lula's shoulders dropped as she let out a groan. *Great*, she thought, squeezing her eyes shut. She closed the door and got ready to go. *Today is going to be a great day*, she told herself sarcastically as she pulled on her long, olive-green dress. This errand would eat into her time with Shea. She put on her new necklace and glared at her reflection.

Get there. Get back. Make it quick.

Grabbing her keys, Doyle followed behind like a silent phantom into the garage.

"Poe knows you are coming. Do not stall in returning with the item."

Lula put all her focus into pulling out of the garage so she wouldn't flip Doyle the bird before tearing off down the street. The last thing she wanted was to give him a reason to cut her vacation short.

Weaving through the shaded streets of Portland, she lost herself in the drive. Tiny businesses nestled themselves between old neighborhoods with even older houses. She navigated the hustle and bustle of traffic until she squeezed the car into a spot in front of a large, nineteenth-century house near the Hollywood district.

Walking up to the front door, Lula raised her fist to knock as the door flew open, revealing a short, paunchy man with a head as round as his body.

"What took you so long?" Poe snapped.

"I came straight here. It's not my fault traffic is always terrible," Lula said, leaning against one of the front columns of the old house.

"Excuses, excuses," he mumbled. "Stay here." He pointed his fat finger at the ground when she made a move to follow inside.

Lula grumbled to herself and took an exaggerated step back from the door as he turned away from her slightly.

"Willow!" Poe bellowed into the house. "Willow, hurry and bring me the briefcase I showed you."

An old woman, her thick silver hair pulled up in a bun, shuffled toward them at a snail's pace. Her hands shook as she gripped the handle so tight her knuckles blanched white.

"I say, do you have to take all day?" Poe threw his arms into the air.

"Apologies, Master Poe, but you never fixed my arthritis. It takes a while for me to get moving." Willow kept her face down as she offered the briefcase to Poe. Her aura radiating a brilliant gold, the mark of a Pet. Lula wondered if her aura glowed just as brightly.

"You worthless Pet. You're not worth the price I paid to get you." He sneered before thrusting the briefcase at Lula. "Here, and make sure you don't take your time getting home. Your master needs this right away."

Lula snatched the briefcase from Poe and glared. She wanted to say something encouraging to Willow but knew if she did, Poe would just make Willow even more miserable than she already was. Doyle could be a cruel son of a bitch, but he had nothing on Poe. Death Gods like him lived to make Pets miserable.

Running down the steps, Lula threw the briefcase into the backseat of the car before driving off down the street. Stuck at a stop sign, waiting for her turn to go, her heart pounded. Alone with her thoughts, she admitted to herself that, based on Doyle's appearance this morning, time was running short. Soon, Doyle would force her to collect souls again. She battled against the thoughts surrounding Doyle and Poe. Before she knew it, they found their way to the mysterious visitor at her house the other night. If he found out about the abilities Doyle had given her, she would be as good as dead—or her version of dead, at least.

Doyle had made it abundantly clear he would never give her up. He would destroy her before someone else claimed her. Even though part of her knew the idea of being destroyed should be a relief—no one should be forced to exist for so long—Lula still longed to find a way out of her arrangement with Doyle. She wanted to be free, even if deep in the pit of her stomach, she knew Max's plan was nothing more than a pipe dream.

Guilt and fear churned in the pit of her stomach as another realization crossed her mind. Sooner or later, Lula would disappear, and Shea would never know why. The wild side of her wanted to find Shea and run away with him. The idea that he would be ready to whisk her away almost had her laughing out loud. They had only known each other for a week. No, for his sake, she needed to say goodbye and resign herself to the fate that had befallen her.

But she did want to have the chance to say goodbye.

Looking at the time, she decided to throw caution to the wind, and instead of going straight home, Lula ended up driving to the park.

When she got out of the car, she walked to the bench while looking for Shea. Children played on the playground. Couples walked hand in hand down a long, winding path that wove through a maze of beautiful rose bushes. She sat and watched everyone but him pass her by, trying to decide what she would say to him if—no, *when*—she saw him again.

Lula closed her eyes and drank in the afternoon sun as she waited for Shea to show. Frustrated with herself, Lula leaned back to look at the sky. Why was she clinging to Shea? They had hung out every day now for almost a week. Warmth filled her as memories of those times played through her mind. Coupled with his strange familiarity, an intoxicating desire to be with him nearly overwhelmed her.

But this cannot last.

Pain, unlike anything she'd ever known, sliced through her, stealing her breath. A hole opened in her chest. How naïve she'd been to get so attached to Shea. Every option led to the same ending. There was no future with him, no matter how much she wanted it. Lula swallowed hard past the lump forming in her throat. She sat so lost in her thoughts she jumped out of her skin when a hand grabbed hers.

"Whoa." Shea held up his hands in surrender. "I didn't mean to scare you."

"Shea." She clutched at her chest. "Sorry, I thought I missed you."

"No way. I wouldn't have missed this for the world." His smile made his eyes twinkle.

Lula smiled, but averted her gaze.

Shea cupped her cheeks, forcing her to meet his dark eyes that blazed in the afternoon sun. "Lula, are you all right?"

His question didn't surprise her. He always seemed to know when she was in turmoil. Her cheeks grew hot as she fought to answer. With Shea here beside her, all her resolve crumbled.

Leaning into him, that vice in her chest eased. "I am now."

Shea wrapped an arm around her, pulling her in close. He placed a gentle kiss on her cheek. "I'm glad."

Lula looked around the park, trying to shore up the courage again to tell Shea what she needed to. Her eyes collided with Max. He was jumping up and down, waving frantically over his head.

"Listen." Lula pulled back from Shea. "I'm so sorry, but I can't stay."

Shea looked around the park before focusing on Lula again. He seemed to pause for a moment in the direction of where Max stood. "Is there something going on?"

"It's my dad." Not the whole truth, yet not a lie. "He needs me to help around the house today."

Shea cupped her cheek. "So, I'll see you tomorrow?"

"I'll try." Lula bit her lip. "Just want to warn you, it might get harder for me to visit you. It might become close to impossible."

"Nothing is impossible. I will see you tomorrow. One way or another."

The certainty in Shea's voice was hard to ignore. The irrational part of her cheered, giving her a sense of hope she normally wouldn't allow.

"I'll see you tomorrow."

Before she could do anything else crazy, Lula stood and walked as calmly as she could toward the car. Halfway there, Max appeared at her side.

"What are you doing here?" she hissed.

They slowed their pace as they reached the car.

"I told you we would meet up later," Max said.

"Right, because now, while I'm coming home, seemed like a good time to drop in." She rolled her eyes.

"Fine, I have a couple of reasons. First, Poe called Doyle as soon as you left his house. When it started looking like you were taking the long way home, I offered to motivate you to hurry so Doyle wouldn't. Glad I did."

"God, I hate Poe. He's such an ass." Lula jerked open her car door and jumped in, slamming it behind her.

Max already sat in the passenger seat. He pinned her with a stern look. "I also wanted to make sure I didn't lose you again."

"You were afraid you would lose me? Since when?"

"Since I couldn't find you that first night. Good thing I came along too. If I hadn't had my eyes on you there, I definitely would have lost track of you."

"You lost me again?" Lula's voice squeaked. How could he lose her when he had his eyes on her?

"Right when you started talking to your guy. I could see you, but I couldn't feel where you were. Who is he, anyway?"

Lula scanned the park to see if she could still see Shea. He had disappeared, and she missed him already. "Why are you so interested in Shea?"

Max raised an eyebrow. "Because if you aren't careful, you'll be introducing him to Doyle."

"Perish the thought." Lula ground out as she took off down the street. If Doyle ever found out she was talking to someone else, especially showing any kind of interest in them, he would freak out. Knowing him, he might also find a way to use Shea against her. Lula wanted to hit something.

"So what did you have to get from Poe?"

"Some briefcase." Lula shrugged as she weaved through traffic. "It's in the backseat."

"Neat." Max grinned like a five-year-old. "Let's see what's in it."

Before Lula could even open her mouth to object, Max popped into the backseat of the car and started messing with the briefcase.

"Be careful. I don't want to get in more trouble because you break something."

Max waved a dismissive hand. "Whatever. I'm always careful."

"Maybe it has information on this 'war' the Death Gods are supposedly fighting."

"Hell, if they are at war, maybe we can join the other side." Max wagged his eyebrows.

"That's not a bad idea." She was prepared to fight.

Lula barely kept from crashing the car while simultaneously watching Max in the rearview mirror. He lifted the briefcase up, examining the outside. The dark leather case resembled a vintage doctor's bag. Two brass buckles flanked the handle, poised at the top. Max popped open the clasps one at a time. Lula held her breath as he carefully opened the top to reveal what lay inside.

"What is it?"

"A book," Max answered, sounding disappointed. "And a broken piece of rock."

"A broken piece of rock?"

"Yeah, it has weird symbols on it." Max lifted it up to show her in the mirror. "Looks like something you'd see in an *Indiana Jones* movie."

Turning down the main road in their neighborhood, she bit her lip. They were running out of time to snoop.

"What does the book have in it?" she pressed, slowing her speed to a crawl.

Max sat quietly for longer than Lula liked as he flipped through the book. She watched his brow furrow, and he shook his head as he continued to turn page after page.

"Earth to Max." Her voice shook. "Traffic is actually smooth. We're almost home."

Max cursed before putting everything back in the briefcase and shutting it.

"Well?"

"I don't know," he said, hopping back up to the front seat. "The words weren't in English, and the pictures were of old, demon-looking things."

They turned down their street and pulled into the driveway. Lula shut off the engine and sighed. So much for finding the secret to unraveling the war. Reaching behind her, she pulled the case to the front, sitting it between the two of them.

Doyle appeared at the front door before Lula could even get out of the car. She could see wisps of smoke at his feet.

Sighing once more, she opened her car door. She dragged her feet all the way into the house, bracing herself for Doyle's wrath.

He yanked the briefcase out of her hand the second she passed through the front door. "What took you so long?" he demanded.

"Traffic," Max answered for her. "I found her stuck in this awful jam on I-5. You know, they should look at expanding it or something."

Doyle's narrowed eyes pinned Lula where she stood. "Traffic?"

"That's all, and also why it apparently took me too long to get to Poe's place."

Doyle sneered. "Poe is rather impatient. That fails to explain why I briefly lost you again."

Lula swallowed hard, dumbfounded by what Doyle was accusing her of. "I don't know what to tell you, Doyle. Maybe your radar is off." Lula pushed past him. "Anything else you need from me?" she asked at the bottom of the stairs. All she wanted was to go lock herself in her room.

"No, you are free to do what you will. For now," he tacked onto the end like an ominous promise.

The clock never stopped ticking, and time was almost up.

Chapter Thirteen

Lula lay in bed, dreaming of Shea. Her body swayed and rolled in time to the music he played for her. Lula knew it wasn't real, even though it was hard to tell between the dream and any genuine memory she had. She still let herself feel it all, deep in her heart, as they sat on a bench and shared a special moment together.

"What's that look for?" Dream Shea asked.

"Is it a bad look?" Lula scrunched her face.

Dream Shea laughed. "No, just very absorbed, I guess."

"I love music. And I love listening to you play." She leaned against him, smiling.

"Then I'll have to play for you more often."

Lula let out a laugh and lifted a shoulder in a shrug. "I guess it also feels like we've done this all before, like some major *déjà vu*. I know how it sounds, but it feels like this isn't the first time we've met." Reaching up, she ran her fingers through his thick hair.

The dream shifted away from the park bench. Now they lay in an open field. Looking around her, Lula gasped as she recognized the field. They were back in England, and her home sat just over the rise. She sat still for a long moment as memories and longing bombarded her. Everything was just how she remembered it, down to the handsome man playing the guitar beside her. Nothing made sense. Then again, it was a dream.

"I think I would remember meeting you, Lula. You're pretty unforgettable," Dream Shea said, a dashing smile lighting his face.

The strange and beautiful dream came to an abrupt end when the bed bounced violently, practically throwing Lula into the air. A startled yelp yanked her awake.

"What are you doing?" Max asked.

She peeked from under the covers to see him lying on her bed, his chin propped on his hand.

"Trying to get some much-needed sleep," she grumbled. "What are you doing?"

He cupped his hand to the side of his mouth and stage-whispered, "Doyle is gone." When Lula just stared at him, he waved like she should know what that meant. With wide eyes boring into hers, he continued, "We have the house to ourselves."

"And?" She raised an eyebrow at him. It took only a moment before she realized. Her eyes lit up. "Oh my gosh. Max, we have the house to ourselves. We should snoop."

"Yes." Max fell back onto the bed in relief.

Lula jumped out of bed, and they ran down the hall. "Let's do this, but remember..." Lula held up a pointed finger.

Max rolled his eyes. "Yeah, yeah, you only have so much time before you have to go meet up with Mr. Wonderful."

Lula's breath caught in her throat. Even though holding on to these precious moments was stupid and risky, Lula wanted them all. She still didn't know how to say goodbye to Shea. A plan would come to her, eventually. Until then, she would enjoy every moment gifted to her.

She glared at Max but continued down the hall. Yesterday, after Doyle disappeared to who knows where, they searched his room. The only thing they found was Doyle's strange addiction to stereoscope cards. He stored hundreds of the 3-D cards in boxes under his bed. Pictures of every kind of landscape imaginable filled most of the collection.

Today, they decided to see if the book they brought home was in the library, but things looked grim after searching for over an hour.

"The case has to be here somewhere. Right?" Lula asked, pulling yet another book on Victorian history off the massive shelf. "What about the Victorian era is so appealing to Doyle?"

"I don't know." Max stepped in front of the next row of books. "I mean, it was kind of ugly." Lula giggled as Max continued on his tangent. "All the furniture was so uncomfortable, and all the knick-knacks?" He made a gagging noise.

"Hey, I like knickknacks."

"Oh yeah, like this one here?" Max reached up and grabbed a small stone bust of a man. As soon as he lifted it off the shelf, the sound of a lock clicking filled the room.

Max and Lula froze where they stood.

Max carefully set it back, releasing it. The entire shelf moved to the side, and Lula's mouth fell open at what lay before them.

"There is an actual room behind this bookcase." Max grinned like a kid in a candy store. "Very Scooby-Doo."

"How the hell do you even know all these pop-culture icons?" Lula asked, moving to stand next to Max.

"It is a very boring existence I lead." He grinned down at her. "Until now."

Lula glanced over her shoulder, sure Doyle would be standing behind them. The room was empty save for her and Max. She took a deep breath before the two of them stepped inside.

The small room wasn't much bigger than an oversized alcove. The two of them only just squeezed inside. If the door were to shut behind them, they would barely fit. A moment passed before Lula's eyes adjusted to the lower light. They looked around, trying to take it all in. Shelves climbed the longest wall from floor to ceiling. Max made an affirming noise before flipping a switch. A small lantern to their left turned on, bathing the room in a low yellow light. Small demonic-looking figures sat next to thick leather-bound books on the shelves. A thick layer of dust covered most of the items on the wall. She took a book off one shelf, sending debris scattering into the air.

"Good thing I don't stain," Max said as he waved his hand in front of his face.

She opened the book, revealing a drawing of a dark, hooded figure holding a man's hand as they walked under a large, golden gate. Lula recognized the Gate that stood between the two Realms. Below the picture, a phrase in Old English had been scrawled across the page.

"'Death shall lead the way to peace and light,'" Lula read aloud.

"Is that...?" Max pointed at the picture.

"It's the Gate leading to the Realm of the Dead. It looks like Death really did used to be a welcoming and peaceful thing. At least according to this old book."

"What happened, I wonder?"

Lula only shrugged. Who knew what had changed the Death Gods into the heartless deities they were today?

She continued to flip through the book while Max turned his attention to another on the shelf below. Lula kept an ear out for Doyle. The more she read, though, the harder it was to concentrate on anything else. She didn't want to think about what he'd do if he found them. Some books were in English, while others were in German, Italian, and even French. It surprised her how much she could read. So far, none of the books were in that strange language Max had seen in the book she retrieved from Poe. All the books divulged stories about the Death Gods.

Over three millennia ago, the Death Gods appeared. Their entire purpose was to escort those souls judged worthy from the Realm of the Living to the Realm of the Dead. The peaceful transition lasted for only one thousand years. A soul who was not ready to leave this world bargained for a longer life. The Death Gods discovered they held more power than they'd realized—they had the power to control and manipulate. A simple favor escalated into control over all those vulnerable souls, helpless to the whims of their Gods. The Death Gods could make not just the souls, but also those attached to the souls, do as they pleased. They loved holding all the power—a power they abused more and more as time passed.

"Man, they really love themselves," Max said.

Peering over his shoulder, Lula read of their greed and how they lavished in the power they held over souls. The way the book described them all with such admiration made her stomach turn. She made a disgusted noise as she slammed her book shut at the mention of a rising of the Death Gods against an opponent who was determined to take them all down. Clearly, whoever it was failed.

Max traded for another book on one of the top shelves. This one, unlike the others, didn't have any dust or dirt on it. He opened the book, and Lula's heart raced. This had to be the book from the brief-case.

Her heart sank as soon as she started reading. "What the hell language is this?" she asked, flipping through more pages.

"It looks like gibberish to me."

"Is this the book you saw in the case?"

Max looked it over before jerking his chin toward the book. "This is the one. I told you it wasn't in English."

"Yeah, but you didn't say it was in hieroglyphics. Or whatever this is."

Max nudged her. "At least we found it."

"I can't believe this. What are we supposed to do with something we can't even read?" Lula stomped her foot.

"Calm down, Lula. We'll figure this out."

"I feel like we just wasted a huge amount of time, is all."

"I know it's a little disappointing," Max said, but Lula barely paid him any mind. "But, I mean, what did you expect? To find *The Complete Guide to Getting Out of Being a Pet*? We just need to keep looking. The answer is in here somewhere. I can feel it."

Reaching out, she picked up a rock from another shelf. It was the same rock from the briefcase and looked like the corner of a large stone tablet. Turning it over, she froze. The carved symbols began to swim and change. Concentrating, she tuned out everything around her. She had almost made out what they said when Max grabbed her arm.

"Lula!" Max shouted, pulling her back. "Do you feel that?"

Lula gasped as Doyle's unmistakable energy slammed into her. "Doyle's back," she squeaked.

"We have to hurry."

In a panic, they put everything back and raced out of the tiny room. They frantically pushed and shoved the shelf, trying to close it as Doyle got closer and closer. In one last effort, Max pulled on the stone bust once more, and the shelf slid back into place just in time for Doyle to walk into the room.

He stood unmoving in the doorway, his eyes darting between the two of them. "What are you two doing in here?" Doyle demanded.

"Looking for a new book to read." Lula picked up the Victorian history book.

"Really?" Doyle drew out the word, disbelief ringing heavy in his tone. Without waiting for an answer, he turned and left them.

"Where have you been?" Lula asked, following him to the kitchen.

"Nowhere you need to trouble yourself with."

Lula went over to the fridge and pulled out a jug of orange juice. She worked to keep her face calm as her heart pounded in her ears.

Grabbing a glass, she maintained a light tone as she poured herself a drink. "My break isn't over, is it?"

"No," he said, getting a glass and pouring some juice of his own. "Not just yet."

Lula eyed him for a moment. "Really?"

"Really. I feel you have earned this time," he said, sipping his drink and holding her gaze. "Tell me, what have you been up to?"

"Nothing. Listening to music. Reading. Nothing." Lula tripped over her words.

"Keep it that way."

She squirmed under Doyle's intense scrutiny. The way he looked at her, she worried he knew what they were up to. Maybe he even knew about Shea. Her mouth dried up fast, so she took a big drink.

Against her better judgment, she tested the waters. "It feels like you're different lately."

"Different?"

"You know, taking Melvin's soul and giving me this break." She dared to glance up at him and immediately regretted doing so.

His eyes narrowed as he took a step closer. "Things *are* different, Lula. They are about to change. Right now, the most important thing is for you to do what you are told. Which is to stay put and mind your own business. Be a good little girl and enjoy this break. It is a gift that will not last forever." By the time Doyle finished talking, thick smoke coated the kitchen floor.

Lula dared another glance at him before she focused on anything else. Her words shook as she pleaded, "Doyle, will you please be straight with me? What's going on?"

She looked up to find herself all alone. Her heart continued to pound in her chest as she thought about Doyle's words. All she wanted was for things to change, but the way Doyle spoke, things were not about to change for the better. That idea terrified Lula to the point she trembled. The giant clock over her head ticked louder than ever.

Things were different and about to change.

Abandoning her glass on the counter, Lula turned and raced back to her room, desperate to get to the park. Desperate to get to Shea, for what Lula prayed was not the last time.

CHAPTER FOURTEEN

The watch around her wrist read two in the afternoon when Lula got to the park. She had arrived four hours late. Her breath came in short pants as she raced to find Shea. He had to still be here, right? Panic gripped her as she turned circles to see he was nowhere in sight. Kicking a rock, she made her way over to sit on a bench. She cursed under her breath as she plopped down.

To rub salt in the wound, Max appeared, sitting beside her. "Where's Mr. Wonderful?" he asked.

Lula slouched on the bench and glowered at the passing masses. "I missed him."

"Bummer."

She raised her head enough to glare daggers at Max. He cringed away from her, but managed to hold a smug grin. Lula opened her mouth to give him a proper tongue lashing but froze. Her eyes widened in horror as the powerful energy of a Death God slammed into her.

"What is it?" Max asked, picking up on the change in her.

"A Death God," she said, fear locking her where she sat.

"Shit. Where?"

They both looked around for any sign of where the deity could be. Carefully, she reached out with her power, hoping to pinpoint their location. Good news—it wasn't Doyle. Bad news—she couldn't find where they were hiding, so she couldn't find out who it could be. The power felt familiar, but not enough to know who they were.

Throwing caution to the wind, Lula stood and looked around the park once more. Gradually, the power of whatever Death God had visited faded away, and through the small crowd of people, Shea appeared. He walked toward her with a determined stride.

Lula's smile grew wider the closer he got to her. "Shea."

Max turned in Shea's direction, and he scoffed. "I'll leave you to it, then. Don't be too late getting home. I don't want to run interference again."

"Sure, whatever." Lula said under her breath.

Max disappeared just before Shea dodged a family of four out for a walk. Shea didn't stop until he had Lula enveloped in a tight embrace.

"God, Lula," he choked out.

Lula hugged him back, taking her first real breath since getting to the park. "Sorry I'm late. My—"

Shea cut off her words with a searing kiss. He held her tighter, and Lula melted into him. Every worry she had flew away. The hot, demanding kiss cooled to a simmer.

"Are you all right?" he asked.

"I'm fine. Better than fine now. I thought I missed you."

Shea let out a hard laugh. "Close. I almost gave up on you." He released her enough to look her in the eyes. He rubbed up and down her arms before cupping her face. "Are you sure you're okay?"

Lula gave a slight nod. "I know I'm late, but you don't need to worry about me. My dad just needed me to help him out today."

"I just—" He averted his gaze for a moment. "Remember what I told you the night we met?"

"That I was in danger?"

Shea nodded. "I wish I could tell you more, but I have my reasons. I think you *are* in danger, and it kills me every time you leave because I can't protect you."

Lula gaped in disbelief and wrapped her arms tighter around him. Of all the things for him to be worried about, her safety was the last thing that should be keeping him up. A little voice inside her reminded her that by sneaking off to be with him, she was putting *him* in danger.

"Listen..." His words pulled at her attention. "I know what you're going to say, and you're right. You *are* very capable and don't need some dude you barely know protecting you."

"I don't know," Lula admitted. "I kinda like this side of you."

Shea pressed his face into her hair. "I also know that what I'm feeling for you is strong and developed fast. I can't explain it other than when I'm with you, I feel like I found the missing piece of me. It wasn't even a piece that I knew was missing."

"Wow." Lula buried her face into the crook of his neck.

"You probably think I'm nuts. I've just admitted too much, and now you're going to go running from me, screaming into the night."

"Actually, I'm thinking I'm glad I'm not the only one feeling this way."

Shea groaned and kissed the top of her head. "You really are okay?"

The pain in his voice kept Lula from giving him a hard time. Instead, she reached up, placing a soft kiss on his lips. "I promise you, Shea, I'm not the one in danger." Lula mentally kicked herself for revealing too much. "You can trust me, you know. With whatever has you so upset."

Shea let out a huge breath that left him hunched over. He looked defeated. Rubbing a hand over his face, he led Lula over to an area of the park where they were alone. "I can't tell you everything. I'm sorry, Lula, but I just can't. My dad has very strict rules about who learns this information, and for good reason, too."

Lula laced her fingers together and waited patiently for him to confide in her.

Shea couldn't seem to focus on any one thing, like he was searching everywhere for the right words. "I can tell you that my dad and I are working to free people."

"Free people?" she parroted.

"There is a group of people out there who are trapped through no fault of their own. They were tricked into working for these horrible...bosses, we'll call them. My dad and I, with the help of some others, figure out ways to help free them so they don't have to keep living under these evil thumbs."

Lula sat in silence for a moment, trying to process it all. It sounded so much like what happened to Lula, even if that was impossible. There was no way Shea and his dad were tied up in her world with the . Still, what Shea and his dad were doing was so noble. A pang of jealousy hit as she wished they could help her escape too.

"That's awesome, Shea. That's..." Lula cleared her throat.

"There's more. We're looking for someone specific right now. This person apparently has connections that could bring the entire system down. Dad says there's a chance these bosses know who we are and are trying to stop us."

"I won't say anything to anyone. I promise."

"I'm afraid being around you has put you in danger. What I *should* do is stay away from you. The thought of doing that, though, guts me."

Lula took Shea's hands and poured her heart out to him even as it pounded in her chest. "Shea, the idea of never seeing you again devastates me. I promise to keep your secret and to be very careful."

Shea pulled her into another all-encompassing hug. They held each other as the sun dropped further into the sky. Finally, they loosened their hold on each other but refused to let go.

"Tomorrow?" Shea whispered.

"Tomorrow," Lula vowed.

Chapter Fifteen

Lula sat frozen in the seat of her car. After arriving home from the park, the power of a Death God had hit her once more. Someone was waiting inside the house with Doyle, and she didn't know who.

Slowly, she got out of the car and stepped into the house. Voices came from the dining area. Doyle was exchanging heated words with the stranger.

Holding her breath, Lula tiptoed past the deities without being seen. At the top of the stairs, Max stood with wide eyes. He frantically waved her to him. She had made it halfway up when Doyle's voice boomed through the house.

"Lula, my Pet, is that you?"

Squeezing her eyes shut, she cursed under her breath. "Yeah, Doyle, it's me."

"I am so glad you finally made it home. Come join us at the table here. There is someone I want you to meet."

Lula's heart slammed against her ribs. "Okay, let me just put my stuff in my room."

"Hurry up." Doyle's voice was saccharine, overly sweet, still holding an edge of warning.

Lula ran to her room and shut the door. She whirled around to find Max shifting where he stood. Could a ghost sweat? Taking in the sheen on his forehead, Lula wondered.

"It's him," Max squeaked. "The guy."

"Who?" Lula stepped forward. They stood practically on top of each other as Max rubbed up and down his legs.

"He's the same one that came over the night you went to the club to get Rage's soul!" His voice cracked with the effort to keep the volume of his voice down.

"Melvin," Lula corrected automatically.

"What?"

"His name was *Melvin*. Rage was only his nickname."

Max rolled his eyes. "Whoever! I'm telling you that Death God visiting with Doyle now is the same one who showed up that night!"

Lula's heart raced in her chest as she shushed Max's rising voice. "What does he want?"

"I don't know, but they pulled out the book that Poe gave you. The two of them have been poring over it for the last half hour."

"Lula, where are you?" Doyle's voice sounded from just outside the door.

Lula stared wide-eyed at Max. Her breath came in short bursts, and she could hear her heart beating in her ears.

Max mouthed, *I'm right here with you,* before disappearing.

Taking a shaky breath, Lula turned and opened the door. Doyle stood before her. His green eyes blazed as one fire-red brow lifted.

"Sorry." Lula brushed invisible dirt off her skirt.

Doyle turned on his heel and led the way back to the dining room. Standing at the large mahogany table, a deity bent over an open book. His tall frame gave way to long arms with fingers to match. A fine, dark blue, long-sleeved dress shirt matched his dark dress pants. A cashmere coat lay neatly draped over a chair. The wrinkles on his face deepened as he seemed to concentrate harder on the pages of the book. White hair exploded out of the top of his head, and the picture of Albert Einstein sticking out his tongue popped into her mind.

"I think I found the passage, Doyle," the man said, his voice a deep timbre.

Lula pulled the stupidest move ever. She reached out with her powers to get a read on their guest. Power slammed back into her, making her stumble. Worse, she realized she had come across this power before.

Earlier today.

Standing up straight, the deity pinned Lula with a knowing look. He hadn't missed a moment of what she'd done.

Doyle placed a hand on her back and nudged her forward one more step. "Lula, I want you to meet Theodrick. Theodrick, this is my lovely Pet, Lulabelle."

"Lovely indeed. My word, you look like you just stepped out of a Jane Austin novel." Theodrick's dark smile slithered across his face. Lula pulled at her dress to try to hide her nerves. "I heard your master has been rather accommodating and lets you have some time to enjoy yourself."

Lula gripped behind her back. Holding all of Theodrick's attention, she had an overwhelming desire to run and hide. She opened and closed her mouth several times, unable to find her voice.

"Have you?" Doyle asked.

"Have I what?" Lula looked at him like the answer would be written across his forehead. Doyle simply widened his eyes and nodded in Theodrick's direction.

"Yes, girl. Have you enjoyed yourself?" Theodrick elaborated. When Lula still didn't answer, he sighed, slumping a little where he stood. "Good lord, Doyle. Is she dumb?"

"Yes. or I mean, no." Lula stumbled over her words. "No, I'm not dumb. Yes, I have enjoyed myself."

"Good to hear."

"Indeed." Doyle smacked her on the back before walking around to join Theodrick at the table and focused on the book.

Theodrick, however, kept his attention on Lula. "Tell me, have you made any new friends out on your adventures?"

"Of course not, Theodrick. How absurd." Doyle scoffed.

A tremor worked its way down her spine. He had been at the park earlier. She recognized his power, but she was sure that he'd disappeared before Shea had reached her.

"Is that true?" Theodrick asked, making her question again how much he had seen.

"I just hang out with Max," she finally answered.

Where was Max? She could really use his help right about now. She thought he would be right there with her. That's what he'd said.

"That's a shame." Theodrick frowned unconvincingly. He then turned his attention to Doyle and the book before them. "Here,

Doyle, this is the passage I told you about. According to *The Book of Enid*, the prophecy states Sephtis can only rise to power if he has the Statera."

Doyle's brow furrowed. "He must already be looking for it."

"True." Theodrick's sinister smile returned. "If we find it first, we can use it against him. However, Enid is a clever Goddess. Its power must be activated before it is useful. One way is for Sephtis himself to release its power. However, there is a way we can do it ourselves. The only issue is it must be done with a bit of force. That said, when the Statera is under our control, we can use it to secure our place on the throne. Then we will rid ourselves of him for good."

"Who are Enid and Sephtis?" Lula asked before she could stop herself. "What are you guys even talking about?"

Theodrick raised his eyes to Lula, and another shiver worked its way through her.

"They are the Gods responsible for all of our creation." Theodrick explained. "Enid is the Goddess of Life. Every living thing in the universe was brought forth by her hand. Her magic. However, where there is life, there is death. Sephtis, Enid's twin brother, is the God of Death. He was the one originally responsible for guiding souls through the Gate to the Realm of the Dead. However, Sephtis may be a God, but he has become a very irresponsible God, and must be dealt with. So now it is up to us. We are simply taking steps to ensure our continued survival and keep the balance as it is. That's fair of us, don't you think?"

"S-sure," Lula stuttered.

"We may need help to make that happen. If Doyle needed your help, you would help him, right?"

"I mean..." Lula trailed off, feeling like she was walking right into a trap.

"Of course she will help," Doyle answered for her. " She will help us with whatever we need when it comes to locating and activating the Statera. She'll even help us bring Sephtis down. After all, Lula knows what is on the line."

Max appeared next to Doyle, looking wildly around him like he didn't know how he got there.

Doyle placed an arm around Max's shoulder and squeezed. He had called Max into the room, making him appear with his power. Message received. Even if she ran, Doyle could control Max, which meant he controlled her too.

"Of course I'll help Doyle," she said, her wide eyes locked on Max. "Whatever you need."

Doyle turned his attention back to Theodrick. "Are you sure?" Doyle asked.

"Positive. It is time for this war to begin."

Lula wilted under Theodrick's hungry gaze. Whatever they had planned for her left her shivering where she stood.

Chapter Sixteen

"Lula?" Doyle's voice rolled in from down the hall.

Lula pulled the covers so every bit of her lay underneath, trying to go back to sleep. She had been having the most wonderful dream starring Shea. They were together in an open field, lying in the tall grass with the bright afternoon sun beating down on them. He had his arms wrapped tightly around her, and he buried his face in the crook of her neck. She could almost feel the touch of his fingers gliding across her skin.

"Lula?" Doyle's voice called again, much closer this time.

The covers flew off her bed in a flurry of cotton, and her eyes popped open to see him standing over her.

"I need you."

"What do you need me for this time? Another package run?" She groaned, propping herself up on her elbows.

"No. I have decided it is time for you to get back to work. You are off to collect a soul. So get up and in something other than your ratty pajamas."

"Are you sure? I mean, I thought I had more time off to enjoy."

"Nonsense." Doyle wagged a finger and glided over to her closet. "You have had a week off. It is time to get back to work. How about one of your flapper dresses today?"

"Is this because of what your friend said?" she asked, ignoring the question. Theodrick's words had haunted her since he'd left last night.

Doyle walked to the end of the bed with clothes in hand. His eyes narrowed, and a small stream of smoke filled the room. "Your duties have nothing to do with my friend and everything to do with the deal you made with me all those years ago. Now get up and do as you are told."

Lula slid out of bed and walked over to Doyle, taking the maroon dress he handed her. "Who is it?"

"A young girl by the name of Melissa. She is playing hostess to a rather nasty condition that will be her end today," he said, turning his back to her.

"You know, you don't have to be so callous about it."

Doyle raised a fiery-red brow. "You now have a problem with the way I address the soon-to-be deceased?"

"You just don't have to be so *blasé* about the whole thing. I mean, would it kill you to show a little feeling for these people?" She dropped back onto the bed, trying to sort out the wadded ball that was supposed to be an outfit.

"I am sorry, Lula," he droned before turning to face her again. Sitting beside her, he let out a heavy sigh. "Truly, Lulabelle, I am sorry.

I have been doing this for so long, sometimes I do not think I could feel genuine emotion if my very existence depended on it."

"Like you've ever felt genuine emotion before," she scoffed.

"Yes, at one point, I very much did. We all did. So long ago. In the beginning, releasing those souls so they could be free filled us with such joy and wonder." Doyle got a far-off look in his eyes before focusing back on her. "That is why I am so very grateful I have you."

He ran his hand from the top of her head down her back in what Lula was sure was supposed to be a comforting gesture. Instead, it left her cold, her heart racing.

"Me?" Lula's entire face scrunched as she put some distance between the two of them.

"Yes, you silly girl. You are still so human. Sure, I have given you immortality and a few other skills that we deities possess. However, you are still very much the young girl I found weeping in the field that day, brimming with innocence and love. You make me want to feel those things, Lula. Sometimes you make me want..." Doyle pulled his hand away and cleared his throat. "Anyway, please be quick about it. This particular soul is very important, so be careful. I will see you when you have collected her soul. Then I will send her off to the Realm of the Dead."

"You'll send her through the Gate?"

"Yes. I feel perhaps I should make more of an effort around here. Not leave everything up to you. I am turning over a new leaf."

"I'll make it quick," Lula said, not sure what to make of this new leaf of Doyle's.

Thirty minutes later, Lula drove near the park on her way to find Melissa. She tried not to think about Shea or how much she wanted to see if he was there right now. Instead, she focused on the road ahead of her and the wind blowing through the open window, cooling her overheated face. Doyle's words echoed in her mind and soured her stomach. Moments like those reminded her of how she'd been tricked into her sentence in the first place. Doyle's warm words and caring eyes had fooled her. Armed with an overwhelming charm, he had easily manipulated Lula into this strong-arm relationship that she hadn't realized she'd agreed to until it was too late.

Lula drove through the grand entrance of the quaint neighborhood in Happy Valley. She didn't stop until she reached the front of the red, ranch-style home with a huge evergreen tree in the front yard. She looked around to see the well-manicured yards lined up in perfect rows. Lula was smack dab in the middle of suburbia. All that was missing was the peppy theme music.

Reaching out with her powers, Lula prayed Melissa was all alone. When she only sensed the presence of the Marked soul, she turned the doorknob, finding it unlocked. Opening the door slowly, she peered inside to find the place sparsely decorated. She tapped, but only deafening silence greeted her. If it wasn't for the pull of the Marked, Lula might have thought no one was home at all.

She slipped inside and looked around. Only a couch and coffee table sat in the living room. There were no pictures on the walls. The tiny kitchen had nothing on the counters except a blue glass chicken. With no sign of Melissa, Lula moved toward the hallway. The first bedroom contained only a few boxes. The second was the tiniest room Lula had ever seen. A small wooden desk with a chair sat beneath a small window. A box sat on top, overflowing with books, paper, and a picture frame. The glass caught the early morning sunlight pouring in through the window, which gave a clear view of the front yard. The third bedroom, at the end of the hall, had to be the biggest of the three. Two tall, antique dressers flanked a full-sized bed. A big, fluffy, white comforter covered the girl she had come for.

Melissa couldn't have been older than her early twenties. Long, blonde hair framed creamy skin with her ruby-red lips parted as she slept. Light lashes lay against her cheeks. Every so often, Lula heard the soft sound of a snore mixed with low, even breathing. The girl reminded Lula of *Sleeping Beauty*. That wasn't what made Lula stop dead in her tracks, though.

The aura of the soon-to-be departed radiated off Melissa. The blue light danced around her, swirling and calling out. However, the longer she stood there, the tighter Lula's brows pulled together as she watched the sleeping girl. Deep green and tiny sparks she couldn't quite make out mixed with the blue in a way she had never seen before. She focused as hard as she could to pull out these hidden colors. Fear crawled up Lula's spine as flashes of red sharpened and sparked at the edges of the blue. Doyle had lied. No affliction was ready to end Melissa's life. She was young and, more importantly, healthy. There was only one reason red would be mixed with the blue of her soul.

Murder.

Poor Melissa wasn't the first person Lula had had to take because of murder, but this was the first time she'd beat the killer to the scene. She used her power to get a read on who this girl was, but for the first time, it was like her powers were blocked. Either that or this girl had no life outside this room, which made no sense. Lula's breath quickened as she strained to figure out what to do. She needed to get out of there before the killer showed up. No way she could stomach being there when it took place and watching Melissa die. That would destroy yet another piece of her.

The sound of the front door closing yanked Lula from her thoughts. The killer had to be in the house now.

Looking around for anywhere to hide, Lula darted into the closet, burying herself among the clothes.

Footsteps pounded down the hall in time to Lula's heartbeat, followed by a hard knock at the bedroom door.

"Melissa?" a gruff voice called. "Melissa, wake up."

Melissa groaned. "What is—What are you doing here?"

"You're okay?" the man asked, panic making his voice rise.

"I'm fine, just tired. What time is it?"

The sound of the mattress squeaking followed the sounds of rustling sheets.

"It's just after nine in the morning. I called but you didn't answer." The man's words poured out of him in a rush.

"I'm sorry I slept so late. What's going on? Why are you even here?"

"You've been Marked."

"Marked?" Melissa's voice rose sharply. "Why? When?"

It was beginning to look less and less like this man was the killer. But if that was the case, who the hell was he? And how could he know about the Mark on Melissa's soul? That was impossible. Right?

Lula felt dizzy as questions circled in her mind. She listened to their retreating footsteps down the hall before slipping out of the closet.

She caught the sound of the man's voice saying, "I don't know. The best I can guess is because of who we are. I think they want to make an example of you."

"Me?" Melissa's voice cracked.

Lula peeked down the hall to find them standing in the living room. The man stood with his back to Lula, and she could barely make him out. Short, dirty-blond hair covered his head. Wide shoulders heaved with every breath as he stood stiffly, blocking her view of Melissa.

"We're at war, Melissa. All the rules go out the window." His words were clipped. "Don't worry, though, that's why I'm here. I came as soon as I heard."

"I just don't understand why this is happening. Do you think it's because we were given the chance to escape?"

Lula leaned forward even more, straining to hear.

He laughed harshly. "Yes, and we're going to fight them. We won't stop until we restore the balance, just like Shea says."

"Does everyone know what's going on?" Melissa's voice shook.

"Yeah, and I've been told that we've found a secret weapon, so to speak. Some great leverage in the upcoming battle. A girl."

Lula leaned against the wall, dumbfounded. They were at war? *Shea* had told them they were at war? And they wouldn't stop until they restored the balance? What on earth was he talking about? The familiar ring had her recoiling. No, there was no way that these two suburbanites had anything to do with her world. They had to be talking about something else. Lula didn't even want to think about what this leverage could be. Whoever the poor girl was, Lula felt sorry for her.

Though Lula knew her job, it appeared the girl wouldn't be dying any time soon. Obviously, Doyle had made a mistake about more than the cause of death. The only thing she could do was get the hell out of there now and go back to talk to him.

As quietly as she could, Lula tiptoed from the back bedroom to the tiny room with the desk. Sliding the window open, she began climbing on the desk so she could make a quick getaway when she knocked the box onto the floor and ruining her chances of a quiet escape. The contents crashed and scattered.

Crap!

Dropping a piano would have made less noise.

"Hey!"

Lula snapped up to see the man looming in the doorway. Without a second thought, she darted out the window, almost falling flat on her face. Running with all her might, she made it to her car. The sound of yelling followed close behind her until she peeled off down the street.

Lula's heart pounded as she struggled to gain her composure. Weaving around slower traffic, she started to process everything she had overheard. Each thing he'd said sent her into a tailspin of questions and fears. The fact that everyone seemed to talk about an impending war did nothing to calm her nerves. Who the hell was Melissa? Why had Doyle sent Lula *before* she was murdered? And for the love of all that was holy, please someone tell her that the Shea they mentioned wasn't *her* Shea? Knowing her luck, they were one and the same.

Lula's stomach twisted into knots the closer she got to home.

Chapter Seventeen

What. The. Hell?

Those words echoed over and over like some kind of sick mantra. She drove without seeing where she was going. Her only goal at the moment was to get as far away from that house as she could. Nerves gnawed in the pit of her stomach. Everything about what had just happened sent her heart racing into dangerous territory.

"How did it go?" Max asked, appearing beside her.

Lula's scream filled the car as she swerved hard to the side, only barely missing a head-on collision and just making it into a parking lot. She slammed on the brakes and took a moment to catch her breath before shifting her frenzied gaze to Max, who looked pale, even for a ghost.

"Jesus, Lula." Max sat smashed against the car door. "What the hell is wrong with you?"

She sucked in large gulps of air, trying to regain control of herself. How did she even put into words everything that had gone wrong?

Max looked her over once more before he frowned. "You didn't get the soul."

The world around Lula swam as she pinned him with sorrowful eyes. "I couldn't do it."

"What do you mean you couldn't do it? You have never had any problems before." Max studied her. The glare she gave him had him backtracking. "I mean in the sense of you physically not being able to take it. I know emotionally it messes with you."

Lula swallowed hard and forced the words out as the scene replayed through her mind. "I couldn't...and then this guy showed up and chased me."

Max's eyes bugged out. "Someone chased you?"

"Max, she was supposed to be murdered. Not die from some disease, but murdered! Then this guy showed up, and I thought it was him, the guy that was supposed to kill her..." The words spilled out of her mouth like water through a broken dam. "I don't know who they were, but then they started talking about how she was Marked, like they knew what that meant. How could they know? Then he brought up the fact that they were at war, so of course she would be a target. I got so scared and confused. I tried to sneak out, but the guy found me and chased after me. I had to just get out of there."

"Oh my God, Lula." Max pulled her into his arms, and for the first time in a long time, she went willingly.

That wasn't even the craziest part—not that she could say those words out loud. How the hell did they know Shea? If they were even talking about the same Shea, *her* Shea. The stab in the pit of her stomach had her doubting it could be anyone else. Pieces of a crazy puzzle she'd been shown were fitting together too neatly.

Max tightened his grip on her. "What are you going to do about Doyle?"

Great question, one that needed a really good answer. It would be a monumental understatement to say that Doyle wouldn't be happy. Lula didn't know how to handle any of this. She focused on the crowd outside the car. Only at that moment did she realize that she had stopped close to a park.

A couple walked by, hand in hand, a scene that punched Lula right in the gut. The couple strolled over to one of the park benches. Sitting down, the woman curled into the man as they sat, holding each other. A torrent of emotions whirled in her chest. The scene filled her with a desire to find Shea that was so strong it left her trembling. Lula needed to get a grip, and now. In a hurry to start the engine again, she pulled away from Max.

"What is it?" Max asked.

"We need to get home." Lula pulled out of the parking space faster than she should have.

Max watched her, worry drawn on his face. "Hey, Lula, if you—"

"Leave it alone, Max!"

Max recoiled a bit but remained silent the rest of the way home. It gave Lula more time to come up with how to tell Doyle why she didn't take the soul he'd sent her for.

They had no sooner pulled into the garage when Doyle appeared. Locking eyes, she released the steering wheel as she wracked her brain to come up with some way to tell him what happened. She took a deep breath before getting out of the car. She could feel Doyle behind her as she made her way into the house, causing the hairs on her neck to stand on end. His deep growl stopped her, frozen in her tracks.

"You did not collect the soul."

On a positive note, that saves me from having to tell him, she thought to herself.

Spinning around to face him, all the blood drained from her body. Never in her entire existence had she seen such a look of pure rage on his face, darkening every feature. Doyle, in that moment, radiated evil.

"Why did you not take the soul I sent you to collect?" He prowled toward her.

With every step he took, she took a step back.

"I told you how important your task was to complete. Why did you not do what you were told?"

"You don't understand, Doyle." Her voice rose as fear tightened around her throat. "There's a very good reason I don't have it."

Doyle took another step toward her. "Enlighten me."

"When I got there, she was Marked for not just death like you told me, but murder."

"So what? You have taken murdered souls before." He continued his pursuit.

"She wasn't dead yet, Doyle, but I could see that you were wrong when you told me how she was going to die. Which I would like to know—"

A wave of power hit her, shutting that line of interrogation down quickly.

Swallowing hard, Lula pushed on. "And then this guy showed up, and I thought he was the one who was supposed to kill her, but he wasn't. He was there to check on her. I didn't know what to do. And then he found me and came after me. I freaked out, Doyle. I mean, I was terrified out of my mind. The only thing I could think about was getting out before he did something to *me*." Her rambling petered out.

Doyle's face softened. "Shhh, do not fret." He gathered her into his arms, running comforting circles on her back. "Everything will turn out as it should, Lulabelle. You will simply go again."

"I can't do it," she whispered. "Please don't make me. Not this one. Please."

"Lula, my dear sweet Lula, you do not have a choice." His warm voice ran like ice in her veins.

"Doyle," she choked out.

"Lula, I have a job to do. And because I have a job, that means *you* have a job to do, no exceptions. That was the deal. You know that."

Lula's whole body trembled as she released a sob. Doyle held her while she cried. A big part of her screamed out, demanding answers to all those questions still circling. Deep down, though, she realized how dangerous it would be to tell Doyle all the details of what happened. How would she even begin to bring up the fact that the man knew about Melissa being Marked? Her mouth went dry.

Pulling away, she started toward her room, her sanctuary.

"Where are you going, my dear?" Doyle's words were soft, but the grip on her arm tightened.

"I'm going to my room."

Doyle frowned. "You are going to get that soul. Right now."

"But she hasn't been murdered yet. What about the killer?"

"Oh, Lula." His head lolled back as if asking for help from above. Meeting her eyes again, he said, "I am so sorry to tell you like this, I should have told you sooner but.... *You* are the killer."

Bile rose in her throat. "What?"

"You must go and kill this girl and collect the soul. Everything depends on it."

She heard his words but still did not understand. "I can't kill someone."

"Yes, you can. You simply take their soul. They cannot live without their soul."

He explained it like he'd asked nothing more than to bring him a glass of juice. She didn't understand any of it. She couldn't.

"But why would you ask me to kill someone? Why?"

He clenched his jaw. "It is not just *someone*."

Sorrow melted into pure despair. Lula was not a killer. She took only the souls of those already doomed. Even then, they were able to live on in the Realm of the Dead. "But why do *I* have to kill her?"

Doyle's eyes narrowed to slits. "You do not get to ask questions."

"Then I'm not going to get her soul."

"You will." Doyle's voice dropped low as his hand slid up her arm and around the back of her neck before squeezing. His eyes lit with something more ominous than Lula had ever seen before. "Or you will pay dearly in a way you never thought possible. I promise you."

Lula stared at Doyle in disbelief. Pain erupted at the base of her skull before shooting down her spine. A small cry escaped her as he forced her on her knees, and he loomed over her.

"Am I making myself clear?"

For the first time in the many hundreds of years since this nightmare began, he threatened more than just seclusion. From the look in his eyes, he would make good on his words if she didn't obey.

Swallowing hard, she forced out, "Yes."

He let her go, and she collapsed to the floor.

"Good girl."

***

Lula lost all feeling on her way back to find Melissa. She sat out-side herself, watching everything take place. Following the call of the Marked, she found Melissa at the same house where she'd left her. Reaching out with her powers, confirmed Melissa was alone once more. There was no attempt this time to be quiet or to hide.

Melissa sat at her little kitchen table, drinking tea and reading a book. What an innocent thing for this girl to be doing.

Lula marched up to the girl, watching with unseeing eyes as Melissa looked up from the book before jumping out of her chair.

"Who are you?" she asked, scrambling back and putting the table between them. "Did they send you to come get me?"

"I'm here because it's time for you to die," Lula heard herself say.

"No, please, wait!" Melissa threw up her arms, trying to protect herself. She stopped and squinted at Lula for a moment before waving wildly. "Oh my God, you're like us. You're—"

Lula cut off whatever Melissa was about to say with a hand to the chest. She heard but did not listen as Melissa begged for mercy. Lula watched herself pull at Melissa's soul, like watching made it less real.

A wave of energy washed over her after the soul ripped free, taking her breath away. The world around her blurred into a rainbow of colors before coming into focus once more.

The light in Melissa's eyes died, and she fell to the floor.

Lula studied the soul dancing in her hand. Warmth radiated up her arm before finding its way to her chest. The soul shrank as the warmth in her chest bloomed. Lula pushed at it, rejecting the warmth. She didn't deserve it. The positive, clean energy made Lula feel dirty, but the energy continued to grow until the soul shrank so small it disappeared. Lula's heart pounded in her chest as her eyes stayed glued to where the soul once burned brightly.

Doyle appeared at her side.

Tears filled her eyes as she presented her empty hands to him. "I don't understand."

Doyle placed a hand on hers and offered a weak smile. "It looks as though Theodrick was correct."

Lula looked around the tiny kitchen where they stood. Melissa lay crumpled, dead, on the floor next to the small table with her mug of hot tea and book.

"What the hell was he right about, Doyle? What the hell did any of this prove?"

"Take your time coming home, my Pet. I feel you have earned whatever it is you choose to do with your last night of freedom. I will see you when you get home."

Doyle took a step back and disappeared.

Wrapping her arms around herself, Lula dropped to her knees and cried out. Her agonized cry broke the heavy silence left in the house. She screamed herself hoarse as she shattered into a million pieces. Finally, picking herself up on shaking legs, she ran to her car and drove.

Max sat in the passenger seat beside her but remained silent, only reaching out to hold her hand. Not that Lula could feel it. She couldn't feel anything anymore. After all, the dead can't feel, and that was what she had become.

Chapter Eighteen

The setting sun painted the park in a deep hue of rich colors. Lula did not know what time it was as she parked the car and stared at the fountain. The place sat empty. Abandoned. Much like her soul. After the morning's events, Lula had driven aimlessly around the city, too afraid to stop for fear she would fall apart. Everything that made her human had dissolved into nothing. She was empty. She should have been stronger. She should have stood up to Doyle more, not that it would have made any difference. However, the fact it happened at all continued to eat away at her. So she drove and drove until, since all roads led back to the park, she found herself watching the few people left wander the paths.

Max sat next to her, unmoving. She could feel him watching her. The sensation made her skin crawl.

"Go away, Max," she said, never taking her eyes off the fountain.

"Lula—"

"Go. Away."

Max remained motionless only a moment longer before releasing a heavy sigh. "I won't be far away," he told her before disappearing.

Lula had no doubt he meant it. While hearing him say that should have given her a certain amount of comfort, all it did was make her even angrier.

Anger—that was the only thing she could muster when she experienced anything at all. She was angry at Max for leading her on all those years ago. She was angry at herself for falling, not just for Max's lines, but Doyle's promises as well. The mere thought of Doyle's name stoked a rage in her that made her skin hot and her whole body tremble. He made her *kill*. He made her *take* a life before it was time. Only when her thoughts found their way to Shea did the pounding in her ebb, melting to pure sorrow. Her time was up. The clock bells had at last chimed, marking the end of her respite. She hoped to see Shea one more time. Maybe it wouldn't hurt so much if she got to say goodbye.

Getting out of her car, she began walking toward the fountain. The setting sun brought cooler temperatures, raising goosebumps along her arms. She allowed Doyle only a passing thought. He had promised to leave her alone and let her take the rest of the day to do what she pleased. One last night of freedom, he had called it. *At least I have tonight,* she thought, rubbing her arms to relieve the cold building inside her. Reaching the fountain, she glanced around her every so often, hoping to find Shea here. Longing for the chance to see him and say her goodbye. He would be long gone by now. Did he think she'd abandoned him?

God, what had she become? Lula's stomach roiled. Every time she closed her eyes, Melissa's face appeared. She wished she knew why

Melissa, of all people, had become Marked. Why on earth had Doyle made her kill Melissa?

Lula hugged herself and picked up the pace as the weight of the day settled over her like a moldy, wet blanket.

Just ahead, a figure appeared, walking straight toward her. She stopped, and the figure did the same. Taking one more big step forward, his dark hair and sweet face came into focus.

Shea.

Lula stood there for half a heartbeat before bolting toward him. Shea's pace quickened as relief painted his features.

"Lula," he said and pulled her into a tender embrace. "You're here. God, I was getting so worried. I've been waiting for you all day."

"Sorry, my dad—" Lula buried her face in his chest and focused on the feel of his arms around her, begging time to stop.

Shea held her tighter and kissed the top of her head. "I know you said it might get harder for you to come, but...I just didn't want to believe it. I've been here all day."

"I'm glad you stayed. I hoped you would be here." She smiled, swallowing hard past the lump in her throat. "I'm so glad I found you." Holding him tighter, Lula took a deep breath in, rejuvenating her and giving a spark of life back to her damaged soul.

"I am too." He pulled back a little. "Are you okay? You look like you've had a rough day."

"I am now."

She watched him search her face. "Are you sure? You look like something's on your mind."

"The only thing on my mind is how glad I am we're together."

A bright smile broke out across Shea's face, and he leaned his forehead against hers. Lula held on tight to him, never wanting to let go.

The sun dropped further, turning the sky a beautiful shade of red and orange.

Shea glanced around them before smiling back down at Lula. "What do you say we go somewhere more private?"

"More private, huh?" Lula raised an eyebrow. "Do you have anywhere specific in mind?"

"Come on," he said, tugging her along. "You're coming with me."

Yes, she thought, *take me away. Far away.*

They followed the trail to the opposite end of the park. Under a street lamp sat a beautiful red Mustang. The classic car made her Plymouth look like an even bigger piece of junk. They climbed in without another word. Shea turned the key, and the engine roared to life. Lula could feel another tiny piece of her soul spark back to life. Throwing the car into gear, he peeled out of the parking spot and down the street.

"Where are we going?" Lula asked.

She didn't care, as long as it was far away from everything she knew. A hysterical giggle slipped out of her and she smiled so big that her cheeks hurt as they made their escape.

"I thought we could go someplace special," Shea said.

She sent up a silent prayer: *Please let it be a place where the dead and deities can't find me.* "I can't wait to see it."

They drove into the sunset with both windows down. Lula's hair whipped around her in a mad dance. She stuck her hand out the window, letting the wind slide over her outstretched fingers. She leaned back against the seat, and her eyes fell closed. Never had she tasted such sweet freedom.

"What are you thinking about now?"

Lula looked over to see Shea stealing glances at her. "I'm thinking that I love the idea of running away with you."

She cursed herself as soon as the words left her mouth. The words were true, but she worried about what Shea would think. Especially now when she had to say goodbye.

To her relief, Shea's grin spread into a full smile. "You know what? I am loving the fact that you're running away with me as well." In a move that melted her racing heart, he reached over and took her hand, lacing their fingers together.

Lula ducked to hide the blush she was sure now painted her hot cheeks. Biting her lip, she stole glances at Shea, feeling her heart pound in her chest. Each beat breathed life back into her soul.

The last of the sun's rays had slipped beyond the horizon when the car slowed. Shea turned past a gate and drove down a dirt road. It stretched out before them, surrounded by open fields. Only the occasional tree broke the clear view of the mountains in the distance. They followed the road until a quaint house came into view. The two-story farmhouse, complete with shutters and a wraparound porch, stood just in front of a tall barn.

"Where are we?" she asked, eyeing the place in awe.

"I live here." He pointed toward the house while parking the car.

"You do?" Lula had a hard time picturing Shea living here, though she couldn't explain why.

"I have all my life."

"It's nice." She grinned, not sure what else to say.

Shea laughed and ran a hand through his hair. A wave of desire washed over Lula, and she wanted nothing more than to run her own fingers through the thick strands.

"It's something. To be honest, country life is not really for me. But I stick around to help my dad out. He's getting up there and could use a hand. Not that you would ever hear him admit he needs help."

"That's nice of you." She swallowed past the lump that formed in her throat as she indulged in memories of her own parents, her real parents.

"I can't imagine you having issues with your parents. I'm sure your dad doesn't fight you tooth and nail for helping."

"No, my father is...he's a bit different."

In truth, it sounded like her actual father had been very much like Shea's. Her father would never admit that he needed help and would always do more than his fair share. The difference seemed to be that her father had expected everyone to pull their weight as well, having no patience for laziness.

"Come on." Shea opened his door and shot her a sly smile. "Let's go inside and get something to eat. I'm starving."

Inside, the house was just as quaint as the outside. It screamed old farmhouse, from the floral-wallpapered walls to the plaid fabric on the furniture. Even the kitchen table looked straight out of a 1940s magazine. The newest things in the house were the appliances in the kitchen, still framed by bright yellow walls with old white cabinets. The door next to the refrigerator led down to the basement, which she was sure housed a boiler that kept the house warm in the cold winter months.

Shea pulled out a large platter filled with slices of turkey from the refrigerator. Lula's mouth watered as he placed a glass dish filled with tuna-noodle casserole in the oven on a low heat.

"Better than a microwave," he said with a wink.

They ate together in a comfortable silence. The whole time, Lula kept worrying Max—or worse, Doyle—would make a sudden appearance. Max would be hard to explain to Shea, so it was a good thing she didn't have to worry about Shea actually seeing him. She just knew he would try to distract her. Doyle showing up would be the end. He would go insane if he saw her here with Shea. Her stomach soured, realizing the danger she had put Shea in, yet again, by being here.

"Is something bothering you?" Shea asked, pulling her from her spiraling thoughts.

"What?" She could barely meet his eyes. "No. I'm fine. Sure. This is great."

He raised a doubtful brow.

"I guess I'm a little nervous." She brushed her hair behind her ear.

Shea took a big drink of his water, a wicked glint shining in his eye. "What are you nervous for?"

Unable to tell him why she was sweating bullets, Lula told him something both believable and true. "It's been a while since I've had dinner with a guy."

"You're kidding me? I figured you would be out with guys all the time."

Lula's cheeks burned. "Yeah, well, thanks for the compliment, but no."

"So which is it? Ex-boyfriend broke your heart, and you don't trust guys anymore, or your parents are too strict and don't let you out of the house?"

"Both, actually." Lula poked at her casserole. "My last boyfriend was... I mean, he wasn't a bad person, and I think he cared about me on some level, but..." She vividly remembered the day she'd learned the truth, the day she'd met the girl Max had been in love with. The memory left a bitter taste in her mouth. "He just didn't love me. Not really. In fact, he was in love with someone else."

"I'm sorry, Lula." Shea looked like he wanted to say more but clenched his jaw instead.

Lula sipped her water, washing down the memories. She didn't want to think of all the betrayals she had been through in her life. She just wanted to enjoy the moment.

"Well, I feel better." Shea pushed his plate away and leaned back in his chair, eyeing Lula. "Are you about done?"

"Why?" She put her fork down, feeling a fresh wave of nervous energy pulse through her.

"Do you like animals?"

"I love animals."

An ornery grin broke out across Shea's face. "Then come with me."

Chapter Nineteen

Shea took Lula's hand and led her out the back door. The cool night air raised goosebumps along her arms. There was not a cloud in the sky. Away from the city, one could see a blanket of stars above them. Lula almost tripped, trying to see them all.

Shea reached out and caught her before she fell to the ground. "Careful there," he breathed in her ear.

"Sorry, I just haven't seen stars like that in a while. They're so beautiful."

Looking deep into her eyes, he sighed. "There's a lot of beauty out tonight."

They made their way to the barn, where Shea stopped and brought a finger to his lips before opening the big wooden door. A musty smell mixed with hay and animals hit Lula before she even stepped inside. Four horse stalls lined either side of the giant building. She could hear heavy breathing inside each of them. Beyond the stalls, the barn opened to a wider area with a tire swing and a pile of hay. Above each stall, a sign had a name carved in the wood. One by one, she read them all: Champ, Flower, Spirit. The last stall on the right gave her pause.

"Rigatoni?" She eyed Shea over her shoulder.

Shea meandered over to stand next to her. "We got him at a year old. He's my favorite."

From the shadows, the horse appeared. His long, white mane fell off to the side but still covered his eye. A thick red coat covered the rest of his body, giving off a shine in the light.

Lula reached her hand up slowly, giving the animal time to object before stroking the side of his neck. "Why Rigatoni?" she asked, keeping her focus on the beautiful creature before her.

"He's Italian," Shea answered with a shrug. "So I gave him an Italian name."

"You poor thing," Lula whispered to the horse, then laughed when Shea elbowed her. "Is he your only Bardigiano, or do you have other Italian breeds?" She watched with satisfaction as Shea's mouth dropped open.

"No one has ever guessed what breed he is. How did you know?"

"I named my Bardigiano Aurora. She was the most beautiful horse you've ever seen. All the heads turned when I rode her through town." Aurora had been a gift from her father. Thoughts of home and the horse she loved so much sat heavy on her heart, but tonight's company made it easier to push on. Tonight needed to be the night she relived the happy times in her life. The times she'd had before she, in all the ways that counted, had died. "Papa told me, 'Lulabelle, I am giving this horse to you. If you treat her well, she will treat you well in return.' Papa always gave good advice like that."

Shea's brow pulled together tight as he looked down. The corner of his mouth twitched like he was holding back a smile. "So, where are you from, Lulabelle?"

Lula smiled through the pain forming in her chest. "I was born and raised in a city in eastern England called Attleborough. I know I told you my father was a shepherd, raising a small flock of sheep. Mama was talented with a loom and spent hours turning wool into yarn. My sister would help Mama out. I did help them when I could, but I enjoyed helping Papa and my brother the most. You know how I love spending all day outside. Back home in the meadows was no different." She looked over to see Shea watching her with the softest eyes. "I'm sorry. I started rambling a bit, didn't I?"

"Don't be sorry. I enjoyed hearing your story. In fact, I want to hear more." He took her hand and led her over to the tire swing.

"I like the tire swing." Lula grabbed the rope above the tire.

"Thanks. My grandpa put it up for me. I used to swing on it all the time when I was a kid."

"Looks like fun."

"Well, hop on."

Shea helped her onto the swing, and she was careful to tuck her skirt beneath her legs so it would stay in place. Lula couldn't hold in her laughter. Holding on tight to the rope, she leaned back and twirled on the swing.

"So, tell me about your family? Did you grow up here?" she asked as Shea watched her.

"Pretty much. My great-great grandparents bought this land to raise horses on. It's a generational thing. Most of the horses are race-horses, but we bred some horses for work. Lately, though, we just rent out the stalls. My dad just wasn't as interested in breeding as my grandpa was. To be honest, if it wasn't for my Uncle Michael, I think my dad would sell this place."

He gave her a push, sending her soaring through the barn. She held on tight, catching glimpses of him through her long hair. Every time she swung back Shea's way, his hand touched her back, sending warmth rushing through her. Feeling as carefree as her days at home on the farm, Lula let her head fall back as she flew through the air. A laugh bubbled up inside her, and for once, there was no reason to fight it.

She hadn't realized Shea had stopped pushing her until she slowed enough for him to grab her arm, bringing her to a stop. Their eyes locked, and Lula's heart sped up. Wrapping his arms around her waist, Shea helped Lula out, never letting her go. She held him close, keeping her arms tight around his neck. His dark eyes held hers, seemed to overflow with equal parts unnamed emotion and hidden secrets. He lowered her, sliding her down his body. All too soon, her feet touched the floor. To her utter delight, though, his arms stayed wrapped around her.

Goosebumps broke out over her body as his breathing kicked up. She could feel the sharp rise and fall of his chest as his eyes consumed her. Every cell in her body called out to him, begging him to bring her back to life. Make her whole again.

"Lula," he breathed as he leaned in.

His lips pressed against hers. A gasp escaped her, and he deepened the kiss. Fire swept over her, breathing life back into her soul. Never had she been more lost in someone, yet at home in the arms surrounding her.

"Shea?" a deep voice called out, interrupting the moment.

Shea broke the kiss and stepped away to reveal a dark figure at the barn door. All the warmth drained away, leaving Lula cold. A man made his way inside. He was tall like Shea, but his shaggy, dark hair, peppered with gray, reached his chin, and deep wrinkles framed his eyes, giving away his older age.

"Hey, what's going on?" Shea shifted from one foot to the other.

"I should ask you the same thing," the man said. He took another step forward, his gaze finding Lula. He stopped, frozen, as his mouth opened and closed a few times.

She bit her lip and resisted the urge to hide. She picked invisible lint off her sleeve and worked to smooth and straighten her skirt, unable to stay still under his intense scrutiny.

He gave his head a little shake before looking Lula up and down once more. "What is she doing here?" he asked, almost stumbling over his words.

"I invited her over to hang out," Shea said, sounding defensive. "This is Lula."

Lula gave him a timid wave, wiggling her fingers. "Hi."

"Lula, this is my dad, Devin," Shea introduced his father.

Lula cringed, realizing what Devin had walked in on. *Great first impression,* she thought.

When Devin didn't even blink, Shea stepped in front of Lula. "What do you need, Dad?"

It seemed to take Shea's father another minute before he found his words and focused on Shea. "We need to talk. Something's happened."

"Sure, just give me some time," Shea said.

Devin's eyes darted to Lula. "We don't have a lot of time, Shea."

Lula rocked back on her heels before clearing her throat. "It sounds like I should go home."

"No, not yet," Shea snapped.

"Shea, my dad will be furious if I'm out too late."

"Lula, wait here for a moment? Let me talk to my dad."

"Shea—" Lula started, but before she could say anything more, Shea dragged his dad outside the barn.

Lula let out a groan and wandered back over to be with the horses. This was turning into a mess. She had just decided she'd demand Shea take her home when she heard arguing right outside the barn. What the two were discussing was private.

Stopping in front of Rigatoni's stall, she bit her lip. She should mind her own business, but curiosity got the better of her. She used her powers to listen more carefully. Reaching out, she began petting the horse while concentrating, focusing all her energy on the men outside.

Lula gasped when their voices came into sharp focus.

"Shea, I don't know that you want your friend around for this conversation." Devin sighed as they came to a stop.

"Dad, she's the one I told you about."

"I figured as much."

She couldn't help but marvel a bit. She had never been able to pull voices in so clearly before. It was like they were standing right next to her.

"She needs to stay here with us. So we can protect her."

"Listen, something happened today. Melissa was killed."

Lula gasped.

"What?"

"They took her soul, Shea."

Lula's eyes popped as her hand faltered while petting the horse's mane. How could she have forgotten about what she'd heard at Melissa's house? They knew each other. The Shea they had spoken of *was* her Shea. And Lula had gone and taken Melissa away.

"I don't understand."

"Thomas called and said he went to check on her earlier today because he found out she had been Marked. He left a little while later when he found some girl hiding in the house. He chased her but somehow lost her. By the time he made it back, Melissa was dead. They killed her, Shea." Venom coated every word.

"Trying to send a message?" Shea growled.

They? Lula's breath caught in her throat as her stomach dropped. She hadn't killed Melissa to send a message. She hadn't even wanted to kill her.

"I think it might be something else, but I need to verify."

Hadn't Thomas also mentioned something about a group they were fighting? He had known Melissa was Marked for death, even though Lula thought that would be impossible. Doyle had expressed how important Melissa's soul was. Did Doyle have her kill Melissa to send them a message? Was Theodrick involved somehow? Were they the ones fighting the Death Gods?

"This is all the more reason Lula needs to stay with us." Shea's voice rose enough that Lula no longer needed her powers to hear.

"Shea, where did you meet that girl?"

"Why does it matter?"

"Just answer me."

Shea took a deep breath. "I met her at the club. The night Rage died."

Devin's voice sharpened. "*Lula* is the girl you met that night?"

"Yeah, is there a problem?"

"No, I just...I didn't expect you to meet so soon. Meet someone so soon."

Shea let out an uncomfortable laugh. "I'm nineteen, Dad. I think I'm old enough to meet girls."

Lula couldn't take it anymore. Self-loathing sat heavily on her chest, making it hard to breathe.

Approaching footsteps pulled her from her thoughts. She strived to hold it together so she could face him again. Her fingers trembled as she continued to pet Rigatoni.

Shea reached her side and gave Rigatoni a pat before grabbing her hand. Devin stood with his arms crossed, eyeing her intently.

Shea started talking before she could even take a breath. "Lula, we want you to stay with us."

"I can't stay, Shea." Lula attempted to get through to him. "For so many reasons."

"You have to," he insisted. "Things are getting dangerous now."

"Even more than they were before?"

"Shea feels that you would be safer if you stayed with us. I don't disagree, but I don't know your situation yet either," Devin chimed in.

Doyle and Theodrick flashed into her mind. Doyle held all the cards with her, and Max would suffer first for her insubordination. Then he would turn his sights on Shea.

Lula's eyes darted all over the barn as she searched for the right words. "My situation is... my dad would never allow it. He's very strict, and it's just better for everyone if I go home. Now."

"Who's your dad?" Devin asked, tilting his head to the side. His sharp eyes never left her.

"His name is Doyle?" Her answer sounded more like a question, but the inquiry had thrown her off.

Devin's eyes widened as his jaw locked. A harsh laugh left him. Shaking his head, he turned to leave the barn. "Shea, take her home."

"But—"

"Trust me, son. Take her home."

***

Tension sat thick the whole car ride back to the park. Neither of them spoke a word, and Lula figured she would drown in her guilt. Shea was upset, and it was all her fault. More than upset, he seemed to be defeated. She could see it in the set of his shoulders and the blank stare that never left the road. When he parked beside her Fury, she bolted from the car.

"Lula," Shea called, following behind her.

"Thank you for a lovely evening." The sentiment sounded so generic.

"Lula, I am so sorry." He ran another hand through his hair.

"What did your dad talk to you about?"

Shea swallowed hard before answering. "Someone I know. She died today."

"Who was she?" Lula asked before she could stop herself.

"Melissa is—was—a girl that was special." He kept his eyes down as he spoke, never meeting Lula's.

"Was she like your girlfriend or something?" She tried to shake the tiny green monster that had no business showing up at a time like this.

"No." Shea laughed without humor. "She was a friend. Dad and I just rescued her. She and her brother. They were some of the people I was telling you about earlier."

Lula nodded, remembering what he'd told her about rescuing people from horrible "bosses."

"We were going to take them somewhere safe."

"I am so sorry, Shea." Tears burned in her eyes, begging to fall. "I wish I could somehow make it better."

"Hey." Shea gathered Lula in his arms. "You have nothing to be sorry about."

Lula snuggled further into Shea's chest, more to hide her shame than to seek comfort. She squeezed her eyes shut and swallowed past the fire building in her throat. Lula had everything to feel sorry about. She would give anything to stay right there and ignore what she had done.

Hiding from the truth wasn't possible, though. "I better go. Like I said, my dad is super strict."

"I'm sure he just needs your help with the sheep." Shea smiled down at her.

Lula swallowed hard and told Shea the truth, at least the part she could. "My papa is dead, along with my mother and siblings. The man I'm with now... I guess you could say he took me in and watched over me."

He cupped her face with his hand. "I'm sorry, Lula."

"It is what it is." Lula gave a little shrug before pulling away.

"Tomorrow," Shea said, leaving no opening for her to say no.

"I hope so." She took another step back and pushed out the words that broke her heart. "Goodbye, Shea."

She got in her car before he could say anything, before the tears began to fall. Whether she would get to see him again hung heavily on what would happen after she got home tonight. What Doyle exactly meant when he said *I feel you have earned whatever it is you choose to do with your last night of freedom.*

CHAPTER TWENTY

Lula turned down her street, exhausted to her bones. Every part of her wanted to turn around and take Shea up on his offer. The thought of abandoning Max to Doyle's rage was the only thing that kept her driving until she found his farm.

"Where have you been?" Max demanded, appearing out of nowhere. "I lost you again."

Lula jumped, swerving a little as she clamped her hand over her mouth. "Holy shit, Max." She turned to see him slumped with his arms crossed in the passenger seat. "Don't sneak up on me like that. You scared me half to death."

Max swallowed hard. "Lula, I would love for you to tell me where you've been, but I need to warn you. Doyle lost you and not like he's lost you before."

Lula's face scrunched as she unraveled what Max was saying. "Wait, you guys have bitched about losing me before. How was this time different?"

"Before, I could feel you were out there, but couldn't lock in on where you were. This time, it was like you were completely wiped off the face of the earth. I'm pretty sure Doyle experienced the same thing. He has been on a rampage trying to find you. The only reason he's not in this car is that Theodrick, of all people, has kept him planted in the house."

Lula turned into the driveway, bringing the car to a crawl as she pulled into the garage. "I don't understand," she said in a broken whisper.

Max reached over and squeezed her arm. "Just brace yourself."

A tremor snaked its way down Lula's spine as she made her way inside. Max stayed close behind her, only making her feel more trapped than she already did. As she shut the door, Doyle charged at her. She backed herself against the door, her wide eyes locked onto him.

Rage turned his green eyes red as smoke billowed all around him. "Where have you been?" Doyle screamed at Lula.

"You said I could take the rest of the day to do what I wanted to."

"Do not get smart with me." Doyle jabbed a long finger against her chest. "You tell me where you ventured off to. Right. This. Instant!"

Lula's face flushed, and she could hear her pulse in her ears. The only thing that made less sense than his words was his rage.

Lula's heart pounded in her chest as she pushed off the door, glaring at Doyle. The hairs on her arms stood on end as she took a step forward. "I went to go blow off some steam. Is that acceptable to you? Today was the first time I committed *murder*, so you will excuse me if I needed some time to myself. *You* were the one that gave me permission in the first place. Where I went is none of your business, and I'm confused how you don't realize that. You will also excuse me if I'm still a little confused about the fact you keep asking me where I was in the first place, considering your stupid deal connects us."

"I am asking you where you were because after you left that house, you completely disappeared." Doyle bit out every word.

"Really?" Lula's heart picked up, and her palms dampened. She remembered in vivid detail the first time she came home to find Doyle outraged he couldn't track her. It made no sense then, and it made less sense now. Where in the world had she gone that broke her connection to Doyle? "But I just went to the park. I've gone there before, and you haven't had a problem finding me. At least Max hasn't."

"Maybe, but you failed to stay there." Doyle stood straighter, so he towered over her even more. "Now, where the hell did you go?"

"I went to the park," she repeated, glaring up at Doyle. It was the truth. She had started her evening at the park. Of course, she hadn't stayed there. She thought back to riding in Shea's car and going to his farm. Could it have something to do with Shea? Could he cloak her in a way that kept Doyle and Max from finding her? That made less sense than anything else.

"Maybe she blocked you," a voice offered instead.

"Blocked me?" Doyle raised a doubtful brow.

Lula looked over her shoulder to see Theodrick sitting on the couch with his legs crossed. The thin smile made him look more sinister than happy. "Tell me, dear." Theodrick sipped the drink he held. "How did you feel after taking that soul?"

"Awful," she spat at him.

"And perhaps, powerful?" He raised an eyebrow.

Doyle backed up a step from Theodrick. His brows pulled so close together they practically touched. "You *expected* this?" Doyle asked.

"That was the hope, my friend. For her to change. Which is precisely what we need for her to do."

"Yeah, maybe I *have* changed. Maybe being forced to kill that innocent girl changed me in a way that now I have new abilities, like I can hide where I am from you." The notion sounded ridiculous, but Lula thought about the energy that flowed over her after taking Melissa. Nothing like that had ever happened to her in all the centuries she had taken souls. Could that be what Theodrick was referring to? Lula's heart stopped and then doubled in speed as it occurred to her that Theodrick could've been the reason Doyle had her collect Melissa's soul.

Theodrick's eyes lit up as the vein in Doyle's forehead pounded. The tension in the room was so thick you'd need a chainsaw to cut through it. Doyle growled as he jabbed a finger in Lula's face when he spoke.

"You listen here, Pet. Even if you have new powers because of what you did, you are *mine*. Do you understand me? I will *always* know where you are, or else." He turned his rage to Theodrick. "And if you think I am going to risk losing her because you have some cockamamie notion that she is the key to you rising to power, you have another thing coming."

Theodrick shot up off the couch and stood before Doyle in the blink of an eye. Doyle stumbled back a step as his eyes widened to saucers. Lula slid against the wall, away from the two deities. A dark energy, so much like Doyle's smoke, yet so much stronger, thicker, now crawled over her skin.

Theodrick's eyes narrowed to slits, but the smile never faltered. "Doyle, as my most loyal friend, I will only remind you of this once.

We have a goal. One goal. And I will take and use whatever I need to achieve it. Anyone who is unfortunate enough to get in my way will pay with their very life. Do you understand me?"

A bead of sweat trickled down Doyle's temple. He wiped at it with a quick, jerking motion. "I...I understand you."

"Good." Theodrick clapped Doyle on the back before turning his attention to Lula. "You did very well today, Lulabelle. Your master is very proud of you." He let out a sigh. "I must go now. Chin up, Doyle. And Lulabelle..." He turned and reached for a coat draped over the back of a chair. "Keep up the good work."

Theodrick disappeared, leaving the house in a heavy silence. Doyle rubbed his face and stared into the distance, his nostrils flared. Lula wondered what the hell he could be thinking. The thought barely registered past her own confusion. Theodrick's declaration had yanked the floor out from under Lula's feet. Her stomach knotted as realization settled heavy on her shoulders, without a doubt, Lula would be forced to kill again.

***

Doyle left her alone for the rest of the night. Lula wanted to find sanctuary in her room. She changed into pajamas and climbed into bed. Curled up under the covers, the hard music that usually calmed her down only played as a soundtrack to the day's events. A war of rage and dread pounded in her head. Light from a streetlamp poured in through her window. The shadows it created played tricks on her mind. Curves turned to faces, and long shadows cast by her knick-knacks became fingers reaching out to grab her. Her whole body twitched with the need to escape the monsters now hiding under her bed. The feeling that she was being watched crawled across her skin. Lula sat up and trembled as she looked around her quiet room.

Slowly, the empty space filled with a presence. It became stronger, something she had never experienced before. The feeling continued to grow until she recognized who it was.

Max appeared, sitting beside her on the bed. He took her head-phones and held one side up to his ear. "I like this band," he said, handing them back.

Lula just stared at him for a moment before Max finally asked, "Are you okay?"

"No." The word burned her throat.

"You gave me a real scare. I still don't know how you disappeared like that."

"I don't know either," she said, then gave a watery smile. "If I'm honest, I kinda like the idea you both couldn't find me. It gives me hope maybe I *can* escape Doyle."

Max scrunched up his entire face. "Not without me, though."

Lula grabbed his hand and squeezed. "Of course, not without you."

Lula studied Max as they sat in silence, trying to figure out how she had felt his presence before he appeared in her room. She swore she'd experienced nothing like it before. How else had he been able to sneak up on her all these years? Maybe Theodrick was right. Maybe she did have new powers? The only thing that had changed was taking Melissa before her time. Lula remembered with chilling clarity what Melissa had spoken.

"Her last words to me were, 'Oh my God, you're like us.'"

He flinched back. "What the hell does that mean?"

"I wish I knew."

Max tilted his head, watching her. "What else is bothering you? You look like you've seen a ghost and not the usual." He touched a finger to his chest.

She concentrated on pulling the thread on the corner of her bedspread, only peeking up at Max. "Something weird just happened. It's probably nothing."

"Tell me."

Lula bit her lip and refused to look at him.

"Come on, Lula. I know things have been rough between us lately because of me not being on team 'Mr. Wonderful,' but I hope you remember, I'm here for you. After all, we're friends." He offered her his hand. Heaving a heavy sigh, she took it, pulling him closer. Because he was right, they were friends. She didn't know what she would do without him.

"Fair enough. And yes, I know you are here for me as my friend," she conceded. "Even if you don't like Shea."

"So you will tell me?"

Lula furrowed her brow while shaking her head, still having no idea what had happened. "It was the strangest thing. Right before you appeared, I felt you."

"What do you mean, you felt me?"

"I felt something in the room, a presence that kept getting stronger and stronger until I was able to recognize it as you. A moment later, you appeared. That's something I've never experienced before."

"So you knew I was coming before I got here?"

"Yeah. Crazy, right?"

"That is weird." He smirked. "Maybe you did change after... you know." Max leaned back and searched her face. Did she look different now, too? "Where did you go tonight? And don't tell me you were at the park." He nudged her.

"I went with Shea," Lula admitted.

Max's eyes narrowed. The way he fixated on her made her squirm, but Max just sat still, like he was putting the pieces of a puzzle together. The corner of his lip twitched like he was fighting a smile. "Wow." Max's eyebrows shot straight up. "It must be serious then."

Lula's cheeks burned. "I think it is."

"Don't worry, Lula. I'll make sure you get to escape with your Prince Charming."

Wouldn't it be great if she did?

CHAPTER TWENTY-ONE

The next morning, Lula went straight to the kitchen and fixed herself some coffee. She looked out the window into the backyard, trying to enjoy the peace, only to be haunted by Melissa's face. Shea had been so devastated upon hearing about her death, and it was all Lula's fault. Self-hatred burned deep and turned her stomach.

Tingles walked up Lula's back. Like the night before with Max, a presence grew stronger and stronger in the room until she could recognize who it was. For the first time, Doyle didn't surprise her when he came up behind her. His abrupt appearance still almost made her spill her freshly poured cup of coffee.

"I need you." His voice held no room for compromise.

It shouldn't surprise her that he already had another job lined up. Lula only hoped this time, the person didn't die just because she was in the room.

Her shoulders dropped on a defeated sigh. "Who is it?"

"His name is Thomas. You should not have any trouble finding him."

Lula focused on her coffee, unable to bring herself to face him. "Please tell me he's going to get hit by a car or something?"

He met the question with only silence.

"Doyle?"

She turned around to see him standing tall, arms stiff at his sides. A brown aura Lula had never seen before swirled around him, looking very much like the smoke that usually gathered at his feet. Taking in the grim expression on his face, her blood ran cold. *Keep up the good work.* Theodrick's words rang in her ear, and all hope drained from her body.

"No." Lula slammed her coffee cup onto the counter, blazing with more confidence than she actually had.

"Lula, you do not have—"

"I'm not taking another life, Doyle. Period. I don't care what you and your creepy friend think I am. I am not killing! Period!"

"Do not take that tone with me. You will leave this instant and take Thomas's soul." With every word he spoke, he stepped closer and closer to her.

"Doyle—"

"You are mine to command."

The light in the room dropped with his voice. Around Lula, the cabinets vibrated. She swallowed hard, trying to keep a brave face even as her stomach dropped to her toes.

"I grow weary of your headstrong defiance. When I tell you to do something, you shall carry it out without question, or you shall endure my wrath—something you have never seen before."

"Deal with it!" Lula shouted as her whole body trembled. "I signed up to help souls ready to pass to the Realm of the Dead, not kill innocent people before it is their time."

"You *signed up* to do as I say."

"No, I didn't."

Lula's heart threw itself against her chest. Never had she been this defiant, but dammit, she wasn't going quiet anymore. Her very soul depended on it. After what she'd done to Melissa, she didn't deserve any happiness. Especially with Shea.

She clenched her fists, determined to redeem herself. For Shea. For Melissa. For herself.

Doyle's snarled and the kitchen filled with smoke. In a quick motion, he grabbed Lula by the arms and slammed her against the pantry door. The force knocked the wind out of her as pain flared through her back.

"Do you know how many humans would *kill* for even a fraction of the power I have bestowed upon you? I have met them and watched as they pined for the opportunity."

Lula gaped at Doyle—at the absurdity of what he was saying. Thinking back on all the people she'd met over the years, there had been some with the blackest of souls. She could only pick out a few who would jump at the chance to hold this power for personal gain, no matter the cost.

"All I would have to do is whisper the prospect, and they would fall to my feet and never give me a day's grief like you have," he continued.

Lula wanted to deny what he was saying, knowing the only reason she had her powers in the first place was because she wanted to save the love of her life. She was different, though. Wasn't she? Maybe Doyle wasn't that far off after all.

"I'm not them," she said.

"Clearly."

"You don't understand." Her voice broke as she pleaded with him, "This is *killing* me. You can't...you just—"

"And you think I could just—*would* just—take all I have given to you back because it causes you pain?"

Lula locked eyes with him, not saying a word, only hoping she was showing him all the pain and destruction the power he'd gifted her was doing. With their eyes locked, his palm gently came to rest on her forehead. Doyle's eyes narrowed, and his jaw locked as his hand stilled. A small tingle raced down Lula's body all the way to her toes. A pulling sensation filled her chest. The air stuck in her lungs, and she struggled to draw in a breath. Pressure pounded in her head as the ripping sensation intensified. Her mind raced, trying to figure out what Doyle was doing. Could he be freeing her? Could he be about to kill her? Lula wasn't sure which would bring her more relief. For a tense moment, the two stood there in the kitchen, locked in a silent battle of wills.

Doyle's hand finally dropped to his side. Sweat glistened on his brow. His wide eyes fell to the floor as he stood there, gasping for breath. A string of curses poured out of his mouth as he pounded his fist on the kitchen counter.

"Doyle, what just happened?" Lula asked while her heart finally slowed.

"There are things you do not understand—that you could never understand, and you do not have to. All you have to do is what you are told, just as I have to do what I am told. Now go, Lula. Go get Thomas's soul. I will take you myself if I have to."

The bitter expression on his face sent shivers down her spine as she crawled inside herself.

"You have no choice. It is your fate."

A shiver raced over her skin as she realized he meant every word. She started to back out of the kitchen, afraid of what would happen if she turned around. Her only goal was to escape to her room and get ready. Right now she wouldn't put it past him to drag her kicking and screaming across the city in her pajamas to kill again. Not that wardrobe choices should be her biggest concern at the moment. However, if she focused on the fact she was about to end another life prematurely, he really would have to drag her there. The very notion made her want to curl into a ball and cry.

"I will meet you there," he called out before disappearing to who knew where.

Lula wanted to die. There was no way she could do this again. Every part of her rebelled against the order given to her. Not if she wanted to keep what remained of her humanity. Maybe that was Doyle's plan all along. He was finally going to kill what made her, *her*.

She shuffled down the hall until she got to her room and softly closed the door behind her, all fight in her gone. After all, there was no point in fighting if he was just going to physically drag her there anyway.

Max stood in the corner of her room, still as a statue. "What the hell was that?"

Lula shrugged her shoulders. "I'm off to murder another soul."

Max's eyes widened as he took a step toward her. "No, Lula, he can't make you do that. Not again." When Lula only gave him a withered look, Max bit out a curse of his own. "I hate Doyle, I really do. I hate him so much. How can he do this to you?"

"Because he can."

Max dropped onto the bed and let out a huff. "Is he so goddamn lazy that he can't do this one thing himself?"

"Apparently, this is my fate."

"Your fate? What the hell does that mean anyway? This is all so messed up."

Lula sat next to Max on the bed. She couldn't argue with that. The events in the kitchen replayed like an awful movie, including the pulling sensation that had robbed her of air. Doyle had looked like he had been concentrating very hard. His hot, sweaty palm on her forehead had burned uncomfortably as he trembled.

Lula pinched her face while a thought took root. She turned the concept over and over, trying to make sense of the reflections swirling in an endless riddle begging to be solved. "When I first made the deal with Doyle, he gave me the power that I have. He told me he was giving me a part of him."

Max scratched his chin. "Think it was a metaphor?"

"I used to, but then later, we came across that one Death God. Do you remember him? He visited us when we were in France. He had asked Doyle to kill his Pet for him."

Max's eyes lit in recognition. "Right, I do remember. He had captured some French noble trying to escape the guillotine. The Death

God couldn't control him because he wasn't powerful enough any-more."

"Doyle admonished him for giving his Pet too much of his own power, making the Pet powerful and leaving the Death God weak."

Max rubbed the back of his neck. "Wow, so they actually give you a slice of the power they hold just so they don't have to work?"

"I wonder how much power Doyle gave me?" she wondered out loud. "In the beginning."

"A lot, apparently."

"A lot, for sure," Lula agreed, searching her memories from when the deal was first made. "How much did he keep for himself, though?"

"Like, he can only have so much, right? I'd bet money that he gave you more than he meant to."

"I think Doyle tried to do something to me in the kitchen."

"What?"

Lula stared at the carpet as she put what happened into words. "In the kitchen, he put his hand on my head, and a pulling sensation started deep in me, like he was trying to rip something out of me." She sighed. "I think whatever he was trying to do, though, didn't work."

"What makes you say that?"

"Because whatever he was pulling at wouldn't budge. Maybe Doyle isn't as powerful as he thinks he is."

"That, or maybe you have officially become more powerful than him. Taking Melissa's soul *did* change you. You said so yourself—you can do things you couldn't do before."

"I could sense when you were coming, and it worked with him too. I don't know if that's a big leap in ability, Max."

But maybe Max had a point. The idea that Doyle had less power than her opened a whole new world of possibilities.

"After last night's conversation," Max said, "it seems like this is what they want. That Theodrick guy seemed giddy that you might be able to block Doyle."

Lula walked across the room and started pulling out clothes to change into. She knew she only had a limited time before Doyle would barge in and wonder what was taking her so long to get ready. As she pulled out the black Victorian-style dress, an image of Theodrick's excited eyes flashed before her. He had been right about her, but what exactly was he right about? Thinking back further, the first evening she met the Death God came to mind.

Narrowing her eyes, she faced Max. "Doyle and Theodrick were looking for something. Weren't they?"

"Yeah..." Max rubbed his chin. "They needed to find the star-some-thing?"

"The Statera," she remembered. "They said it was the one thing that could stop Sephtis."

"Whatever that is."

If they were looking for the Statera, then why were they focusing so hard on Lula? Making her, a lowly Pet, change into something more powerful seemed like a dangerous game. Why would a Death God risk such a thing?

"Why would they change me?" Lula whimpered.

"Maybe they need you to find the thing they're looking for. This change could make you like a homing beacon or something."

Max didn't sound crazy. Lula could see the Death Gods beefing her up and using her as a tool to get what they needed.

"Lula..." Doyle's voice rumbled down the hall and the door to her room quaked.

Time was up. She needed to leave to find Thomas. The question was, what would she do once she found him?

Chapter Twenty-Two

Lula found Thomas in a small bar at the far end of town as easily as she had found Melissa. The dimly lit establishment radiated with the sounds of jazz and the smells of cheap beer and delicious food. With no windows, the early afternoon sun was completely hidden from the patrons. The bar ran along the left side of the joint with a doorway to the right leading down a tiny hall. Tables sat scattered throughout the place, with high-backed booths lining the right wall. The loud chorus of lotto machines against one wall was in contrast to the smooth music playing.

Sitting in the last booth before the back exit, facing her, Thomas sipped his drink. It had to be him, despite only being able to make out the top of his dirty-blond hair. A vibrant red aura, mixed with the blue glow and flecks of gold and green, surrounded the man, a beacon that demanded attention. Lula was shocked to see how much stronger his Mark shone compared to Melissa's. His aura was practically on fire.

Thomas chugged down the last of his drink. Lula nearly tripped over the heavy fabric of her ankle-length skirt as his face came into view. Thomas—the man whose soul she was there to take—also happened to be the same man who had chased after her when she went after Melissa.

A sinister voice deep inside her suggested that maybe ending his life by taking his soul wasn't such a bad idea after all.

She blinked rapidly, trying to clear the unclean thought. Lula was better than that. She was only doing this because Doyle was forcing her to.

Thomas raised himself higher in his seat and looked around the bar. Lula panicked and bolted back out the door to avoid him discovering her. She made it two steps outside before running smack into Doyle.

"What are you doing?" Doyle asked, looking her up and down. "Get back in there and take the soul."

"It's complicated, Doyle."

"Complicated," Doyle deadpanned.

"Yes, Doyle, I'm going to have a real hard time getting this soul—" she worked to explain.

"I warned you, Lula," he interjected, not interested in hearing more. "You know what will happen if you dare to defy me."

"I understand, but—"

"Now get back in there!"

Before she could open her mouth to try again, a strong chill crawled up Lula's spine, stronger than ever before. She turned and watched as the tall, slender man slid out of the shadows.

Theodrick sauntered up, wearing a deep burgundy suit with a matching top hat. He narrowed his eyes on Lula, and she could feel his gaze on her like a touch, leaving her feeling dirty. She knew he was powerful, but now, with her new powers, Lula got a whole new read on him. A chocolate brown aura, much like what surrounded Doyle, flared as he joined them. Her body locked up as her breath froze in her lungs. He had to be the most powerful Death God she had ever been around. What the hell was she seeing now? More importantly, what the hell was he doing here? She stared back at him as another chill rocked her to her core, and something in her soul shifted.

Doyle tipped his head in greeting. "Theodrick."

The Death God touched his own hat. "Doyle."

"Why are you here?" Lula pushed out.

"Do not concern yourself with him," Doyle answered. "You stay here while we go talk."

The two walked to the street corner, not fifty feet away. Doyle glanced over at Lula, and the glint in his eyes told her he was going to block the powers she had, so she couldn't listen in. He'd done it so many times before. She braced herself for the small, sharp pain that accompanied him, blocking her powers. Only, the pain never came, and he didn't seem to realize. Doyle began talking, and she could hear every word they said.

"What are you doing here?" Doyle's voice sounded as tight as he looked standing there. Lula watched him clench his fist at his side.

"I think your darling little Pet has led us to our jackpot." A sly grin slid across Theodrick's face.

"The soul. Yes, she is here to get it like we planned," Doyle said.

"Not just the soul. Sephtis."

"He is here?" Doyle squeaked.

"Shhh." Theodrick smashed his finger against his lips. "I'm not positive, but I think there may be a chance he is at least nearby."

Doyle turned back towards Lula but seemed to look right past her doing her best impression of being disinterested in the world around her. Clearing his throat, he turned, focused on Theodrick again. "I do not sense him."

"No one has sensed that coward in centuries. However, going over *The Book of Enid* again today, I am convinced he is close."

Doyle shifted his stance. "If he *is* coming out of hiding, we should prepare. This war is about to get ugly."

"Oh, Doyle, it is hardly a war. Not when the other side is so outmatched. Especially when their army is nothing but a bunch of renegade Pets." He chuckled darkly, and then his face fell as his eyes pinned Lula. She acted intent on picking invisible lint off her skirt instead of hearing every word they said.

Renegade Pets? Lula could feel more puzzle pieces falling into place. Shea had spoken about him and his father freeing people tricked by "evil bosses." Theodrick was using her to find this Statera. Melissa's and Thomas's Marks were almost identical. Finally, Melissa's last words. *You're like us.*

Renegade Pets.

The Death Gods were fighting Shea and his family. Melissa and Thomas were runaway Pets. Could that be what was happening? Crazy as it seemed, everything in her knew it had to be at least close to the truth. It still begged the question, what was so special about her?

"Speaking of Pets, is she under control?" Theodrick's voice rumbled.

Doyle sighed. "Yes, I believe I have her back under control."

"Are you sure? Because mark my words, Doyle, either she proves herself useful to us, or I'll destroy her myself."

"I am telling you, Lula is completely under my control."

Lula couldn't breathe. Her head spun so fast that she pressed up against the side of the building to keep from falling over. *Damned if you do, damned if you don't.*

Something deep inside her rebelled against everything. Either that or she was just flat over it. There was only one option left for her to do.

Step one, save Thomas.

"Then let's not waste any more time." Theodrick made a sweeping gesture.

Doyle deflated before turning to join Lula where she stood.

Opening the door to the establishment, Theodrick smiled, sweeping his hand once more. "Shall we?"

Lula held out her arms. "Wait!" The two deities froze to look at her like she had lost her mind. Maybe she had. She shifted to stand a bit taller and cleared her throat, ready to put her plan into action. "You two need to stay out here."

Theodrick's eyes narrowed.

The vein in Doyle's forehead pounded.

"Why would we need to do such a thing?" Doyle asked.

"Because Thomas is in a bar?" The two continued to gawk. "A crowded bar. With lots of people who shouldn't see a girl in a steampunk dress rip a guy's soul out."

"She has a point, Theodrick."

Theodrick sighed and let the door close. "What would you have us do, then? We need to be there when you do it."

Lula's face pinched like she smelled something foul. "Why?" she asked and immediately regretted it.

"Because I want to see what power it will bestow you with next," Theodrick said.

Lula swallowed hard. "Fair enough. If you think that will even happen." She looked up and down the street, her eyes touching where her car was parked. "Out back," she offered. "The alley is usually secluded enough that I can collect souls without being noticed."

Theodrick crossed his arms and strolled over to stand right in front of her. Out of the corner of her eye, she saw Doyle's eyes widen. He made a move to put himself between them, but Theodrick elbowed Doyle back.

"Go in. Get Thomas to follow you out back. I will give you five minutes to accomplish this before we come in and help you." Theodrick left no room for negotiation.

She raised her chin. "I'll see you out back."

Lula yanked at the door and slipped inside. She wasted no time making her way to the booth where Thomas sat. His eyes widened when he noticed her. To her horror, Thomas was not alone. Shea sat right across the booth from him.

"You," Thomas growled.

Shea turned and looked up. His eyes popped as he took her in. "Lula?"

"Do you *know* her?" Thomas asked.

"Do *you*?" Shea asked in return.

Lula forced herself to concentrate. Casting a glance around the bar to make sure Doyle or Theodrick hadn't followed her inside, she bent over, leaning against the table. "You need to come with me. Now,"

Lula said, tapping her finger against the tabletop, punctuating each word.

He leaned forward in his seat, leering up at her. "Why would I go anywhere with you?"

Lula glared. "Trust me, you want to come with me. Right now. Both of you."

"Trust you? The girl who broke into Melissa's house?"

Shea's eyes darted between the two of them. "What's he talking about?"

"It's a long story I would love to tell you all about after we get out of here." She grabbed Thomas's arm and started pulling, trying to get him to stand.

Thomas held his ground, refusing to even budge. How in the hell was she going to convince him? She slumped over the table, banging her head a couple of times for good measure.

"Please, you are in danger if you stay here," Lula explained.

Shea slid out of the booth to stand beside her. "Thomas, let's get out of here. Dad said Melissa would just be the start."

"I don't trust her," Thomas said.

"I do, and I say we go with her."

Thomas cursed under his breath, but finally stood up from the booth. Lula was going to kiss Shea as soon as they got out of there.

She motioned for them to follow her. "I'm parked out front."

"Well, I'm parked out back." Thomas stayed put.

"We need to take my car. We can't—"

"There is no way I'm getting in a car with you behind the wheel."

Lula took a deep breath, ready to beg at that point, when a rush of energy hit her in the back.

"Holy shit, those are two Death Gods," Shea said in a hoarse whisper.

So much blood had drained from Shea's face he could almost pass as Max's twin. She turned toward the front of the bar. Theodrick and Doyle stood blocking the front door, hands clenched at their sides.

"Oh man," Thomas's voice shook.

"Your car it is," Lula squeaked.

Thomas grabbed her and yanked her to him. His nails dug into her arm. "Did they come with you?"

Lula gasped, answering through the pain, "I can explain."

Her thoughts raced, trying to think of any way to keep them safe, anywhere these two deities could not get.

"No time for explanations." Shea motioned behind them. "We need to go. Now."

As Theodrick and Doyle began making their way through the crowded bar, the three of them ran out of the back exit. Lula ran behind Thomas toward a car sitting in the back corner of the parking lot. She almost fell as she plowed into the car. Thomas yanked out the keys and unlocked the doors. Theodrick and Doyle didn't go around back, and they didn't stay outside. Now the two were charging toward them like raging bulls. Lula hated what she had to do but knew it was the only way to give Thomas a chance to escape.

"Go back to your farm and stay there. Do you hear me? Do *not* leave that property for any reason," she ordered Shea.

"My farm? I don't understand."

"They won't be able to find you there, trust me."

"What about you?" Shea asked. His eyes stayed transfixed on the exit behind her.

"Don't worry about me." When he still didn't move, she shoved him with so much force that he stumbled back several steps. "Go now, before it's too late."

"Come on, man. Let's get out of here!" Thomas called.

"But—" Shea reached for her. She could practically see the wheels turning as he seemed to still be weighing his options.

This hadn't gone the way Lula wanted it to at all. She longed to jump in the car with them and escape, but she knew the consequences.

"You have to. It's not safe for Thomas. He is Marked for death, but we can't let that happen. You have to keep him safe."

"I can't leave you. I have to keep *you* safe."

When he still refused to move, she reached up and gave him a quick but searing kiss. Shea groaned and wrapped his arms around her. A wave of energy crashed over her, filling her up, every cell in her body coming alive. She felt invincible.

"I'll be safe, I promise. I'll find you when this blows over, but you have got to get Thomas away from me and them right now if you want any chance of beating the Death Gods."

Shea looked at her, a plethora of emotions playing across those dark eyes.

"I promise they won't hurt me. They can't," she grabbed his arms and tried to push him away.

It wasn't the whole truth, but she hoped it would be enough to get him out of there.

Just then, the two deities burst from the bar. They whipped their heads around as they scoured the parking lot until they narrowed in on Lula.

"Go!" Lula screamed.

It was enough to jar Shea out of his trance, and he jumped into the car. Thomas revved the engine before peeling out of the parking lot.

She turned, ready to face the Death Gods alone, when Max appeared next to her.

"Lula, I have something I need to tell you," he said.

Theodrick let out a bone-chilling cry. Doyle charged toward her, only stopping when he was inches away from her face.

"Woah!" Max jumped back at the sight of the two deities.

"What do you think you're doing? You let the soul get away!" Doyle's hand flew toward her, hitting her with enough force to knock her to the ground.

"Leave her alone," Max demanded as he strived to put himself between Lula and Doyle.

"She didn't let him get away, Doyle. You heard it yourself," Theodrick hissed at Doyle's side. "She helped him escape. I told you she would betray you."

"Damn you, you willful Pet. After all that I have done for you, this is how you repay me?" Doyle reached down, shoving Max out of the way and pulling Lula to her feet by her hair. A small cry slipped from her. "How could you betray me?" Doyle slapped Lula again. Pain blossomed across her entire face, and the bitter taste of blood filled her mouth.

"She won't kill people for you anymore," Max said. He lunged at Doyle, and Lula winced at the pain pulsing in her scalp as Doyle's fingers continued to grip her hair while Max desperately tried to pry them off.

"Stop it!" Lula screamed, struggling to get away.

"How could you?" Doyle repeated, rearing up and hitting her again.

"I said, stop it!" Lula shoved at Doyle as hard as she could. A pulse of energy burst from her hands, sending Doyle flying across the parking lot.

"She is even more powerful than I thought," Theodrick said, "and with only one soul."

She didn't know if she had whatever power Theodrick was talking about or not, but she had to try. Focusing on Theodrick and all the evil that he stood for, she released another burst of energy. The resulting wave shattered a bunch of windshields and sent Theodrick flying.

Exhaustion hit her like a brick.

Max dropped down next to her and, clinging to him, she thought about the only place in the world where she knew she would be safe and happy—the car with Shea racing down the street. Her hand in his. She wished with every fiber of her being that she and Max were there, seeing them in the car with them. The vision was as real as if they were actually there.

Another wave of energy pulsed from her right before she found herself lying in the backseat of Thomas's car.

"What the hell?" Thomas yelled.

The car swerved as Thomas fought to keep it on the road. He pulled the car over, and the two turned to look in the backseat. Shea's eyes widened as he faced the passenger seat, leaning toward her.

"Lula." Shea reached out and cupped her face. "Where the did you come from?"

She opened her mouth to answer, but darkness overtook her.

Chapter Twenty-Three

*L*ula lay in the grass, watching the clear summer sky. Big, white, fluffy clouds lazed away overhead. A slight breeze blew through the meadow, tickling her bare feet. The sound of the guitar playing beside her filled her ears, bringing a smile to her face. She looked up to meet a pair of warm, dark eyes twinkling in the sun.

"What's that smile for?" he asked.

Lula's smile widened as her eyes fell shut. "I love listening to you play, that's all."

A chuckle mixed with the cheerful tune. "Is that the only reason you keep me around?"

"Pretty much." Lula sat up and turned, facing him. "I have seen you with the sheep. So helping me watch the flock is out."

He changed to a more somber tune. "Fair."

"I could teach you." Lula poked his knee. "It's not that hard to herd a bunch of sheep."

He stopped playing to brush the long, black hair out of his eyes and stared across the meadow. Hope pounded in her chest at the idea of him staying. Every day they spent together left her happier than the last. She knew in her heart that she loved him more than anyone in this world. Lula waited in impatient silence, wondering what thoughts could be churning behind his distant gaze.

"I would love nothing more than to stay here and have you teach me. Being here with you, Lulabelle, is more precious than anything else in this entire world."

A warm hand cupped Lula's cheek. Letting out a moan, she turned into the palm holding her.

"Lula," the voice called out to her.

She knew that voice but was still far too gone to care. All she wanted was to go back to her dream, back to the man who'd made her heart race. Lula cared about him, loved him even, yet somehow, had forgotten about him. *How,* she couldn't imagine, but she'd found him in her dream and didn't want to lose him again.

Cool fingers traced across under her eye, wiping a stray tear she hadn't realized had fallen. Lula blinked before she could focus on the face in front of her. Shea hovered above her, looking down at her with a tight jaw and pained features etched in his expression.

"It's you," she breathed as the last bits of the dream flashed before fading away.

"Yes, it's me," he whispered back, brushing a strand of hair behind her ear, giving her a strained smile.

"I—"

"Lula, you're awake," Max interrupted. "You scared the crap out of me. Are you okay?" He maneuvered himself between Shea and Lula.

"Hey, back up, will you?" Shea snapped.

Lula's jaw dropped open as she watched the two men scowl at each other.

Max narrowed his eyes at Shea. "I'm just making sure that Lula is okay. Okay?"

"No, not okay. I have no idea who you are or even *what* you are. So until I know, you aren't going near her."

"I'll tell you who I am. I'm—"

"Max." Lula reached out to squeeze Max's arm. "He can see you?"

Max planted himself on the end of the couch by Lula's feet and crossed his arms. "Yeah, apparently, both of them can. Threw me for a loop too."

Shea raised a brow. "You are really hard to miss."

Lula continued to look dumbfounded between the both of them. "He usually is. He's kinda..." she trailed off, not sure how to explain.

"I'm a close cousin of Casper the Ghost's," Max offered, and Lula smacked her hand over her face.

"Wait." Shea pointed at Max. "Are you... are you dead?"

"Great," Thomas piped up. Lula turned to see Thomas standing by the fireplace. His posture was so stiff a solid hit would break him. If looks could kill, she'd be dead. "Looks like your new girlfriend also hangs out with poltergeists."

"Who are you calling a poltergeist?" Max moved to jump off the couch.

Lula threw her leg in front of him, keeping him in place.

"Calm down, Max."

"Don't tell me to calm down," Max grumbled under his breath.

Lula's cheeks burned as both men watched her sit up on the checkered couch. With a sigh of relief, Lula took in the living room of Shea's farmhouse. Out the window, the evergreens of the Cascade Mountains seemed to glow under the midday sun.

"Now that you're awake, maybe we can get some answers," Thomas clipped. "You can start by answering who you are and how the hell did you get in the backseat of my car?"

"I don't know how that happened. I don't know how any of this is happening. I wish I knew," Lula confessed.

"And we're just supposed to trust you?"

"Thomas, what's wrong with you, man? She just saved our butts," Shea said.

"I'm just wondering why we're with a girl that hangs out with not one but two Death Gods, is all," Thomas said, giving a half-shrug.

"She's one of us, can't you see?" Shea countered. He maneuvered himself onto the couch next to Lula, placing an arm around her shoulders.

"How do you know about Death Gods?" Max asked, squeezing onto the other side of Lula.

"What do you mean 'one of us'?" Lula asked at the same time.

Thomas locked his jaw. "Don't say anything."

"Why not?" Shea challenged.

"Maybe she is one of us, but this is also the same girl that broke into Melissa's house," Thomas said.

Lula stiffened.

"What are you talking about?" Shea turned to Lula. "What is he talking about?"

"I can explain," Lula whispered.

Thomas crossed his arms over his chest. "I'm all ears."

"I'm not…" Lula swallowed hard, trying to find the right way to tell them so they would understand. "Yes, I work with *a* Death God. I wouldn't say that I'm *allied* with them, at least not voluntarily."

"Yeah, yeah, because you're a Pet." Thomas rolled his eyes. "That only explains the *one* Death God loitering over you. There were two, though, and they looked pretty close to you."

"You know that I'm a Pet?" Lula's voice cracked.

"Yes, just like I am. Just like Melissa was."

"*Unlike* you and Melissa," Shea's voice vibrated with fury. "Dad and I got you away from your Death God."

Lula's wide eyes bounced between Shea and Thomas. They were Pets? *Renegade Pets.* He knew what she was this entire time? Lula thought about all their conversations. It had scared Shea to think that she was in danger. All that worry made sense now. The bite of betrayal stung as she focused on Shea. He could have helped her. The whole truth soured her stomach. It wasn't like she was the picture of honesty and openness, either. Keeping him in the dark had been to protect him, though. Lula would bet money that it was the same reason Shea had kept her in the dark. He'd even told her as much. That's what she told herself.

Letting out a long breath, she sank back onto the couch and closed her eyes for a moment. God, she wanted to believe that. What a mess.

Max slumped back next to her and crossed his arms over his chest. Scratching his jaw, he looked between Shea and Thomas.

Shea shifted in his seat, pinning Max with a glare.

"What?" Max asked, indignant.

"You want to tell me what the hell *you* are? Because you're *not* a Pet, and leaving it at Casper's close cousin isn't going to cut it," Shea said.

"He's a long story," Lula offered.

Thomas snorted. "I bet."

Max flipped Thomas the one-fingered salute.

Shea took her hand. "Will you tell us your story?"

"Which story do you want to hear first?"

"Start with how you became a Pet," Shea said before Thomas could speak.

Lula shivered at the flood of memories filling her. "When I was nineteen, a spooked horse trampled someone I cared for. Everyone did all they could to save him, but in the end, it was clear he wouldn't live. It devastated me. At the time, this person meant the world to me." Lula glanced at Max, who kept his face down. "I wandered out to a field and gave myself over to my grief, praying for a miracle, some way to save him."

"And this person was..." Shea leered at Max.

Max gave a tiny wave with a sheepish smile. Lula rubbed her forehead before jerking her fingers through her hair.

"*Him?*" Shea choked out.

"Hey, I may be dead, but my feelings are very alive. Thank you very much." Max harrumphed.

"*Anyway.*" She cleared her throat and continued, "A man I'd never seen before appeared. He smiled down and told me he was there to take Max away. I begged him not to, but he said it had to be done. It was the way of things, and to play with fate in such a way would only lead to more sorrow. I poured my heart out to him, and when that didn't work, I told him I would do anything to save Max and keep him by my side. We struck a deal. Max could stay with me, and in return, I would repay the debt now owed."

Lula paused her story, daring a look up to gauge Shea's and Thomas's reactions. Thomas looked bored by the whole thing. Shea, however, appeared frozen. His eyes remained locked on Max.

"You struck a deal with Death to save him." Shea motioned toward Max. It wasn't a question, but Lula felt the weight of his words settled in her chest.

"Yes," she breathed. "As soon as I made the deal, everything changed, and not in the way he led me to believe. Max died the next morning. After the funeral, Doyle came to get me."

"Your Death God's name is *Doyle*?" Thomas choked out a laugh. "So lame."

"He informed me that my time to repay the debt had begun. When I questioned how he could say that since Max was dead, he smirked. Max appeared beside him, a ghost now, forever linked to me. As long as Max is with me, I belong to Doyle. Until today, no one but Doyle and I could see him. I guess, other Death Gods can see him too, but no mortals for sure. I'm still trying to figure out how you can."

"So you're, what, devoted to this ghost?" Thomas asked, ignoring her last statement.

Shea paled.

"What?" Lula burst out laughing. She couldn't help it. "I am not even devoted to Max, not romantically anyway."

"I thought you just said you loved him? Why wouldn't you be?" Shea asked this time.

"I said I cared for him, and that was a *very* long time ago." Lula's laughter faded away. "Max has been more my curse than anything."

"How can you say that?" Shea asked.

"Yeah," Max chimed in. "Am I that bad?"

Lula took a deep breath and laid it all out on the table, ignoring Max's comment. "The funeral was when I learned Max had been in love with someone else, the butcher's daughter. She was beautiful." Lula sighed as Max got up and walked across the room, away from everyone. "Anyway, I guess she was losing interest in him, so he'd started pursuing me to make her jealous, hoping she'd want him back. Apparently, it worked because, at the funeral, I learned they had just gotten engaged when the accident happened."

Thomas chuckled. "Harsh."

"He is also my closest friend now, but it's because of the deal that we are bound together. That's why I said curse."

"How long ago did you make this deal?" Shea asked.

She squeezed her eyes shut and confessed, "It's been two hundred and seventy-three years now since that night in the field."

"Whoa."

Lula opened her eyes at the sound of Thomas's reaction. He stood watching her with his head tilted. She slowly turned to see Shea staring off across the room. She touched his arm with a trembling hand.

"Shea," she said his name softly, as if doing so would keep what they had from breaking.

Shea blinked several times before putting his hand over hers and offering her a smile. "I knew Pets were immortal because of the Death Gods' powers. I guess I never considered..." he huffed out a laugh. "You look good."

Lula let out a shaky laugh and leaned against his shoulder. "Thanks, I guess."

"What all did your Death God make you do?" Thomas asked, sounding more curious than anything. His wording piqued Lula's curiosity even more.

"The biggest power he gave me was the power to see souls and collect souls."

"You can see them? Like all of them?" When Lula nodded, he asked, "What do they look like?"

"New souls are yellow. The older a person gets, the more green begins to show until it becomes a dark forest green. As a person's body begins to fail, they begin to die. The yellow bleeds out, leaving the soul blue. Once a soul turns completely blue, they create a sort of pull that Death Gods can feel and follow. My biggest job has been to follow that pull and retrieve those blue souls, ready for death, and take them to the Realm of the Dead," she answered.

"He actually had you take souls?" Thomas cocked his head to the side, staring at her. "I thought that was a big no-no?"

"Well, Doyle is a special brand of lazy." Lula gave Thomas a tight smile.

"That's nuts," Thomas scoffed.

"And also, while technically it's not a no-no, giving a Pet that much power is dangerous, at least to the Pet."

"Why?"

"Death Gods will fight over Pets. The more power they have, the more another Death God will want them so they can use them for any and everything the sick assholes can think of. The Pet is usually destroyed in the fight."

The color in Thomas's face faded a shade.

"I'm surprised you don't know this," Lula said.

"Yeah, well, Melissa and I weren't Pets for long."

"How long were you Pets?" she pushed. "Tell me your story now. What the hell is this war you and the Death Gods are going on about?"

"What makes you think we're at war with the Death Gods?" Thomas asked defensively.

Lula raised an eyebrow. "First off, you guys aren't the only ones talking about this war. The Death Gods know you're planning to make a move against them."

"And secondly?" Thomas took a step toward her.

"The other Death God you saw today? I'm sure he's losing his mind right now because it seems they need me to find something that will turn this war of yours in their favor."

Chapter Twenty-Four

Thomas stood beside Shea, eyeing her. Based on the rigid way he looked down at her, Lula would have believed he hated her. The glint in his eyes made him seem more baffled than angry, at least for the moment, which she could understand. She had dropped one hell of a bombshell.

"So, how do you guys know about the Death Gods' war?" she asked again.

Shea stood, a still statue, his shoulders tight as he stared at the floor. Thomas ran a hand through his short, blond hair as he bounced from one foot to the other.

"My family has known about them for generations. My dad has ways for us to find Pets and free them," Shea answered.

"Are you both Pets?" Max pointed at the two men. "I'm confused."

"He's a Pet." Shea gestured to Thomas. "I'm a normal human, but like I said, I have connections to this. Now, what did you mean by 'the Death God needs you to find something?'"

"Did you know I was a Pet when we met?" Lula asked instead.

Shea's eyes danced around the room, avoiding hers. "I knew."

Okay.

"Did you think about trying to free me?" Lula asked before she could stop herself.

"Lula…" Shea sighed.

The way he seemed to curl in on himself spoke volumes. He didn't have to say *no*. She already knew. Lula crumpled in her seat, feeling utterly defeated.

"Told you," Max whispered in her ear.

He had, hadn't he? *He will only hurt you.* Max's reminder stung. Shea had promised to keep her safe. Wouldn't that mean freeing her from the Death God he knew controlled her?

Panic flashed across Shea's features as he dropped to his knees in front of her, reaching for her. "It's not what you think." His wide eyes implored her to listen.

Lula opened her mouth to respond, but the words got stuck in her throat. Every vow he'd offered, every affection he'd uttered, dissolved in a sea of feelings she couldn't name.

"My dad gave me strict instructions. Melissa and Thomas were the last Pets to be saved. We were moving into the next phase of this war, and we couldn't risk saving anyone else."

"Sure, buddy," Max scoffed.

"I don't understand why you're groveling like this," Thomas said.

"Because I can see in her eyes Lula thinks I didn't save her from her Death God because I didn't want to—or worse, didn't care. That is so far from the truth. Lula means everything to me, and I would do *anything* for her. I just couldn't free her, even though I wish to God I could have."

Shea never looked away from Lula. Every word he said, his eyes stayed locked on hers, imploring her to believe him.

She took a sharp breath. It still hurt, but she believed him. Besides, they had bigger things to focus on. "What is this next phase?" she asked.

"We're also looking for something."

"You know, I wonder if you guys are looking for the same thing?" Max tapped his chin.

"What are you looking for?" When Shea only stood back up and walked away, she threw her hands in the air and groaned. "Shea, I want to help. That's why I told you guys to run. That's why I'm here now. If I'm freed, if I can help others become free..." Lula swallowed hard past the lump forming in her throat. "Please." She jumped off the couch and stepped toward him. "Trust me."

"It's not that I don't trust you." Shea grabbed Lula when she looked away. "I mean it. We've reached a point where we need my dad. He's the one who knows more about it."

"Sounds like you should get a hold of your dad," she said.

"I'll bet money your dad is looking for the same thing as that Death God, Theodrick, is looking for," Max chimed in. "The thing they mentioned in that book you got from Poe's."

"Who's Poe?" Thomas asked, entering the conversation.

"He's another Death God that's also friends with Doyle. He has that sweet old lady for his Pet. What's her name, Lula?"

"Willow."

Lula tried to remember if Willow had any outward signs of being a Pet. Nothing came to mind as she pictured the old woman. Studying Thomas now, she took notice, for the first time, of the details in his aura. Flecks of gold light mixed with the blue and red she had always known. Did Willow have gold around her, too, and she'd just never noticed?

"What did you get from Poe?" Shea asked.

"There was this weird rock, along with a book that had a strange language in it," Max offered freely. "We went looking for it a couple of days later, didn't we?"

"We hoped it would help us break the deal I have with Doyle."

"Did you ever find it?" Shea seemed to hold his breath.

"Did we ever!" Max's entire face lit up. "Still couldn't read it, so not super helpful."

Lula hugged herself as memories of meeting Theodrick washed over her. She told them about coming home to find Doyle and Theodrick pouring over the book. Theodrick held more power than any other Death God she'd ever come across. Drunk on the idea of even more power, he was focused on only one goal: bringing down this Sephtis and securing the throne. She still didn't understand what role she played. Sure, apparently, she was the one who could find this thing, but she didn't understand how.

"Who is Sephtis?" Thomas asked.

"Apparently a Death God himself? I'm still not exactly sure, but if Theodrick doesn't like him, I want to help him." Lula huffed out a humorless laugh.

Shea rubbed his face. "Yeah, I think I need to call my dad. Right now." Shea turned on his heel and marched out of the room.

Lula straightened and pulled at her long skirt, wishing she had chosen a short-sleeved blouse. Raising her chin, she dared to let her gaze land on Thomas. "How did you become a Pet, Thomas?" she asked.

Thomas leaned against a wall and ran a hand through his hair before answering. "It wasn't three hundred years ago or whatever, and it wasn't for something sappy like love. My sister was an avid hiker. She loved to challenge herself. The harder the trail, the better." Thomas's whole body sagged as he continued. "We were on a mountain, and she fell and took me down with her. We were hurt, really bad. The Death God tricked her, tricked us. We were only his playthings, though. Our Death God never gave us any power except to see other Pets. And other Death Gods."

"Who was your sister?" Lula asked, a knot forming in her stomach, even though she already knew.

"Melissa."

"The girl you visited the day you found me?" Lula asked, only just able to keep her voice from breaking.

Thomas nodded, and Lula squeezed her eyes shut against a fresh wave of guilt that threatened to overtake her. She sat back down on the couch and hugged herself. The conformation was like a spear to the chest. At least she knew why Thomas was in the home. He wasn't there to kill Melissa for sure—he was there to protect her.

"Who was your Death God?" Max asked.

Thomas kicked the floor with the toe of his shoe. "His name was Arthur. He had an affinity for collecting forbidden objects. I guess we counted towards it."

"What is it with Death Gods and their collections?" Max scoffed. "It's always something. Doyle has boxes and boxes of those stereoscope cards."

"Stereo-what?" Thomas turned to look at Max.

"You know, those old-timey 3D cards."

"And he had boxes of them?"

"So many boxes. He has to have thousands of those stupid cards. Lula and I found them as we were searching for the old books and the stone we got from Poe."

"For all the good finding it did." Lula groused.

"So, how were Shea and his dad able to get you away from your Death God?" Max asked.

Thomas smiled, and Lula guessed it was the only genuine smile she would see from him. "They were able to trick the trickster."

Max returned the smile. "Do tell."

"As I'm sure you know, a Death God is hard-pressed to pass up on their passion. They just had to find out what our Death God was into and bribe him into letting the two of us go." Thomas's face fell. "All for nothing now." Thomas kept rubbing at his temples, like he was trying to erase the memory.

Lula's stomach soured. "I'm sorry."

Thomas said nothing, just clenched his jaw and looked away.

Shea came back into the room. "Dad is on his way," he said, taking in the scene. "Everything all right?"

"Way better now that you're here." Max beamed up at Shea with a cheeky smile.

Lula rolled her eyes. "When will he be here?"

"Soon."

Shea took a seat beside Lula. Though hurt still gripped her, she didn't resist when he laced his fingers through hers. Smiling, he placed a kiss on the back of her hand.

"Tell me, what are you and your father planning besides saving Pets?" Max pushed.

"We're going to fight the Death Gods so we can restore balance."

Lula turned so she was facing him on the couch. "What do you mean, 'restore the balance?'"

"My grandpa knew someone like you, Lula, and Thomas. They sold their soul and became a slave to a Death God. Digging deeper, he learned not just about them but the origins of the Death Gods. A millennium ago, a benevolent Death God was overthrown by the other Death Gods. Forced into hiding, he could only sit back and watch as the Death Gods threw the Realms of the Living and Dead into chaos, with their greed for power and slovenly ways. They knocked the two realms completely out of balance."

Lula slumped back onto the couch. The rumors she'd heard were true. How had she been so close to a Death God and never known all of this until now? Even after reading those books in Doyle's secret room, she always assumed this was how it always was with Death Gods.

"Anyway, Shea's grandpa figured out a way to free the Pets and taught his son. Devin expanded on the things he had already learned. He knew things couldn't continue the way they were," Thomas continued for Shea. "They had to be set right. His mission became to free anyone else trapped by the Death Gods and find any means necessary to bring them down."

"He wanted to find the Death God that had gone into hiding. Once we find him, we'll fight to put him back in power. Then, with any luck, balance will be restored." Shea said.

"How do you even know who's a Pet and who's not?" Max asked. "I mean, if you aren't a Death God or a Pet, how could you find any of them?"

"My father gave me the ability to see the difference," Shea said.

"How's that?" Lula asked, but Shea just stared at them, not answering.

Lula sat quietly for a moment, trying to absorb everything she'd learned. If what they said was true, then they were the key to her freedom. Hell, they were the key to everyone's freedom. How amazing would it be to live without fear? She closed her eyes and indulged in the thought, just for a moment, of what that could feel like.

Her breath hitched. Opening her eyes, she looked right at the two of them. "How many have you freed?"

"Hundreds," Shea said.

Lula gasped, feeling dizzy with excitement while her stomach twisted with worry.

"Where are they?"

"Hidden," Thomas answered this time. "They're getting ready to fight when the time comes."

"Do you think this war will happen soon?" Lula asked.

The front door opened, and Devin walked in. Boots clanked across the hard floor. He strutted up and stood in front of the couch. Everyone stayed frozen where they were. Max looked as though he was trying to fade out but couldn't. Lula grabbed his hand, trying to give him a reassuring squeeze.

The side of Devin's mouth lifted in a half smile. "My lady, the fight has just begun."

CHAPTER TWENTY-FIVE

D evin stood in his worn jeans and a plaid flannel shirt under a jacket. His hands rested on his hips, giving off a certain air about him. The ball cap that covered his salt and pepper hair sat high giving Lula a clear view of his face. The muscle in his cheek twitched as his eyes raked over the living room, taking in the small group before him. A green darker than any Lula had ever seen on an adult saturated his aura. It seemed to pulse with a hidden color as his eyes narrowed on Max for a moment before settling on her. An array of emotions flashed across his face, too fast for Lula to register, before he seemed to catch himself and cooled his features once more.

"Lula," he greeted with a nod. "Fancy seeing you here again. And so soon."

"Dad," Shea jumped in, "we need to talk."

"Sounds like we do."

Devin turned and disappeared into the kitchen before returning with a beverage in hand. Leaning against the wall, he took a long drink.

Everyone seemed to hold their breath, waiting to see what would happen next. Tension sat thick in the air. Lula fussed with her long skirt, waiting, but she didn't know exactly for what.

Lowering the glass, Devin tilted it toward Max. "Is that something we should worry about?"

Shea furrowed his brow. "No, I don't think so."

"Who the hell are you?" Devin asked after looking Max up and down.

"I'm with her." Max pointed timidly toward Lula.

"I gathered." The low timbre of Devin's voice left no room for sarcasm.

"I'm Lula's ex-boyfriend." Max cleared his throat as he explained himself, making Lula cringe. "I died, though, so now I'm just a ghost."

"Her ghost ex?" Devin repeated.

Max winced. "So to speak."

"I thought it was crazy, too, when I heard it," Thomas said, moving to stand next to Devin.

Devin pinned Lula with a sharp look. "Let me guess, he's the reason you ended up a Pet?"

"Yes," Lula answered. "And I would love to know how you can see him."

"Not many can?" Devin asked.

Lula crossed her arms over her chest. "Only myself and other Death Gods can."

Devin took a step forward, gulping down the last of his drink. "My family and I have been armed with special tools to help us. Making ghosts like your ex here visible is just one of the many I have at my disposal. This entire house is warded and guarded against anyone or anything that would threaten us." He raised an eyebrow, "Clear enough?"

Lula and Max both nodded as their wide eyes stayed locked on Devin.

Devin deliberately placed his now empty glass on a table. "Tell me this, Lula. How did you get away from your Death God? Because I'm also guessing he didn't just let you out of your deal and set you free."

"He didn't. I—" Nerves stole her voice. Lula crumpled in her seat, overcome with grief over what Doyle had forced her to do.

"You what?" Devin pushed.

"Doyle made her take souls," Max answered for her. "They were souls that weren't supposed to be taken yet. At least one of them wasn't supposed to be. Today, though, she fought back, and we were able to get away."

Max lifted his chin, and the look on his face made Lula think he was almost proud of her.

"What souls?"

Lula took a steadying breath. Until this moment, she had dodged Thomas's question about why she was at the house with Melissa. This was going to be the hardest thing to say because she now had to confess to Melissa's brother that she'd killed his sister. Her stomach rolled as she opened her mouth to speak. There was no way Shea would want her after this.

"I...I took Melissa's soul. And I was supposed to take Thomas's soul as well." The words came out just above a whisper.

"You what?"

Thomas's voice sliced like a knife. His entire frame vibrated. Clenching his fists, Thomas charged across the room straight at her.

Chaos erupted. She jerked back in her seat. The men jumped in to intercept him. Shea locked his arms around Thomas, leaning in to stop his advance. Devin grabbed his arm as it swung wildly in the air. Thomas flung insults and threats like daggers straight at Lula. She sat silently, accepting them all. She deserved them all for what she had done. Max joined in the melee, shouting excuses to calm the hysteria.

"I knew you were trouble!" Thomas shouted, his eyes wide with rage. He lunged at Lula again, dragging Shea and Devin forward a step forcing them to adjust their hold on him.

"How *do you* know her, Thomas?" Devin asked.

"I recognized her," he answered, pausing his struggle. "I saw her in the house where we were hiding Melissa the day she died." His voice slowly dropping to a growl.

"It's not her fault." Max jumped up, placing himself between them and Lula. "Theodrick was the one who told Doyle it was a good idea."

Devin froze. His eyes widened, and some of the color drained from his face. "Who?" His question bounced off the walls and brought everyone to a stop.

Max's form faded a bit as he took a step back. He looked to Lula, silently imploring her to help. "Theodrick." Max's voice cracked and he stumbled while retreating further as Devin took a giant step forward. "He started showing up at the house a week or so back. He's the one who convinced Doyle he needed to make Lula do it so they could help him secure a stupid state-thing and get rid of what's-his-name."

Devin closed his eyes. His knuckles turned white from the force of his clenched fists, and harsh-sounding words poured from his mouth in a language she didn't understand. With movements so stiff they had to hurt, Devin went over and sat next to Lula.

Cold, gray eyes pinned her where she sat. "I need you to start over, and this time, start at the beginning."

Lula's wide eyes stayed on Devin as she spoke. Starting with the night she met Shea, she relayed how Doyle had shown up to take Melvin's soul through the Gate—something he hadn't done in a long time. The encounter had left her uneasy. Then she came home to find out from Max about Theodrick's first visit and then how Doyle had lost track of her. Shivers raced over her skin as she recalled how enraged he'd been, but it had led to her time off. That night wouldn't be the last time he would lose her, either.

"It was because you were with me," Shea confessed.

"How?"

"Shea has a special mark on him that keeps him hidden from anyone who can sense and track souls. The thing covers a decent radius, so as long as the two of you were close to each other, you were hidden as well," Devin explained.

Shea pulled down his collar to reveal a black line with a V close to the top. It looked a lot like a stick figure with its arms in the air.

"But we're connected because of the deal she made with Doyle. Why couldn't *I* find her?" Max asked.

"It's a powerful mark." Devin shrugged. "When did Doyle send you after Melissa's soul?"

Lula shot Thomas a glance. He stood by the fireplace, staring holes into the wall.

"About five days after my time off began, I think? Right after one of Theodrick's visits. They were going over the book I brought back from Poe's."

She told Devin all about her trip to see Poe and bring back the case. She lost herself for a moment, recalling the book with the strange writing. At the mention of the piece of rock she and Max had found in the case, his eyes widened.

"What did it look like?" he pressed.

"The book? Just a brown, leather-bound book. It had strange writing in it that kinda looked like hieroglyphics."

"The rock?" His voice dropped, "What did it look like?"

"It looked like a corner of something bigger, with some of the same strange writing on it. Maybe the corner of a tablet?"

"Which corner?" Devin sounded like he was bracing himself for the answer.

"Which corner?" Lula asked.

"You said it looked like the corner of a tablet. Which corner did it look like it came from?"

"I'm not sure. Maybe a bottom corner?" Lula looked to Max for help.

"Left corner?" Max offered with a shrug.

Devin squeezed his eyes shut and bowed, slumping against the wall.

Max shrugged again. "I don't know the language written on it, so I don't know which way would have been up. Besides, he didn't seem very interested in the rock but more interested in the book. He mentioned finding the Stat-something."

"Statera." Lula clarified.

"What the hell is it?" Thomas asked.

"Wait." Devin's head popped up. "He said they found the Statera, or they're looking for it?"

"The way they were talking? They were looking for it. But the way Theodrick would look at me? Especially after I took Melissa's soul?" A chill walked down her spine. "He thinks I'm the one who can find it, but only after I become powerful enough. That's what he said was written in the book."

"I need to get a hold of Michael," Devin said.

He jumped off the couch and pulled a phone from his coat pocket. Placing the phone to his ear, he marched down the hall. She could hear only a "hello" before a door slammed shut.

In the silence, all eyes turn to Lula, the weight of everyone's stare sitting heavily upon her. She struggled to keep her head up and not crawl as far into herself as she could. A part of her worried Thomas would try to come at her again. It sure looked like he wanted to. Swallowing hard against the tears, she fought against the urge to run. Especially as Shea sat frozen beside her, struggling to offer an encouraging smile.

In a room full of people, Lula sat isolated, right next to everyone but miles away from a friendly face. Grief ripped at her heart, stealing her breath.

This was where she lost him.

Chapter Twenty-Six

Lula fidgeted while waiting for Devin to reemerge. No one spoke. Shea sat beside her on the couch but stayed at a distance. Outside, the sun had slipped lower in the sky as the first signs of evening changed the mountains to a darker shade of green. Devin had spoken of a mark on Shea keeping them hidden, but nerves threw her heart against her ribs. Was that the only thing keeping them hidden? She remembered the wards Devin spoke of, but were they truly enough? Lula shivered as the list of questions she needed answers to only grew. For the moment, she prayed whatever power made them invisible held. Lula practically panted as she sucked in big gulps of air in an attempt to calm herself. She closed her eyes and recalled the dream she'd been having before waking in this farmhouse, but she was too distracted. She could feel Thomas staring at her.

"How did you find Melissa?" Thomas demanded.

Lula's eyes shot open, and she gasped. Thomas had moved to stand right in front of her.. His bright-blue eyes were slits as he glared down at her. His short, dirty-blond hair looked lighter under the glow of the lit room.

"I, uh, followed the call of the Marked soul."

"But how did you know Melissa was Marked?"

"I told you. Doyle gave me the power to see them."

"That's not...that's not what I'm asking."

"Then what are you asking?"

Thomas rubbed his face before turning away. Lula thought he would leave her alone, but instead, he squatted in front of her.

"I guess I just want to know what a Marked soul even looks like. I mean, I know you're a Pet, and Melissa was a Pet because of the gold light coming off you both. I assume I also have a golden glow."

Lula sat back and took Thomas in. He still had the blue hue surrounding him, signifying his status as a Marked soul, and mixed in with it, there were the gold flecks of light. Strangely enough, the red had vanished.

"I see it." Lula frowned. "I wonder why I never saw it before?"

"You never saw another Pet, maybe?" Thomas offered.

Lula tilted her head. "No, I've actually met quite a few."

"Maybe you're just not that observant." Thomas sneered, and Lula glared back at him. "So...?"

Shaking her head, Lula looked over at Max. He wandered around the room, looking at pictures and knickknacks. He looked over at her, giving her a reassuring smile.

"Marked souls, good souls, are a bright blue. The closer their body is to giving out, the brighter the color and glow. Melvin was entirely *bathed* in the blue light."

"Good souls?"

"Souls that led a good life and earned a place in the Realm of the Dead. They spend an eternity in paradise as a reward."

"What's it like?" Shea asked.

Lula's eyes slid closed, conjuring the Realm of the Dead in her mind's eye. "The first thing you notice is the beautiful fragrance filling the air, a mix of wildflowers right after it rains. The meadow stretches out forever, filled with the softest grass that tickles your feet. Then you look up..." Lula smiled and looked up, not seeing the ceiling but living the memory she held of the tranquil Realm. "A kaleidoscope of every color you can imagine spreads above you, churning and swirling but never quite mixing. I would raise the soul high above me and watch as it floated off. The colors would shimmer when the soul would reach the sky."

"It sounds wonderful." Thomas's eyes took on the shine as he looked past her into the distance.

"It is." Lula brought her eyes down to his. "The most overwhelming calm and sense of belonging you've ever known fills you. I always struggle to tear myself away and come back here."

"I wish I could see it. I wish—" Thomas broke off, swallowing hard. "Do you think we can get Melissa there? She was a good soul, right?"

"She was, and she deserves to be there. I don't know if we can, but I promise I'll try to find a way."

Even as the promise fell out of her mouth, she knew it would be impossible. Melissa was a part of her now.

"What about the bad souls?" Thomas asked.

"They're black and thick like tar when pulled out of the body. Releasing them into the Realm of the Dead would be dangerous, so they're immediately destroyed."

"What color am I?" Genuine fear sparked in Thomas's eyes. Lula couldn't understand what would make him ask this question. Then again, as she thought about her own life and the decisions she'd made, she could imagine asking the same.

"Blue." She smiled reassuringly. "You are a beautiful bright blue."

Thomas sagged with a sigh before getting up and wandering over to the end of the hall. Shea got up and joined him. The two began talking, but Lula didn't pay any attention to what they were talking about. With everyone busy and no sign of Devin coming out of the backroom, Lula slipped out the door and made her way to the stables. She went straight to Rigatoni's stall and greeted the sweet horse with long strokes of his mane.

"Rigatoni, what am I going to do?" She leaned her forehead against the horse's soft neck. "Can I tell you a secret?" she whispered. "I'm scared."

"Don't be," Shea's voice drifted in from behind her.

Lula turned to see him standing in the barn doorway. A shiver ran down her spine as she took in his tight expression. A beat of silence fell between them, threatening to bury them in everything they needed to say but couldn't find the words.

"Shea." Lula cleared her throat. "I didn't hear you."

"I didn't mean to startle you." He strolled over to stand next to her but she could tell it was a fight to look casual. Clearing his throat, he stroked Rigatoni's mane. "I'm sorry about everything you've had to go through. And not being able to free you."

"And not telling me you knew I was a Pet?"

"Yeah, I should have been more honest with you. Dad's orders be damned."

"Well." Lula swallowed hard. "I know how demanding dads can be sometimes."

"Are you talking about your papa or Doyle?"

Lula gave a small smile. "Both, but I was thinking more about Doyle. I wish I could have told you about him. I was worried that if he found out about you, he would kill you. Literally."

"He has the power to do that, doesn't he?"

Lula couldn't bear to answer, so she changed the subject. "I'm also sorry about Melissa. I swear I didn't want to do it, but that doesn't change the fact that I did."

"I'm sorry, too, but trust me when I say I don't blame you."

Lula ducked her head and blinked away the tears threatening to fall. Now was not the time to break down. Instead, she focused on petting Rigatoni and what she had learned. "I still can't believe you're in a war with the Death Gods. I guess there's a lot I still don't know about you."

Shea gave a shrug. "That's fair. No one has been completely open and honest with each other. Not a great way to start a relationship," he admitted with a crooked smile.

Lula huffed out a laugh while keeping her focus on Rigatoni. "Yeah, well, I guess we can just start over again. This time, no more secrets."

"I can get behind that." Shea sighed. "I'm just not sure where I fit into this love triangle. I know you're devoted to that ghost." His lip twitched like he was fighting a smile.

Lula's eyes nearly rolled out of her head. "Oh my god, please don't even joke about that."

"I can't believe he used you to get to another woman. What an idiot." He let out a huff of a laugh before cupping her face. "If it had been me, I would have forgotten all about what's-her-name the second I looked into your beautiful eyes."

Lula smiled. "Nice line, Don Juan."

"It's no line." His eyes shone as they searched her face. "I meant what I said in there. I care a great deal for you."

"You do?" Lula's heart threatened to beat out of her chest.

Shea took her hand and pulled her away from the horse's stall. "What is it about you?" Even though this wasn't the first time he'd asked this question, it was the first time it made her breath hitch.

"You told me once I remind you of someone."

"It's more than just that."

In a swift move, Shea pulled her flush against his body. He brushed the hair from her face and lowered his mouth to hers. The first soft touch shot straight to Lula's toes. Her heart raced in her chest as her whole body quivered. He teased her and playfully nipped at her. Lula's hands slid up his arms and into his hair. Tentatively, she opened her mouth, and he deepened the kiss. Shea wrapped his arms tighter around her body and let out a moan as his tongue danced with hers. Every time they shared another kiss, another taste, Lula's entire body warmed in the most delicious way. Nothing had ever been this good.

"Shea," she moaned as he trailed kisses along her jaw.

"God, Lula." He buried his face in the crook of her neck. When he pulled back, his eyes were full of desire. "Is it possible to feel this much for someone so fast?"

She knew what he meant, but it didn't matter. The only thing that mattered was that she needed him like she needed her next breath.

"All I know is," she told him, holding his face, "with you, I know I'm safe. I feel more alive than I ever have in my whole life. You are the only one who has ever made me feel this way."

Shea's chest heaved as he listened to her speak. She couldn't believe she had confessed those things to him. The words were so right but still left her nervous and vulnerable.

Instead, he reached down and swept her into his arms. Without taking his eyes off her, he walked over and laid her on a pile of hay. "You're so beautiful, Lula," he said, showering her face with kisses. "Inside and out."

Happy tears sprang to her eyes. Never had anyone bestowed upon her such affections. Being with Shea brought her more joy than anything else in all her many years. His lips met hers once more, and pure bliss consumed her.

A door slammed, and voices began speaking in a flurry of curses.

"Shit." Shea leaped to his feet. "My dad." He reached down and pulled Lula up. "I was supposed to just come out here and get you. Dad is off the phone with my uncle, and they have a plan, I think."

Lula giggled as the two of them brushed at all the hay on their clothes, failing to get it all off.

Shea looked down at her and smiled. He reached out and began pulling bits of hay from her hair. "Sorry."

"I'm not." She grinned up at him. "I rather enjoyed it," she confessed as heat warmed her cheeks.

Shea leaned down, giving her one last, slow, toe-curling kiss. "I must admit, I rather enjoyed it myself."

Lula burst out laughing. Despite everything caving in on her, she had never been more free and alive as she was right then. "Come on, let's go find your dad before he finds us." Lula giggled again at the look of pure horror on his face.

They walked hand in hand back through the barn, but before they went out to meet his dad, she stopped. "Shea." She pulled on his hand.

"Yes?"

"I do want to help you. I want to help bring balance."

He gave her hand a squeeze. "We will, Lula. Together."

Chapter Twenty-Seven

When Lula and Shea stepped out of the barn, hand in hand, Devin was leaning against the railing of the small back porch. His relaxed pose belied his calm demeanor. He stood every bit as imposing as he had in the farmhouse. By the look on his face, Devin seemed to know what had taken them so long. His expression left Lula wondering what he could be thinking. He didn't seem upset. More than anything, he looked amused by the sight. Those dark eyes, so much like Shea's, bore into her as they made their way to the backdoor. It was like he couldn't believe his eyes as he stared at her, his mouth lifted in a half smile. Her being wound tight, she sought to shrug it off.

"I was wondering if you two were going to join us."

Shea covered a laugh with a cough and gestured toward the door. "Let's go inside. I can't wait to hear what you and Uncle Michael talked about."

Entering the house, they all stopped short. Lula eyed Max standing by the fireplace, surprisingly close to Thomas. The two looked like they had just been caught with their hands in the cookie jar. Lula gaped at Max.

"Hey, everyone." Max grinned, giving a little wave. "We were just chatting."

"Everyone in the kitchen. I'm grabbing something, and I'll be right there." Devin gestured as he marched down the hall.

Lula slipped over to Max and smacked his arm.

"What?" He laughed.

"Making friends?"

"Someone has to." Max said, unrepentant. "We were just bonding over the ridiculous figurines they have around here. I mean, really, it's worse than your collection."

Max laughed harder as Lula swung at him but missed after he ducked out of the way. They did as they were told. Lula took a seat next to Shea, with Thomas sitting right across from him. Max opted to lurk behind Lula, leaning against the counter. Devin returned to the kitchen with an enormous book.

"After a long talk, Michael and I have come up with a plan."

"What is it?" Shea asked.

"First, we want to make sure we fill Lula in." He looked right at her. "I'm going to explain everything that I can to you right now."

The massive tome looked older than any Lula had ever seen, including the ones she and Max had stumbled upon in Doyle's library.

The black hard cover appeared frayed at the spine, with the title worn away and hard to read. She could see the brown string fighting to keep the pages together. When Devin opened the book to a place marked by a faded gold ribbon, the yellowed pages crinkled as if made of tissue paper.

"My family has known about the Death Gods for a long time. Our knowledge comes from generations of studying them. Not everything we've learned made us thrilled. One thing we learned, though, made us downright furious. The Death Gods, as I'm sure everyone here already knows, are a bunch of lazy good-for-nothings. They have one job: take souls at the end of their lives and guide them through the gate to the Realm of the Dead. It seems to pain them to do that one simple task. My grandfather, through means all his own, discovered that their laziness had taken a turn for the criminal. Over the years, through hard work and tons of research, we have accumulated not just a treasure trove of knowledge about the Death Gods but some of their artifacts. We were able to learn about using and activating special markings like the one Shea and I have that keep us hidden from other Death Gods. We also have physical talismans that can not just hide us and locations, like this farm, but act as weapons. We've actually managed to destroy several Death Gods ourselves."

"You've killed a Death God?" Lula nearly fell out of her chair.

"Yes." Devin stuck a hand in his pocket. "Using a very powerful and very old spear especially designed to take down Death Gods. "

"How long have you been fighting Death Gods? I'm asking because Theodrick made it sound like the battle had just begun. I'm not sure if he knows who is behind any attacks either."

"That doesn't surprise me. Theodrick is a very powerful Death God, but he doesn't pay attention to anything unless it directly affects him."

"Well, he may not know who you are, but he does know you are recruiting Pets."

Devin leaned forward, rubbing his forehead. A curse slipped out under his breath.

Shea leaned forward. His brow pulled together in concern. "Dad?"

"They were bound to find out, eventually. I guess I just hoped we had a bit more time before they did."

"And you're doing this just because they are tricking people into becoming Pets?" Lula asked.

"Liberating Pets is one of the reasons." Devin sighed. "The other is what these deities are doing to the souls of the dead. They rip them from bodies before destroying them instead of taking them to the Realm of the Dead, like they're supposed to. Now, before you jump in, I know the souls of those like killers and abusers do not deserve to carry on. But these deities are destroying even the most innocent of souls without a second thought because it's too much work for them. No matter how you slice it, that's wrong."

Lula had been wondering what they were doing with the souls. She had overheard more than her share of conversations between Doyle and other Death Gods. Hearing how lazy they were and how determined they were to do as little as possible, she had worried they were doing something they shouldn't be. Devin's explanation made her blood boil. She thought of all the souls she had taken—the girl from the restaurant, Melvin. Her cheeks burned as her nails bit into the flesh of her hand. It was bad enough that she had to endure the control and isolation that came with being a Pet, but to find out these monsters were destroying innocent souls was unbearable. Her only solace lay in knowing that the souls she had taken were safely in the Realm of the Dead—most of them, anyway.

Lula bowed and clenched her fists harder until she was sure the skin would break. "They're destroying souls for no reason."

"Well, not for no reason," Devin corrected. "It's one of the biggest reasons we need to stop them."

"Laziness is not a reason," she pointed out.

Devin shifted in his seat, looking guilty as sin as he avoided looking her in the eyes.

"What aren't you telling me, Devin?" Lula pushed.

Letting out a defeated sigh, he explained, "Every time a Death God destroys a soul, they gain the power that life held. This strengthens them."

"Wait," Max interjected. "Doyle didn't destroy *any* souls."

"How do you know?" Thomas challenged.

"Because he made Lula take them through the Gate after *she* collected them. Remember?"

"He's right that not all Death Gods take part in this. Only the strongest ones."

"Great," Thomas grumbled.

Melvin passed through her thoughts like a phantom once more. Grinding her teeth, Lula would have bet everything she had that Doyle had turned his poor soul over to Theodrick.

"What is that?" she asked, motioning to the book, trying to keep focused on the here and now.

"It's one of the many books and artifacts we've collected over the years. This one is the *Book of Sephtis* and talks about the prophecy of Enid."

Something about that name rang a tiny bell in the back of Lula's mind, something Doyle and Theodrick had talked about. Was Enid somehow tied to the prophecy? Lula couldn't exactly remember how, though.

"Tell me."

"Enid speaks of the rise of Sephtis, the God of Death. Only after he has found the Statera will he be able to reclaim his throne."

"How did he lose it in the first place?" Lula asked.

"That is a long story." When Lula just continued to stare at Devin, he sighed and began the tale. "There are two deities that created our universe. Enid is the God of Life. Everything from the stars in our sky, to the planet we live on, to plants and animals all around us, she created. Her entire existence is bringing forth new life. Her brother is Sephtis, the God of Death. His sole purpose is to end the life that Enid created."

"That sounds harsh," Thomas scoffed.

"It's not harsh. It's balanced and necessary. You can't have one without the other. Sephtis only ensured that there would be room for a new life to grow. And those with souls didn't parish, but were instead guided into the Realm of the Dead so they could exist in peace."

"So the *Book of Sephtis* is what? A book about the God of Death?" Thomas asked.

"The *Book of Sephtis* is an account of his life and a testimony of what happened. He knew he needed to right this wrong." Devin tapped the book. "Sephtis is a loving god, despite what he does. He always enjoyed the company of Enid's creations, especially humans."

"He made friends with humans? Did they know what he was?" Max asked.

"Of course they didn't. He knew how they would react. Still, any chance he got, Sephtis would talk to them and learn about them. He said—or it's said in this book that he said—it helped with the loneliness he would feel. The only problem was they would eventually die, and Sephtis would have to guide them through the Gate to the Realm of the Dead. In desperation for company, he made the first Death God. They got along well, and Sephtis was so happy, he made more."

"How many Death Gods did he make in total?" Lula asked.

"Fifty. And they were all like him—immortal with all the powers he possessed so they could help escort souls from around the world through the Gate."

"What...does it say how they guided the soul?" Lula asked the question that had burned in the back of her mind.

Devin peered at Lula for a moment before answering. "When a soul was ready to pass through the Gate, their aura would turn blue, and it would leave their body. Sephtis and the others would then collect them and escort them through."

Sephtis had created many Death Gods for such a selfish reason. Then, those Death Gods resorted to barbaric means of collecting souls for even more selfish reasons. Lula closed her eyes and forced herself not to curl into a ball. Fifty.

"Why are you asking?"

"Let's just say that's not how souls are collected anymore." Lula's voice shook.

Devin turned his uncomfortable focus to the table. He cleared his throat before continuing.

"For a time, everything was peaceful and perfect. Sephtis had friends who would never die, and they helped him guide souls that had passed. One day, however, he noticed some of the Death Gods weren't exactly like him. They were immortal and had power, but he had not made them. More alarming, their numbers were skyrocketing. He learned that a few of his original Death Gods had made Death Gods of their own. Then he learned they'd developed the power to bargain with souls, so instead of basking in the Realm of the Dead as they should, some were being destroyed while others were turned into slaves for the Death Gods to order around and abuse. Horrified and desperate to regain control, Sephtis took away their ability to make more Death Gods. Enraged by what he had done, the Death Gods revolted. Overpowered by the rebel Death Gods, Sephtis fled. He went to his sister Enid and begged for her help."

Devin slid the book in front of Lula and pointed to the words on the page. She read along as Devin continued to explain. "Enid could not help. Her power was in giving life, not taking it. She devised a plan so Sephtis could reclaim his place as the God of Death. Enid would create the Statera, the one thing that would give him the power to restore the balance that the Death Gods had thrown off. It's a living force with great power. In the end, with the Statera, the true God of Death will come forward to reclaim his Realm."

She sat in silence, letting the words roll over her.

"Hey, Lula," Max leaned in and whispered. "Doesn't that book look familiar?"

Lula looked harder at it. "It does look like that book I brought back to Doyle's."

"Doyle has something like this?" Devin pointed at the book.

"Yeah." Max's eyes danced with merriment. "Doyle has a hidden room in his library full of books. You even pull a special bust to open the door. There were lots of old books in that little room. I don't remember the name of the one like yours, but I remember it was the strangest out of all of them. We couldn't read it because it was in this strange language. Another of the books we found revealed all sorts of history about the Death Gods—that one had to be written by them. Right, Lula?" Max elbowed her.

Lula rolled her eyes as she remembered a section spewing about the glory of their existence. "I can't imagine anyone else writing such over-the-top flattery, all about how amazing the Death Gods are. They really love themselves."

"We mean, they *really* love themselves," Max declared with exaggerated outrage.

Devin's eye twitched. "If we could focus, please?"

"Sorry," Max muttered.

Devin's scowled as he stared Lula and Max down. "But there *was* a book that looked just like this one?" He tapped his finger on the book in front of him.

Lula sat up straighter in her chair. "Yes, and they called it *The Book of Enid,* I think. It's also the same book Theodrick read from when he mentioned the Statera."

Devin's wide eyes locked with Lula's. "We need that book. Can you take me to Doyle's house?"

Lula's eyebrows pulled together. "I mean, I can, but don't you think that's a little dangerous? He's looking for me, and he's working with Theodrick. I'm still his Pet."

"It *is* a risk," Devin confirmed. "However, if that book is what I think it is, it'll change everything."

"Why is *The Book of Enid* worth this amount of risk?" Thomas piped up.

"If Doyle has *The Book of Enid*, he basically has a guide on how to find and activate the Statera, effectively becoming the God of Death."

The room went still. The only thing Lula could hear was the pounding of her own heart in her ears. Obviously, that book needed to be as far away from Theodrick as they could get it, but something in Devin's eyes made Lula's palms sweat. Lula didn't know Devin, and he was hard to get a read on. Something felt different about him. This man's aura was too dark. Still, she trusted Shea. She would just have to learn to trust Devin.

"This won't be easy," Lula reminded him.

"Never thought it would be," Devin answered.

Shea tilted his head back. "We can do this."

"Sounds like we have to," Thomas added.

"Lula, please." Devin leaned forward and placed his hand on her arm. "Take us to Doyle's so we can get that book."

"If it's even still there," Max hedged.

"It has to be. Please?" Devin pleaded.

Lula let out a long breath, looking over to Max, who shrugged. "Fine, let's go break into Doyle's library."

"Thank you, Lula," Devin said.

Everyone got up from the table and started making their way outside. They were out the door when Lula stopped next to Devin as he locked up the house.

"Devin, how is the Statera activated?"

His brow furrowed as he slowed his pace and looked at her. "What are you talking about?"

"Theodrick read in that book that the Statera needs to be activated before it's useful. He said there are two ways. One, Sephtis activates it. The other is something they can do, but he never elaborated. I was hoping you knew."

Devin rubbed the back of his neck and looked toward his truck. Lula had a feeling he wasn't watching them pile into the vehicle. A few expressions passed over his face before he looked back at her. "I don't know exactly. That's why we need *The Book of Enid* so badly."

"Do you have any clue?"

"The clues we've been able to gather over the years are that it has to be powered up with energy. Sephtis has the energy to do it on his own. Enid made sure he did before proceeding with the Statera. The Death Gods don't. The only energy that we know of that would be enough is the power generated by a soul."

"How would the Statera get the energy from a soul?" Lula asked.

Devin regarded her for another heartbeat. Reaching up, he nudged her toward the truck. "Later. We have to focus on getting the book right now."

"But—"

"Later, Lula, I promise. Like I said, I don't know anything for sure. Not yet."

Lula sighed but relented. She guessed it was only fair he wouldn't know if all the answers were in *The Book of Enid* anyway. The two walked over to the truck, Lula dragging her feet. She took a deep breath as she got to the truck and climbed into the back, where Shea sat waiting. She slid in beside him and took his hand, giving him a smile.

"I was wondering if you two were going to stay behind," Shea said.

"No, I just needed a minute to build my resolve. Little secret, I'm not looking forward to going back to that house."

Shea brought her hand up and laid it on his chest. The most tender smile lit his face. "Don't worry, Lula. I won't let anything happen to you."

Lula returned the smile and leaned against Shea, feeling the safest she had been in years. She caught Devin looking at them in the rearview mirror. Oddly, he was smiling at them.

The car took off down the road, and Lula braced herself for whatever awaited her back at the house she'd once called home.

Chapter Twenty-Eight

An uncomfortable silence settled over the car as they weaved through the evening traffic toward Doyle's house. Devin's steady gaze stayed locked on the road ahead as they made their way into Portland. Thomas stared out the window, sitting in the front seat with his head in his hand. Lula sat in the middle, flanked by a stiff Max and a possessive Shea. Shea never let go of her hand, earning him some serious side eye from Max.

Unable to take the deafening silence anymore, Lula broached the question weighing heavy on her mind, especially since they were heading back to her house. "Devin, how are you freeing Pets?" she asked.

"We made a few deals in our time. The difference is, we make sure there's a big enough loophole that we can get out of serving them for eternity."

"So, there's a way for you to free me from Doyle?"

Devin sat quietly for a heartbeat before letting out a long sigh. "I'm not sure there is."

Lula's heart sank. He claimed to free so many Pets, so why couldn't he free her? Rubbing her eyes, she had to wonder if Devin *couldn't* or, for some reason, *wouldn't* free her. Maybe after confessing to taking Melissa's soul, Devin had deemed her not worth saving.

Devin looked up at her in the rearview mirror and smiled. He glanced toward Shea before letting out a huff that sounded very close to a laugh. "Lula, you don't need to worry. You don't need me to free you from Doyle. You have all but freed yourself from him when you fought back, helping Shea and Thomas escape. I can all but guarantee there's no way you'll ever be back under his control."

"But you don't know that," Lula insisted. "We're getting ready to break into Doyle's house. If he finds me, he'll never let me go. Especially if Theodrick is with him."

Devin's smile raised a notch as he turned at a traffic light. "Trust me," he called over his shoulder. "No one is taking you away. Not without a fight."

Lula pointed to the house she'd called home for so long. Nodding, Devin kept driving, opting to park in a spot further down the street. Everyone got out and slowly made their way back down the street. The closer they got to the house, the harder it was to pull air into her lungs. Almost all the hate that burned inside her seeped out as panic grabbed her by the throat. Having tasted even these few fleeting moments of freedom, the idea of seeing Doyle and falling back under his control made her dizzy with fear.

"What are you thinking?" Shea whispered in her ear.

"I'm thinking that I don't know what I'm going to do if I have to see Doyle again."

"Don't tell me you're getting ready to back out on us?" Thomas whined from the front seat.

Lula threw her hands up as the last bit of patience she had for him drained out of her. "No, I'm just having a moment. I know it sounds dumb, but I can't help it."

"It's fine, Lula," Shea reassured her. Leaning over, he kissed her cheek.

"I'm scared," she told him honestly. "He still has me. I'm not free of his deal. What if he shows up? What if-"

Shea squeezed her hand, pulling her out of her spiral. "If he shows up, we are going to battle our way out. We can do this, Lula."

"But..." Her eyes darted to all the people around her. She swallowed hard past the lump in her throat. It took everything in her to keep moving forward.

Shea pulled Lula to a stop. His face locked in hard determination. "I'm not going to let you go. Not without a fight."

His confidence did wonders to ease her fears. Taking a step forward, Max brushed by her. She steeled herself for what awaited them. She would get out of this. They were all getting out of this and with that book.

Everyone slowed their pace even more, searching all around them as they moved closer to the front door. Lula reached out with her powers, searching for Doyle, but he was nowhere to be found inside.

Shea leaned in and pointed, "This isn't the house I dropped you off at."

Lula gave an unrepentant smirk. "I had some strange hot guy I'd never met before driving me to my Death God's house. Pardon me for not being completely forthcoming with my exact address."

"You thought I was hot?"

"Still do."

At the front door, Lula took her place at the front of the group, but she couldn't bring herself to walk in. She wasn't sure if she could handle this in more ways than one. Even though she was sure Doyle wasn't home, fear that she would freeze in the face of him were like heavy shackles around her wrists. While she was standing there trying to find her courage, a wave of power slammed into her senses like a train. Lula trembled where she stood. Reaching out, she found someone lying on the floor somewhere in the house. Their power, weak as it was, didn't feel entirely unfamiliar.

"Someone is in there," Lula squeaked between frantic breaths. "A Death God."

"How the hell do you know that?" Thomas asked incredulously.

"Doyle?" Devin asked from right behind her.

Unable to speak, Lula shook her head. Taking a deep breath, she slipped through the front door, the others close behind. She reached out with all her senses to make sure she hadn't missed anyone, and only the *one* Death God waited for them.

"There's only one Death God here."

"Are you sure?" Devin seemed on higher alert now.

"Yeah, and it's definitely not Doyle," Lula reassured herself most of all.

"You can feel if it's your Death God?" Thomas asked.

"After spending so many years with him, I know when it's him. Whoever's back there *isn't* Doyle. I recognize them, but I'm not sure who it is."

"What do you want to do?" Max asked.

Lula and Max shared a knowing look between them. Where there was one Death God, more were bound to appear, but they had to get that book.

Lula spoke to Max. "Take everyone to the library and get everything we need. I'll see who's here and deal with them."

"You aren't going alone." Shea stepped in front of Lula and took her hand.

"I'll be fine," she insisted.

"Take him, Lula," Max said. "As a backup. I'll take these two to the library, then we'll meet back here. Deal?"

"Fine," Lula relented with a sigh. "Just stay behind me." She pointed at Shea.

"Lead the way."

Making their way up the stairs, the first room they checked was her bedroom. Everything sat just where she'd left it. Once a welcome sanctuary, though, it now sat cold and uninviting. Shea wandered through the small space, stopping at her dresser. Lula couldn't take her eyes off him as he went over the things she'd surrounded herself with. He picked up a small skeleton figurine, fighting a smile.

"You're judging me, aren't you?" she asked, half teasing.

"No, I like skeletons too." He smiled at her.

"It just seemed fitting, you know? To be surrounded by the deceased."

"I get it, really. Besides…" He gave a shrug. "They're cute, just like you." He put the figurine down. Something new seemed to catch his eyes. The hairs on the back of her neck stood up as he picked up her necklace. He held it reverently in his hand and stroked the silver chain. "This is pretty."

"Thanks. I've had it for a while. It's the one I told you about that reminded me of the one you gave me." She placed her hand on her neck, stroking her precious gift. "It's literally the only thing I have from when I was alive in England. You know, besides Max," she joked.

The corner of his lips pulled up for a moment, but he kept his attention locked on the delicate piece of jewelry. "Who gave it to you?"

"I don't remember. I used to wear it all the time, but after the chain broke, I decided I didn't want to risk losing it. Now, I just wear it when I get home. It comforts me." Lula's cheeks warmed as the confession poured out of her.

"It doesn't look broken."

"No, I got it fixed. I just didn't want to risk it getting broken again. More specifically, I didn't want Doyle to break it again. I keep it hidden from him."

Shea frowned, and he ran a finger over the jewels. "Why would he break it?"

"He didn't like it for some reason. When he saw me wear it, he would always get upset. Who knows why? Doyle has always been weird."

"Well, you can wear it now. Let me help you put it on."

"Two necklaces. I'll feel so fancy."

Lula pulled her hair out of the way, and Shea slid the necklace around her neck. The second his fingers touched her skin, the room around her was yanked away. One moment, they stood in her room. The next, they stood in an open field. The sun beat down on them as the soft grass under her bare feet tickled her ankles. The long, brown dress she wore danced around her as the wind blew.

Shea finished putting the necklace around her neck. A warm smile never left his face. His dark eyes twinkled as he took her in. "It looks beautiful on you," he said.

Lula looked around, taking in the familiar field. Sheep grazed in the distance. She looked up at Shea once more, but the name didn't fit. She knew him—but by something else. Something she couldn't remember. It was just on the tip of her tongue. Everything about this moment, on this hill, rang so many bells. She knew this place. A memory from so long ago. A strong one that she had forgotten?

Lula opened her mouth to speak, only to be jerked back to her room in the present. She blinked a few times and focused on Shea, who seemed to be locked, wide-eyed, in place before her.

"What..."

"...was that?" Shea finished for her.

"You? Did you just have—"

"A strange vision? Yes," he answered.

A vision? Lula stared into his eyes. Was that what had happened? "It felt so real," she said softly. "More like a memory. Only, a memory that I had completely forgotten."

"How, though? I only just met you. There's no way I have a memory of us standing in a field in England together, no matter how real it seemed."

Lula's breath came in short, shallow gasps as her heart warred with her mind over what had just happened. "I don't know."

Shea hugged her shoulders. His chest rose and fell on a sigh. Leaning forward, he gave her a soft kiss. "Vision or memory. It has to mean we're on the right path. That we're supposed to be together."

Lula stroked the stone now sitting at her throat. "Come on, we need to keep looking," she said.

They stopped at the next door, Doyle's room. The energy of a Death God radiated from behind the door. She opened it to find the Death God on his back, lying on the floor beside the bed. His blood-soaked clothes were torn, and one of his feet looked like it could be pointed at an odd angle. He looked up at her and let out a long, painful groan.

Lula's face contorted as she pieced together what was going on. "Poe?"

"Lulabelle," he croaked. "You're back. I knew they just had to be patient, and you would come to them." He stopped when he saw Shea, and his eyes widened. "Lula, what are you doing? Who is this person with you?"

"None of your business," Lula snapped. She leaned down beside Poe, looking him over. "What happened to you?"

"Theodrick and I came here to talk to Doyle. Doyle has tried everything to find you, but he can't. You somehow fell off the grid. He can't even conjure Max. Theodrick is *obsessed* with finding you and took his frustration out on me. He believes you are the key to this whole thing."

Lula raised a brow. "You mean the key to finding Death and this whole prophecy thing?"

"How do you know about the prophecy? You're just a worthless *Pet*," Poe said, spitting the word at her.

"Watch your language," Shea snapped. "Otherwise, I may have to destroy you."

"Like you could." Poe panted, blood dripping down his face.

Lula's eyes widened as Shea pulled a silver knife out of his boot. The smooth blade led to a wide hilt with an etched grip. His jaw clenched, and he pointed the tip at Poe's face. Lula couldn't help but wonder if it was something he had been carrying the whole time.

"You're not the first Death God I've faced off against," Shea's deep voice left no room for doubt.

Poe's eyes mirrored Lula's as he squirmed, trying to put any space between him and his impending doom. "What are you doing? You can't do this to me! Do you know who I am?" he squealed.

"I know what you're about to become—a faded memory," Shea threatened.

"You can't win!" Poe kept babbling. "Theodrick is too powerful. You won't be able to stop him from getting the throne. Not even Sephtis himself with his army is any match for him."

Footsteps in the hall caught Lula's attention just before Devin, Max, and Thomas' voices reached her. Lula breathed a sigh of relief as they entered the room.

"We have what we need," Devin said, then froze.

Poe squirmed even more under his harsh glare. He squealed and rolled from side to side like a turtle stuck on its back. His whole body trembled as he worked to right himself. Any attempt to get up only led to him falling back to the floor. Whatever Theodrick had done to him had left its mark. Lula looked back and forth between the two as her mind reeled, searching for a reason they were acting this way.

"You stay away from me, you hear? You can't hurt me. I mean it! Stay away, or else."

Devin took two steps forward, as his now cold eyes tightened. "You son of a—"

Poe screamed at the top of his lungs, "I have Katy!"

Devin let out a cry of his own as he charged forward. In one swift move, he wrenched the blade from Shea's hand and pressed it against Poe's throat. All Poe did was sweat as Devin yanked him by his shirt.

"Where is she?" Devin's deep voice rumbled.

"I can't tell you," Poe cried. "They'll kill me."

"You sniveling little rat, what do you think I'm about to do to you?"

Poe only whimpered in response, trying to curl his oversized body into a ball.

"Tell me where she is now." Devin pushed the blade harder against Poe's skin, and Lula watched a new stream of blood trickle down his throat.

"My basement," Poe gave in a blubbering confession. "She's in my basement."

"Why are you keeping someone in your basement?" Lula couldn't stop from asking the question.

"We knew he would want her back. She was going to be leveraged for his part of the stone."

Lula's stomach turned. She didn't know who Katy was, but no one deserved to be held against their will. The thought of some helpless person trapped in a basement and used as a pawn only strengthened her resolve to help Devin see this through to the end. The world would be free of these malevolent deities.

Another wave of energy slammed into Lula, almost knocking her off her feet.

"Devin, Doyle is here, and he's not alone."

Devin glanced at her before glaring once more at Poe. "This isn't over." He shoved Poe to the floor before turning and ordering everyone to move.

The five of them raced through the house. The power around them grew with every step they took. Lula began to tremble. *He's close. Doyle is so close.*

They made it to the entryway, their escape feet away, when the front door burst open.

Doyle stood, taking up the doorway. A sinister smile slid across his face. "Welcome home, Lulabelle."

Chapter Twenty-Nine

Lula froze at the bottom of the stairs, trying to process the scene before her. Doyle loomed at the front door.

A catlike grin slithered across his face as a small cloud of black smoke circled his feet. "I knew you would come back, my Pet. There is no way you could stay away from me. After all, I own you." Doyle's gaze drifted over to Max, standing beside her.

"Of course she came back," Theodrick said, coming out of the living room off to the left. "She also brought the next soul, just like the good little Pet she is. Now we will get to watch as she launches us even closer to our goal."

The two Death Gods stood side by side in the entryway, blocking their way out. Lula couldn't think past the fear gripping her. She couldn't go back to Doyle, never again. Devin had promised she would never have to go back. Shea had vowed to keep her safe, but how? They were no match for Doyle and Theodrick. They were mere mortals.

Then again, Lula wasn't. She had power now, and she shouldn't be afraid to use it.

"Max," Lula whispered, not taking her eyes off the deities in front of her. "Get them out of here."

"Lula?"

She heard the uncertainty in his voice.

"I mean it, Max. I'll cover you."

"Lulabelle."

Lula turned her wide eyes to Max's. Despite all the years they'd been forced together and the resentment they'd sometimes held toward one another, Lula knew Max would do anything to help her. The sentiment was mutual, and Max knew it.

Taking a deep breath, he gave a nod. What happened next was a blur of chaos.

Max turned and screamed, "Everyone, head towards the back!"

Lula focused her energy on Doyle. Letting out a scream, she released a blast into the entryway. Doyle ducked, narrowly missing being hit, while Theodrick threw himself back into the living room. It wasn't a stretch to guess where Theodrick would go. Lula ran through the house to cut him off before he could make it to where the rest had gone. Her sweat trickled down her temples as she released another blast just as he peeked out from the room.

"Don't fight us, Lula. You belong with us!" Theodrick called out.

"No, I don't!"

Lula shot another blast of energy, this time through the wall, leaving a giant hole. With her energy drained, she had to bend over and brace herself on her knees for support. She sucked in each breath, trying to stay focused.

"You do, Lula. You belong to me," Doyle said from close behind her. "We made a deal, remember?"

She peeked over her shoulder to see him towering over her. "Killing people was never part of the bargain."

"I told you there might come a time when you would be forced to do the unpleasant."

Devin appeared behind Doyle. "Leave it to you to be vague."

Devin grabbed Doyle by the arms and threw him back into the entryway. He then pulled Lula behind him before charging into the living room.

A moment passed before Lula regained her wits enough to follow. She made it two steps before a hand clamped down on her shoulder. Shea stood beside her, a fierce expression on his face.

Looking down at her, he left no room for argument. "We've got this," he said before lunging forward to join the fight.

Lula opened her mouth to protest, but she couldn't get the words out. She was completely spent.

Thomas and Max came up beside her. Thomas held a large leather bag in his hand. She focused on the two, but the room spun.

Max caught her before she hit the floor. "Easy there," he said in her ear.

"They can't..." Lula managed.

"They're stronger than you think. Don't forget, they've tangled with Death Gods before," Thomas reminded her.

Max helped her stand straighter. Lula closed her eyes and tried to slow her breathing. It felt like she'd just finished a marathon as her breath sawed in and out of her tight chest. She needed energy, or Devin and Shea were toast. Taking a moment to reach out with what power she had left, Lula found an energy source near her. On instinct, she dipped into it, pulling it into her body. The more she pulled, the better she felt.

"What the hell?" Max's voice ripped her from the energy source.

"Are you okay, man? You look paler than you did, and that's saying something." Thomas squinted at Max.

"I think so." Max tightened his grip on Lula. "It just felt like the life was being sucked out of me, so to speak."

"Oh my god, I think that was me." Lula stepped back in horror.

"You sucked his life force?" Thomas's face scrunched in revulsion.

"I'm sorry, I—"

Lula was cut off when Devin came crashing through the wall, leaving a hole right next to the one she'd made. "Is that all you got?" he snarled as he pulled himself to his feet. Spitting a mouthful of blood onto the floor. "I always knew you were a weakling, Doyle."

Doyle stepped through the hole in the wall. Lula's eyes widened as she took the two in. Doyle's bottom lip seemed bigger than usual, and his face was smeared with blood. The two stared daggers at each other. Clearly, they knew each other, but Lula couldn't fathom how.

"And I always knew you were a thief." Doyle sneered.

Lula stepped in front of Thomas, offering him cover, as the two men began trading blows once more. She braced herself, ready to protect Thomas and the book from whoever came their way.

Shea slid across the floor behind them. Lula turned and saw him hit the wall.

Theodrick strolled in from the living room with a smug look on his face. He glanced over at Lula. "This is so pointless, my Pet." He spread his arms wide as if presenting the ridiculous situation before them. "Leave them now and come back home to Doyle. We'll make sure you are taken care of when this silly war is over, I promise."

"Liar. And I am not your *Pet*," she spat at Theodrick.

"But you *are* mine," Doyle said, standing over Devin's now-still body on the floor. "And it is time for you to come home."

Lula swallowed hard as her eyes darted between the two of them. Shea and Devin were down and not moving. Max and Thomas were beside her but defenseless against the Death Gods unless she came up with a plan fast. Her heart pounded in time to her frantic breathing. There had to be something she could do.

Lula's eyes widened as she watched Doyle take a step towards Thomas. "Wait!" Lula cried out.

Doyle stopped and narrowed his gaze while Theodrick moved a step closer to her. Behind them both, Devin slowly rose to his feet while pulling something out of his pocket.

Lula's whole body slumped. "I'll come with you," she said.

"No, Lula!" Max cried out, but she held up a hand to stop him from doing anything.

"But you have to know..." Lula pointed her finger at them. "This won't end well."

Doyle cocked his head to the side. "I do not understand what you are saying."

A small smile slid into place. "You don't have to get it."

"You just have to keep your eyes on her," Devin finished for her.

Before anyone could react, Devin stabbed Theodrick with the silver knife he'd taken from Shea. Theodrick screamed as the site around the entry wound turned red, and small wisps of smoke rose from the blade. Devin was able to throw Theodrick with enough force that he landed back in the living room. Lula concentrated on what she wanted to do. With her new powers, she mustered enough energy to transport herself in the blink of an eye right behind Doyle. Grabbing his hand, she locked onto his energy source and pulled, draining as much as she could before shoving him across the entryway.

Devin took the opportunity to kick Doyle away from the front door. With the path to the front door clear, she made a run for it.

Lula turned back in time to see Shea struggling to get to his feet. "Shea, are you okay?" she asked, kneeling beside him.

"Just got the wind knocked out of me."

"Come on, we have to go."

Making their way toward the front door, she saw Doyle get up from the corner of her eye. Devin and Max were at the front door yelling something, but Lula couldn't hear past the panic threatening to consume her. Lula began dragging Shea beside her.

"You will not leave me again!" Doyle shouted.

Wide-eyed, Lula turned and was shoved as Shea stumbled through the open door, and Doyle released a blast of his own. Someone's cry filled her ears as she braced for an impact that never came. Instead, a sharp pain lit in her chest, like something was being ripped from her body.

Clutching at her chest, she met the horror that poured over Doyle's face.

"No! You fool, what have you done? Your deal is over! She is now free!" Theodrick's cry confused Lula even more until she looked down.

Max kneeled before her, his form flickering. He looked up and smiled at her. "I think we're even now."

Only when he spoke did Lula realize what had happened. Max had taken the blast directly to the chest. Doyle had destroyed him.

"No, Max!" Lula reached to grab him, but her fingers went right through him.

Lula was grabbed and pulled while voices yelled in her ear. In the back of her mind, she knew she should listen. All she could focus on was Max and how he just kept fading, and the more he faded, the sharper the pain became. She screamed his name and begged him to come with her.

"It's okay, Lula. Go be free and be happy. For me." Max winked before disappearing for the last time.

Lula watched the front door get farther and farther away as her feet scraped the cement of the walkway. She cried even louder as someone slammed the car door. Her chest, now hollow, ached as they sped off down the road. She thought she heard people talking around her, but none of them were who she wanted most at that moment. None of them were Max. She pulled on every bit of energy she had in her, trying to call him and conjure him with her new powers, just like she had when they had appeared in Thomas's car. Hard as she tried, Max never appeared, and the gaping hole in her echoed with the truth.

Max was gone.

Chapter Thirty

Lula couldn't breathe. Grief crushed her chest as she kept picturing Max fading into nothing over and over again. Only one question repeated itself: *why?* Why had Max done that? Why had he taken the hit? He should have let her take it. She could have handled it. Tears streamed down Lula's face as she cursed Max's name. Why did he have to die?

"Lula."

Shea's voice sounded so far away, even as his breath brushed her ear. He spoke to her, trying to calm her, Lula was sure. Nothing he said or did registered. Only the hum of the truck speeding down the road calmed her enough to lull her into a fitful sleep.

Lula jolted awake when the first truck door slammed. Dazed, she sat up, only to have the arm wrapped around her tighten. Shea's face pinched as he looked down at her. Lula averted her gaze, knowing he looked so distressed.

"Lula." His rough voice sounded like gravel to her ears.

Shaking her head, Lula broke free of Shea's hold and looked out the window. The farmhouse sat silhouetted by the setting sun. The sky was fading to a deep orange shot through with pink.

"I think we're supposed to go inside." She said in a voice she barely recognized.

"We don't have to hurry."

Lula stared out the window as Shea rubbed tiny circles on her back. "We should, though. We don't want them to start the party without us," she joked bitterly.

She waited as silence filled the truck, waiting for that witty retort only Max would have been able to give. *They can't start the party without us.* That's what he would say, right? That, or something equally dumb, because he was the king of stupid one-liners. Lula couldn't stop herself as she laughed with no humor.

"What's funny?"

Refusing to answer, Lula's chin quivered as got out of the truck. She trudged her way toward the door with feet heavy as lead. The only thing giving her strength was Shea's ever-present hand in hers. Inside, they found Devin and Thomas standing around in the kitchen. Thomas pulled a book out of the case and dropped it onto the table.

"Careful with that," Devin said.

Thomas grumbled to himself, pulling out the next book and placing it on the table while sneering at Devin.

"You do understand those books are hundreds of years old?"

"Yes, Devin."

Lula's eyes popped as she took in the growing stack, then barked out a laugh as she pictured the tiny room in Doyle's library now empty. "What all did you take?" she asked.

"Whatever we could get our hands on." An unrepentant smile lit Thomas's face.

The last thing pulled from the bag was the stone. Lula gasped as memories threatened to overtake her. She closed her eyes and could see herself snooping in the tiny, hidden room with Max. She pushed back the wave of tears that threatened to fall. Shea squeezed her hand, bringing her back to the present. The small smile they shared helped ease the ache in her chest, even just a little.

"Did you get the book we were after?" Shea asked.

"Max grabbed it after showing us which rock you guys brought back from Poe's," Thomas replied, running his fingers through his hair.

Hearing Max's name sent a fresh wave of pain through Lula. She closed her eyes and worked to keep breathing. Shea squeezed her hand and said her name, or at least she thought he did. Everyone sounded a million miles away. Lula squeezed her eyes tighter. She had to get out of there. Moving away from the group, it took her a moment to realize Shea was guiding her out of the room and down a tiny hall. They entered the first door on the right.

Few things decorated the small room. Simple white curtains framed a window with a view of the backyard. Red numbers cast an eerie glow from the clock on the bedside table next to a lamp. Shea pulled her down next to him on the soft quilt covering the full-sized bed. Lula went straight into his open arms, and the two lay together in a heavy silence. She watched the calm Oregon landscape while a torrent of anger and sadness raged inside her. The only thing holding her together was Shea. He held her close and ran his fingers through her hair. She didn't know how long they stayed there, silent, before Lula spoke.

"I can't believe he's g-gone." Her voice broke on the last word.

"I'm so sorry, Lula. I know how important he was to you."

"This isn't right. We were supposed to get out together. He promised me we would find a way to free ourselves from Doyle together. How could he leave me like this?" Tears ran down her cheeks.

Shea's chest rose and fell with a sigh. Guilt gave her a hard punch right in the stomach as she realized what she'd said.

Before Lula could formulate an apology, Shea kissed her forehead. "I can't believe he stepped in front of the blast, either. I swear, I was about to step in front of you myself when Max shoved me back. I think he... I don't know what he was thinking outside of protecting you."

Lula's face grew hot as rage boiled over. Max should never have been in that position. He never should have been *here* at all. Max should have crossed through the Gate years ago.

"That ass."

Movement jostled Lula, and she looked up to see Shea shaking in a silent chuckle.

"He *was*," she insisted.

"Huge ass. You should have seen him after the fight you had with Doyle. He ended up passed out in Thomas's car."

Lula smiled as she pictured the only way she could see Max acting. "I bet you wanted to call the Ghostbusters."

"That, or a priest."

Lula burst out laughing harder, burying her face in Shea's chest. He held her tighter and shared in the amusement. When the laughter died down, she stared out the window once more.

"I loved him," she confessed. "I mean, I wasn't *in* love with him, not like I was when I made that stupid deal, but—"

"He was your friend and companion through a hard time in your life."

Lula raised up on her elbow and looked into Shea's eyes. "I don't know what I would have done without him. He was such a pain sometimes, but he really looked out for me."

Shea reached up and cupped her face. "I'm glad you had him."

"I didn't deserve him. I never should have made that stupid deal with Doyle. I should have accepted fate and let him go. Instead, he was robbed of eternity in paradise. It's all my fault."

In a swift move, Shea sat up on the bed and pulled Lula onto his lap, holding her in a tight embrace, her face nestled in the crook of his neck. Tiny hairs on the top of her head danced in Shea's warm breath.

"Lula, you have nothing to feel guilty about. Doyle manipulated you, tricked you. He made sweet promises he never intended to keep. In the end, *Doyle* was the one to destroy Max. If anyone should feel guilty, it's him." Soft lips pressed against her forehead. "I will say, while I'm not happy about what you went through, I am happy the path you took led you here, to me."

Lula took comfort in the warmth of Shea's words. She knew his sentiment. Pulling back just enough, Lula gently kissed Shea, trying to give back all the warmth he so willingly gave her. To show him all the love she held for him. Without a doubt, she knew she loved Shea.

When the kiss broke, Shea smiled down at her, and Lula watched as love filled his eyes. It had to be. Nothing else had the power to make someone shine. Only one other time in her life had she been so immersed in someone, and they had been so lost on her. Her memories floated off to England when the young girl she had once been sat in the long grass next to her handsome man.

The clearer the picture became, the more puzzling it became. Not Max, but another had held her heart along with all of her attention, sitting beside her, playing a guitar. His thick, dark hair whipped in the breeze. A smile lit his face, making his dark eyes sparkle in the sun. Not Max, but...

Shea's eyes widened as they stared at one another. Lula could practically hear the wheels turn as another puzzle piece fell into place. This had to be a fantasy. No way could it be a memory. It was impossible.

"Lula, I—"

The door swung open, and Shea and Lula squinted against the bright light pouring in from the hall. Thomas knocked on the door even though he stood in the open doorway.

"Geez, why don't you guys turn on some lights in here? It's so dark."

"I told you I was bringing Lula here so she could have her moment."

"Right." Thomas ran his hand along the back of his neck. "Listen, Lula, I'm sorry about Max. We all are."

"Thanks," Lula said, her voice rough.

"Well, I'm supposed to let you know that Michael is coming. He should be here by morning. We're supposed to be up when he gets here to go over things. Recap."

"What time?" Shea asked.

Thomas shrugged. "I think he said to be up and in the kitchen by nine?"

"We'll be up."

Thomas closed the door, plunging the room into darkness once more. Shea reached over and turned on the bedside lamp. He went to a long dresser and pulled some clothes from a drawer. He turned and handed a white t-shirt and pajama pants to her.

"If you want, you can change in here, or across the hall is a bathroom. I just figured this would be more comfortable to sleep in."

Lula took the nightclothes and hugged them to her. "Thank you."

Slipping across the hall, she changed, taking care to fold her skirt and blouse, gently laying the black vest on top. She splashed some water on her face before finally looking at herself in the mirror. The girl staring back at her had wild hair and bloodshot eyes, but such resolve was set in her high chin. Lula almost didn't recognize herself. If she listened hard enough, she could hear Max. *If anyone can get through this, it's you.*

Lula went back to the bedroom to find Shea in his own sleepwear and under the covers. He sat up taller as she came to a stop at the side of the bed. Offering her a shy smile, he scooted over, giving her space to slide in next to him. The low light bathed the room in a soft glow while they peered at each other. As they lay together in silence, Lula wondered whether her memory of England could be real or not.

"What do you think..." she trailed off, not knowing what to ask first.

"I don't know." Shea said, knowing what she was talking about.

"It's impossible. Right? These, whatever we are seeing, are impossible."

"Completely. There's no way we met before."

"Certainly not in England."

"I've never been."

"It's just…" Lula searched for the right words.

Shea studied her for a heartbeat. "I wish I knew."

Lula bit her lip and looked at the bedroom door. "Should we mention to your dad we keep having visions about meeting about three hundred years ago?"

Shea kissed Lula softly before snuggling further into the bed, holding her tighter. "Let's decide in the morning."

"Shea," Lula said with her heart pounding in her chest. "Thank you. For… you know. Everything."

Shea beamed and cupped her face. "Anytime, Lula. Anything for you."

Chapter Thirty-One

Lula held Shea tight as they stepped into the kitchen just after nine in the morning to find everyone poring over the tall pile of books. Thomas leaned back in a chair, engrossed in a large black book. Devin stood next to a tall man with broad shoulders and long, blond hair. The two were hunched over an old brown book that looked almost identical to the *Book of Sephtis*.

Shea cleared his throat, and the three pairs of eyes shot their way.

"Good morning," the blond man said.

Lula offered a small wave, "Good morning."

"Lula, this is my uncle, Michael." Shea gestured to the man. "This is Lula."

Michael saluted her. "Nice to meet you."

Under the fluorescent kitchen light, Michael's eyes sparkled as he looked back at the book in front of him. He ran a hand through his hair before his finger traced over the page.

Shea guided Lula to a chair at the table before taking a seat to her left. A tight smile pulled as he glanced around at everyone. Lula made sure her chair was as close to Shea as she could be. He held her hand, resting it on his leg, while his thumb ran small circles over the back of her hand. The gesture worked wonders at keeping Lula relaxed enough to pay attention. As it stood, she couldn't decide if she wanted to sit long enough to learn what they'd found or run and scream out the door.

"Find anything useful?" Shea asked.

"Depends on your definition of useful," Thomas said as he turned the page in his book.

"We *are* finding some very useful things," Michael said.

"We have the *Book of Enid*," Devin confirmed. "This is also the corner from the tablet I asked about earlier."

"You think it's important? The corner rock, I mean?" Thomas asked.

"It's very important." Devin's voice became a deep baritone as he enunciated every word.

"What tablet is it?" Shea asked.

"When it's complete, it will reveal Sephtis," Devin explained.

"Reveal him? What do you mean? Isn't he already fighting this war?"

"He was for a long time. Things became too dangerous, and he had to go into hiding, at least until we could find the Statera."

"Hiding?" The book Thomas held slid from his fingers. "Why the hell is a god hiding?"

"Like I said, it became too dangerous to be out in the open. The other Death Gods were relentless in attacking him. The tablet sealed him away so they couldn't find him anymore. When the four pieces are reunited, Sephtis will be released and lead us into battle with the Statera."

"Do we need to find the Statera first before putting the tablet together?" Lula asked.

"Not necessarily," Devin said.

"In fact, we can put together what we have. That way, we can start the process of releasing him." Michael grinned as he turned toward the door. "I'll be right back with my piece."

"Wait, Michael."

Devin dropped the side of the book he held and took off after Michael. Their voices faded as the door closed behind them.

Lula let out a long breath and looked over the stack of books as Thomas filled Shea in on the history of Death Gods he'd learned from his book. From the sounds of it, he was reading the same book she and Max had read.

Lula's eyes suddenly burned, and she blinked several times before she could see clearly again. Maybe she needed some coffee to even her out. Leaning forward, she pulled a book from the middle of the stack. She recognized it from Doyle's hidden room. However, she didn't remember reading this one at all. Opening the book to a random page, she froze. Her eyes popped wide open.

"Lula," Shea's voice pulled at her, but she couldn't look away. Her eyes remained frozen on the page.

Thomas and Shea crowded around her to see what she had found.

"What the hell is this?" Thomas asked.

On the page, a picture of Doyle stared back up at them. Beside the photo, a biography told everything about the Death God, from a physical description and a designation to the region he was in charge of, as well as a list of strengths and weaknesses.

Shea turned the page and revealed another Death God, picture and all.

They continued to flip through what appeared to be the complete directory of every Death God. There were some Lula recognized. Shea recognized a few of the Death Gods himself. Thomas even picked out a couple he knew. Lula's eyes widened more and more with every page turned.

Shea practically vibrated as a smile spread wider across his face with each page they turned. "I can't believe we have this. A complete guide to the Death Gods. Who they are, where they're supposed to be. This is incredible."

Halfway through, everyone's mouths dropped. On the page, a picture of a Death God with a slender face, dark hair, and familiar features filled the top corner of the page. Shea stiffened as they read the impossible.

Devin: In charge of all of Europe and most of Asia. High proficiency in power with the ability to blend in and work with souls. Developed a keen sense and is able to track and properly handle wayward souls. Appears to lack the ability to prioritize tasks. One of the original Death Gods and confidant to Sephtis.

Thomas broke the silence first. "Is that—"

"Dad?" Shea replied.

"It can't be your dad. Right? That doesn't make any sense."

"There is an explanation." Devin's sudden appearance caused Lula to jump in her seat.

They turned to see him standing in the doorway. Behind him, Michael appeared to be holding a stone in a white-knuckled grip.

Glaring up at the men, Shea rose to his feet. Lula's heart pounded as the tension in the room became palpable. She grabbed Shea's arm, and the muscle flexed under her fingers, but he didn't sit.

Shea jabbed a finger at the page. "Why the hell are you in this book?"

Devin held up his hands. "Again, I can explain."

"Are you a Death God?"

"Shea, it's a long story, but you will have to listen."

"Tell me why you're in this book." Shea's eyes blazed. "Answer me!"

Devin keeping his hands up, he took a small step forward. His mouth opened and closed several times, fighting to come up with a good explanation.

Watching him struggle, Michael stepped in front of Devin and gestured toward the kitchen table. "The short answer is yes. If you will all calm down, I promise we will tell you everything you need to know. Trust me, you're going to need to sit down to hear this."

As Shea sat back down, Lula and Thomas scooted closer. Sharp eyes tracked the two men as they took a seat across from the three of them.

Clearing his throat, Michael spoke. "I know you three must have a lot of questions and need a reason to trust us—"

"A good reason," Thomas said.

"Which I'm happy to give you, along with the full story," he finished.

"Please," Devin interjected, "just keep an open mind."

Lula took Shea's hand and squeezed tighter as she braced herself.

"The first thing to know is a brief history. Two gods look over this world. Sephtis and Enid are siblings, and they created this entire galaxy," Michael started to explain.

Shea ran a rough hand through his hair. "We know all this."

"Fine." Michael rubbed his brow. "Then, to refresh everyone, while Enid busied herself with creating planets and life, Sephtis bonded with humans. He loved humans."

"Perhaps a little too much because he would always end up getting attached to them," Devin added, glancing at Lula. "Especially the ones that interacted with him. Then, when they died, he would have to take them to the Realm of the Dead. The whole thing left him sad. It was a depressing loop that left him lonely."

"Again, things we already know." Thomas sighed.

"Yeah, well, it was from that grief that he created the first Death God. He created...me," Michael said.

Lula couldn't take her eyes off Michael as she processed what he had just confessed. Shea's hand became damp as he squeezed hers even tighter. Placing her free hand on his back, she soothed Shea enough to feel some of the tension ease out of him.

"So both of you are Death Gods?" Thomas asked.

"Yes," Michael confirmed. "Sephtis created Devin after me."

"And he did all this out of loneliness?" Thomas rolled his eyes and snorted out a laugh as Shea cursed under his breath.

The two would never understand. How could loneliness be the catalyst of things being out of balance? Lula knew, though. She knew all too well what it did to a person. Thinking of Max, she remembered all she had done in the name of loneliness.

"If this is all true, and you're a Death God, then how can you possibly be my father?" Shea asked, turning his glare to Devin.

Devin rubbed his eyes. Michael shifted uncomfortably. The tension rose like the tide to the point of suffocating. Any second, the wave would overtake them all, and they would drown. She braced herself as the wave threatened to destroy the person she cared about most.

"You aren't technically my son. But it has been my job, all of our jobs, to keep you safe. You are very important in this war, Shea."

Shea opened and closed his mouth before pushing finally asking, "If you aren't my dad, who is?"

Devin winced. "It's complicated."

"Complicated," Shea parroted. "My parents are complicated."

Devin threw a hand up in defeat. "I know that's not what you want to hear. I don't know what to tell you."

"Well, what *can* you tell me?" Shea reached out toward Devin, pleading.

"Nothing right now except you'll know everything when the time is right." Michael said.

Shea's face turned red. "What the hell is that supposed to mean?"

Michael simply remained stoic in the face of Shea's anger. His whole body vibrated as Lula hugged his arm and grabbed his hand. She decided to try to keep the conversation moving forward since they weren't going to be forthcoming after dropping that bomb of information.

"All of your jobs? Are there more than just you two?" Lula's eyes darted between the two men, Death Gods, as she held her breath.

"There are four of us, the original Death Gods. All of us pledged allegiance to Sephtis and vowed to keep him safe and fulfill the prophecy."

Thomas leaned forward in his chair. His eyebrows pinched together, and Lula could practically smell the smoke rolling out of his ears as he digested all of this.

Shea smashed his lips into a thin line as his cheeks turned a dark shade of red. Veins stuck out of his arms from squeezing her hand so tight. Slits for eyes shot daggers Devin's way.

"This isn't possible," Shea declared.

"It is, though. It's all true," Devin said.

"I don't know what to think. I don't even know if I should trust you. It feels like we have no choice," Shea said.

"You can, Shea," Devin said, his voice shaking.

"You've lied to me my whole life." Shea whispered. His eyes, the size of saucers.

Devin went over and kneeled in front of Shea. He reached out as if to touch him but pulled back, seeming to think better. "Shea, I'm so sorry I lied to you. I promise, once this is over and you know..." Devin gestured wildly in front of him, and Lula could almost swear she saw tears in his eyes. "There is a reason. Every step we've taken over the past millennium has been for a damn good reason. All of this is to fulfill the prophecy and ensure we restore balance. It's my duty, one I would die for."

"Any of us would," Michael added.

"My whole life, you've told me that Death Gods are the enemy." Shea leaned in towards Devin. "Now you want me to trust you—both of you—after confessing you're the very thing I've been raised to hate?"

"I understand how hard this is. I only ask you to remember that I've been there for you the whole time. You *can* trust us," Devin said.

Shea turned to Lula. She squeezed his arm as she met his gaze. Shea pleaded with his eyes, and Lula offered a small smile as she brought her hand to his cheek. He leaned forward until their foreheads touched.

He closed his eyes. "One chance," Shea said, finally sitting back up and looking at Devin. "That's all we're giving you."

Devin stood, shoving his hands into his pockets. His focus bounced around the room as he bowed at Shea in acceptance.

Michael stayed unmoving but nodded at the scene before him. "We accept, and on my honor, we won't let you down."

Chapter Thirty-Two

Lula took in Michael's declaration. The resolve on his and Devin's faces made it hard for her to doubt their sincerity.

Michael moved next to Devin and gave him a hard smack on the back. "First thing we need to do is get all of our stone pieces together. That way, we can work on getting Sephtis back. After that, we look for the Statera," he said, turning his attention back to the *Book of Enid*.

"What are we even looking for?" Shea asked.

"According to the *Book of Enid*, she created someone to help Sephtis restore and maintain balance. The person has distinct characteristics. They balance him out. They'd also have enough power, giving them many abilities that Death has. What we need to do is find out if they've been born and then find them."

"Michael, we already have them," Devin said, glancing in Lula's direction.

Michael froze where he was, page in hand. "We do?"

Devin only nodded.

"Well, don't hold out on me, old friend. Who is it? One of the unfortunate Pets we rescued?"

"It's Lula."

A chorus of disbelief echoed in the kitchen from everyone but Devin, who held his ground. "Lula, I've been looking into you for a while now."

The blood drained from Lula's face, and she swallowed hard to keep from losing her last meal all over the kitchen floor.

"The first time I came across you was when you took the girl from the café. I watched you take that girl's soul, and then I watched you open the Gate to the Realm of the Dead. I easily picked up on how much power you had then, and I feel how much power you have now. I listened to what you can do, and I'm willing to bet there's more you can do that you haven't shared."

Devin had been the Death God stalking her in the shadows, the one she had been so scared of. He took one of her trembling hands, but Shea reached out, taking her hand back.

"Don't touch her."

Devin frowned at Shea. "I won't hurt her. I would never hurt her. She's too important."

"I don't understand. I mean..." Lula fiddled with the hem of the nightshirt, trying to gather her thoughts. "How could you know it's me? If you knew it was me all along, why didn't you take me that day?"

He could have saved her from all the pain of taking Melvin's soul. Hell, he could have made sure she didn't have to take Melissa's soul. Tears burned her eyes as she fought to breathe past the rising anger.

"That first time, I only noticed you. It wasn't until later that I knew for sure who you were."

"What happened later? Why are you so sure now?" Pressure built in her chest.

"And what if you're wrong?" Thomas threw in for good measure.

Yes, what if Devin was wrong? She would still join the fight. Lula would do anything to make sure no one went through what she had endured these almost three hundred years. The Death Gods needed to be stopped, and she would give anything to make sure that happened.

"I'm not wrong," Devin reassured them all. "I can't go into the details right now, but trust me, you are the Statera. I think Theodrick knows it too. That's why he wants you so bad. If he somehow convinced you to join their side, I'm not sure we could win this fight."

"Maybe, but there's no way in hell I'll let him near her," Shea spoke with such conviction it almost made Lula cry.

"He has to get past all of us," Michael said sharply.

The look of devotion on all of their faces overwhelmed Lula. Even Thomas had a look of awe. She knew Devin believed what he was telling her. She just wasn't sure she believed it herself. Either way, she would fight.

Michael wagged his eyebrows. "Now, we put this stone together."

Devin turned to leave the room. "I'll go get my piece of the stone," Devin said.

Michael moved to block his exit. "You have it right here."

Devin's entire frame stiffened as he closed his eyes, frozen where he stopped in the doorway. "That's not my piece. It's Katy's."

"Katy's?" Michael stood up straighter. "Is she here? Have you talked to her?"

"That piece came from Doyle's house, with the books." Devin swallowed hard. "Apparently, they have her at Poe's house."

Michael dropped onto one of the kitchen chairs as Devin left the room. An unease fell over the group as they sat in silence. They way she could practically see the wheels in Michael's head turn made Lula's stomach dip.

Shea broke the silence. "Who's Katy?"

"She, uh..." Michael struggled with his words. "She's one of the original Death Gods, one of the original four who swore to protect Sephtis. She's our friend."

"And now Poe has her locked in his house?" Thomas let out a harsh breath. "I gotta say, if you're supposed to be the ones that help with this prophecy, you're off to a banging start."

"Watch it, Thomas," Michael scolded.

Devin reentered the kitchen with a stone in hand. The large corner piece had the same strange writing found in *The Book of Sephtis*. They shimmered and swam as Devin walked by Lula and placed it on the table next to the other piece. Lula, Thomas, and Shea joined them around the kitchen table and watched. Michael helped Devin push the three stone sections together.

As soon as they touched, a stream of golden light raced along the seam, joining them into one. The words on the talisman came into focus, and Lula found that she could read at least some of it. Surprise gushed out of her with a breath. Beside her, Shea shivered.

"Shea?" Lula nudged him a little, taking him in.

Shea glanced at Lula. "Just got a chill, I guess."

"You two okay over there?" Devin asked.

"Yeah, I just..." Lula swallowed hard. "I can read some of the talismans now."

Michael's eyes popped open.

"Told you she's the one," Devin said with a cocky smile.

"How many stones are there?" Thomas asked as Devin put the stone talisman into a bag.

"Four. Each of us took a piece," Michael said.

"Each of you? So that's you, Devin, and Katy. Who's the fourth?" Shea asked.

"Albert. I talked to him recently. He's at the cabin with the rest of the liberated Pets." Michael answered, gathering up all the books on the table.

"Right." Devin hoisted the bag loaded with everything onto his shoulder and looked at everyone in the kitchen. "A few things need to happen fast."

Michael shot Devin a wink and a smile. "I'm already ahead of you. We can get a hold of Albert on our way to my cabin. He has his piece hidden there. It's only about an hour's drive from here."

"Good. First things first." Devin turned to face Lula. Pain and desperation shone in his eyes. "Lula, can you take us to where Poe lives?"

Lula understood what he was asking and why. Katy seemed like more than just an important member of this team, and she was cared for. The only thing she could think about was they were going to be walking right into the lion's den again. There was no way that Poe hadn't ratted them out. Theodrick and Doyle were almost guaranteed to be there. Thinking about going to Poe's made her nauseous until she remembered who else was trapped there.

"Yes, under one condition. We bring Willow with us. She is Poe's Pet, and I can't go there and then leave her behind."

"Lula, we can't just take a Pet."

"You took me."

"That's different. We didn't take you. You came to us. And we wouldn't be able to keep you now if Doyle hadn't broken your deal."

"I thought you said she had already freed herself?" Shea challenged.

The sheepish look that crossed Devin's face outed him as a liar. Lula bit her tongue to keep from sounding off on him.

"P-please." Lula braced herself to continue to beg.

Devin's head dropped forward as he ran his hand through his hair, and Michael chuckled.

Lula held her breath, willing him to help her. Lula had no right to make demands, but the idea of leaving Willow behind didn't sit right with her.

"I can't promise anything, but..." Devin paused as he took her in. "When we get there, we will do everything that we can to free her from Poe."

Lula's shoulders sagged a little as she let out a sigh. "Thank you."

"Don't thank me yet."

Everyone raced around the house, getting ready to leave. Lula grabbed her clothes and went to change. Shea appeared in the doorway. He held a short-sleeved maxi dress with large buttons down the front. She pulled on the long skirt, admiring the soft cotton. Big yellow daisies easily stood out against the white background.

"I found this in a closet. It was my mom's," Shea's arms dropped a little until the bottom of the skirt touched the floor, "or I think it was."

"I'm so sorry, Shea."

He raised the dress higher once more. "Either way, I thought you might like something new to wear."

Lula took the dress from him and held it up to herself. "Thank you. I love it."

She quickly changed and found Shea waiting for her in the bedroom. She smiled while giving a little twirl. The end of the dress tickled at her ankles. Somehow, her old black Mary Jane's didn't look that bad.

"You look beautiful."

Lula took his hand and leaned in, placing a kiss firmly on his lips. "Let's blow this joint."

Following everyone out the front door, Lula found a large black truck with an extended cab parked next to Devin's. Michael strode right up and hopped into the driver's seat. She watched as Devin and Thomas loaded the bags containing all the books and the talisman into a locked cargo box in the truck's bed. Taking a deep breath, she searched for her courage. Going to Poe's house for Katy, she knew they would run into Theodrick and Doyle again.

"Are you okay?" Shea asked.

"No," she answered honestly. "I'm not."

He reached for her face, pulling her to him until their foreheads touched, then kissed the tip of her nose.

She gave her head a little shake. "I'm sorry. I just can't believe everything that's going on. I feel like I'm changing, like *everything* is changing, and not for the better."

"You know what I think?" Shea whispered in her ear. "I think you *are* changing, and it *is* for the better. I think you're not being given a choice on things that you normally wouldn't have anything to do with, but because of that, you'll come out the other side stronger and more compassionate than you ever thought you could be." Then Shea smiled with a sparkle in his eyes. "Not that you aren't the most caring and compassionate person I've ever met already, because you are."

The cheesy sentiment had Lula cracking a smile, if only for a moment before she lost herself in the melancholy once more. "I'm so tired of all this. I want this all to be over so we can live our lives in peace."

"We'll get there. I promise we'll get there together," Shea vowed.

A horn sounded, and they both looked to see Michael waving at them. "Hey, you two. We've got to go!"

In no time, they were speeding down the road. Lula sent out a silent prayer and braced herself for what they were about to face.

Chapter Thirty-Three

Michael weaved through the Portland streets, following Lula's directions to Poe's house. Devin sat in the passenger seat with the window down. His salt and pepper hair danced wildly in the wind. Lula sat sandwiched between Thomas and Shea in the back. Thomas wiggled in his seat, trying to put more distance between his large frame and Lula's smaller one. Shea wrapped himself around her as much as he could. The late morning sun reflected off cars like an ominous beacon, warning Lula she would face Doyle for what she hoped would be the last time. Her heart pounded harder in her chest the closer they got to the old Victorian home. A tense silence filled the truck, allowing Lula's thoughts to spiral out of control. She needed to learn more about her role in the prophecy to avoid going crazy.

"Can you explain what exactly this Statera is?" Lula asked.

"The person who will help Sephtis bring balance once again," Devin answered.

"I know, just... I don't know how I'm supposed to do it?"

"Sephtis will unlock all your powers. Then you will be able to fight alongside him."

"Theodrick mentioned another way to unlock the Statera, or, I guess, my powers."

Devin rubbed the back of his neck. "The *Book of Enid* spoke of another way, by absorbing energy. As we said, Sephtis has the energy to do it on his own. Enid made sure of it. The Death Gods don't. The only energy that would be enough is the power generated by a soul, but not just any soul. It has to be a special soul."

"What special soul?"

Devin glanced back at her, pity etched on his features. Lula's eyes widened as realization turned her stomach. Shea held her tighter and said something she couldn't hear past the whooshing in her ears. She had absorbed Melissa's soul. Doyle had then sent her to get Thomas's soul. Her wide eyes locked onto him sitting beside her. Would she have absorbed his soul as well? Was that what Theodrick had talked about the first night?

Thomas shifted again in his seat under her gaze. "What are you looking at? Planning to rip my soul from my body, like you did my sister's?"

"Knock it off, will you?" Shea glared at Thomas.

"You took another Pet's soul?" Michael asked.

Lula squirmed in her seat. How many times would she have to relive that nightmare? "Yes, but you have to understand. I didn't want to. Doyle made me."

"Did you absorb it?"

"Wait." Thomas braced his hand against the seat and faced Lula. "I thought you took her through the Gate."

Lula turned watery eyes on Thomas. "I didn't mean to. Doyle was supposed to meet me and take her through the Gate."

"I doubt that," Michael mumbled.

"That's what he told me," she insisted.

"Have you gotten any new abilities since then?" Devin asked, but Lula was still staring at Thomas, who was turning red.

Shea took her hand and squeezed, offering Lula a lifeline against the raging storm now brewing in the truck. "Why are you even asking?"

"By absorbing the soul, it sounds like you unlocked some of your powers. I have a feeling if you did it again, more powers would un-lock."

"I would never absorb an innocent soul for any reason." A tear ran down Lula's cheek.

"Not even if it gave you power?" Michael challenged.

"Never." Lula's bottom lip trembled. "Thomas, I'm so sorry."

"You're sorry? You ripped out my sister's soul and *absorbed* it, denying her eternity in the Realm of the Dead, and you're *sorry?*" Thomas's nostrils flared as he stared, hatred pouring out of him.

"I—"

"I don't care!" His fist connected with the car door. "You can say sorry until you are blue in the face and that it wasn't your fault. I know all about how your evil Death God *made* you do it, but I just don't give a shit. My sister is dead, robbed of her chance at paradise because of what you did. And then you lied about it. Top dollar says that's why you showed up yesterday at the restaurant."

"Yes." Lula's voice cracked.

"Figured." Thomas scoffed before he faced forward again, glaring out the window.

Shea opened his mouth to speak, but Lula grabbed his arm and squeezed. She swallowed hard as she vowed to somehow make amends.

"Sounds like whatever you have is all you'll get until we release Sephtis," Michael said.

"Fine with me."

It took another ten minutes before they reached Poe's neighborhood. The closer they got to the house, the more Lula's stomach twisted and turned with nerves. She reached up and ran her fingers over her necklaces at her throat. Feeling the cool chains against her skin helped to steady her erratic heart.

"Do you think Doyle or Theodrick will still try to get me to join them?" Lula asked. The whole idea sounded crazy, but it wouldn't surprise her if they did. "They have to know I won't go with them, right?"

Devin turned in his seat to face them. His eyebrows pinched together as he sat in silent contemplation for a moment longer before answering. "I'm willing to bet that was plan A. Now that Doyle broke his deal with you, I'm not sure what they'll do."

"Maybe they'll try to kill you," Thomas offered.

"No one is going to kill her," Shea declared. "They won't get near her if I have anything to say."

"Shea, I can take care of myself. Like it or not, I have some new, very handy powers since I'm this Statera. That has to mean I'm able to help, right?"

"Of course you can help," Michael said, turning deeper into the neighborhood. "Enid knows what she's doing. According to the prophecy, you are a badass."

"What if Death—the real Death—doesn't like me?"

"Like you?" Devin asked.

"I mean, I'm supposed to be his other half, right? His counterbalance? What if we find him and we don't get along?"

"Wouldn't that just mean that she's not the Statero?" Thomas asked.

"Statera," Devin corrected. "Trust me, he'll love you."

Shea clenched his jaw tightly as he glared out the window.

Lula leaned closer to whisper in his ear, "You know I only have eyes for you, no matter how many fancy titles they give me."

Shea peeked at her before smiling out the window. "You better."

***

All the lights were off when they pulled in front of Poe's house. Lula stood frozen, looking up at the house, unable to move. She reached out with her powers to see who was waiting for them inside but found the house empty. Shea took her hand, allowing her to put one foot in front of the other. Keeping their eyes open, they made their way up the steps to the front door and found it locked.

Michael stepped forward, pulling something from his coat pocket. "I've got this."

Lula watched in amazement as Michael picked the lock and opened the door.

Inside, the stillness made Lula's skin crawl. Every book and knick-knack sat neatly on the shelves, covered in dust. A musty aroma filled the air, and cobwebs ran from wall to wall in the corners of the room. If she didn't know better, she would think it had been months since anyone had set foot in that house.

"Where did Poe say she was being kept?" Michael asked, straining to look up the stairs.

"The basement," Devin answered as he peeked through a cracked open door before moving on. "Lula, where is the entrance to the basement?"

"I don't know. I've never been in here."

"I thought you said you came here before?" Thomas snapped.

"I've been *to* his house. I was never let inside."

"It's around here somewhere. We'll just keep looking," Devin said.

The group moved slowly through the first floor of the house, checking every door they came across. Most of them revealed small closets. When they got to the kitchen, a large door with a bronze handle caught their eye.

"I think we found something," Lula called.

Shea turned the handle easily but had to give two big tugs for it to open. An old wooden staircase led into a dark basement. Michael pulled a small flashlight from another pocket in his coat. Lula couldn't help but wonder what other fun gadgets he had hidden in there. He clicked on the light and aimed the beam down the stairs, which was followed by a faint rustling. Devin pushed his way to the front of the group and led them into the dark. Groping around, Lula found a string hanging from the ceiling. Giving it a careful tug, she turned on a long fluorescent light. Looking around the dimly lit room, Lula gasped as her eyes landed on a large metal cage with vertical bars in the basement's corner. Curled up on the bottom was a small figure with long, brown hair spread over the dirty floor.

"Katy?" Devin's voice broke.

The woman stirred. She turned toward the group with wide eyes. She reached up a hand and opened her mouth as if to speak, but nothing came out. Lula shuddered to think what this poor woman had gone through. Death God or not, no one deserved to be treated like this.

"Katy!" Devin launched himself at the door, almost ripping it off the hinges. He knelt down and gently scooped her off the floor and into his arms. "Katy, please be okay," he whispered into her hair.

Footsteps sounded on the stairs, a steady thump.

Reaching out with her senses, the icy grip that could only be Doyle slammed into Lula. "Doyle's here," she announced as fear choked her. Lula backed up with every step until her back pressed up against the wall.

"Is he alone?" Michael asked.

"No."

Shea moved to stand in front of her as the footsteps made their way down the stairs. "Stay behind me," he ordered.

Lula braced herself for a fight. It would be different now that she was free. He no longer held any power over her. At least, that's what she told herself while working to slow her breathing.

The figure stopped at the bottom of the stairs, and blinding lights flooded the room.

Willow stepped forward and gave a slight bow. "Hello, Lula, it's good to see you." She smiled at everyone before her. "My master and his guests would like to have a word with you upstairs."

Lula and Shea exchanged glances before looking to the others for their reactions. Devin slowly stood while cradling Katy in his arms. Michael shrugged as Thomas looked like he was sucking on a lemon while staring Willow down. Bracing herself, Lula led the charge, following the old woman back up into the main house. Lula never let go of Shea's hand. In the living room, Poe stood with Doyle and Theodrick.

Doyle's eyes narrowed on Lula as she entered the living room. "Hello, my Pet," he said, giving her a tight smile. "You have been a bad girl. Poor Max never stood a chance, did he?"

"You're going to pay for destroying him." Lula's whole body shook.

"Come now, it's not Doyle's fault that Max is gone," Theodrick said in a soft, velvet voice. "Do you think Doyle would really do anything to risk the bond you both share?"

"He—"

"I made a mistake, Lulabelle. That is all. A mistake. After all I have done for you, will you abandon me now?"

The room blurred through hot tears threatening to scorch their way down her cheeks. What happened to Max wasn't a mistake. It was a tragedy. There was nothing Lula could do to make it right. The only thing she had left in her was a fight.

"I'm not going anywhere with you."

"Impudent child, you shall pay for this."

She let out a roar before launching at Doyle. The punch she landed sent Doyle flying across the room. Shea jumped into action, aiming straight for Theodrick. The room descended into chaos. Poe dove behind the couch to avoid a blast of energy from Michael. Lula made her way over to Shea, grabbing his arm. All she could think about was how she could protect him. A warm sensation tingled like pins and needles down her arm and to the hand holding on to Shea. Pushing past him, she landed a punch of her own, hitting Theodrick square on the nose. He dropped like a rock, hitting the floor with enough force to make the whole room shake. She'd just raised her hands to hit him with a blast when Doyle slammed into her. Shea cracked him in the jaw, knocking Doyle to the ground.

Lula reached down and grabbed him by his shirt and yanked. "Rot in hell." Lula placed her right hand in Doyle's face and prepared to release a massive burst of energy.

Doyle's eyes widened for a moment before a smile slithered across his face. "You first."

Lula turned at the sound of Shea's scream. She came face to face with Poe's wide eyes. He held a knife high with the blade pointed right at Lula.

The two stood frozen, staring at each other. Lula couldn't figure out why Poe had hesitated until he crumpled to the ground at her feet. Looking up, she saw Shea standing over Poe, his chest heaving. In his fist danced the bright amber flame of a Death God's soul.

"You destroyed Poe, you insolent boy!" Doyle bellowed.

"How?" Lula whispered.

Across the room, Theodrick's scream shook the walls.

Doyle twisted with such force in Lula's grasp he broke free and disappeared, along with Theodrick.

Lula turned right into Shea's arms. She had to reassure him several times she was in one piece before she could survey the rest of the room. Devin leaned against the doorway to the kitchen, still holding Katy. Her hair covered her face, and one arm was wrapped around his neck. Thomas had himself positioned right in front of Willow, clutching a silver knife in his hand. Micheal stretched and rolled his shoulders before taking in the damage himself.

"Lula?" Willow peeked from behind Thomas. "Lula, what is going on?"

"You're free, Willow. Poe is dead, so you're no longer bound to him or this world," Lula explained.

"I'm free? Does that mean...?"

"You are free to pass on," Michael said. "Come with me. I shall make sure you see paradise. If you would like, of course."

"Oh yes, sir, I would like to go very much."

Willow's eyes sparkled as she smiled up at Lula. She hugged the sweet old woman as they said their goodbyes.

Without another word, Michael took Willow's hand and led her through the Gate to the Realm of the Dead.

Chapter Thirty-Four

Devin moved across the living room, gently laid Katy on the couch, and brushed her long, brown hair out of her eyes. Michael ran off, only to reappear with washcloths and towels. The two men fussed over her, cleaning her face and murmuring to her.

Katy stirred, and her eyes fluttered open. She froze, and her bright green eyes settled on Devin. She reached up and touched Devin's hand, still holding the washcloth. Thomas cleared his throat. Katy bolted upright and looked frantically around the room.

Devin restrained her against flailing around. "Katy, calm down, you're safe."

"What's going on?" she asked.

"We came to rescue you," Michael said, reaching to help steady her.

"Poe!" Her eyes bulged. "He's working with Theodrick and Doyle. We need to leave before they come back."

"It's all right, Katy," Devin consoled her.

"Poe put me in that cage. I don't want to go back!" She sobbed.

"No one is putting you back. It's over." Devin held her close.

Michael bowed. "What happened? How did you even end up captured?"

Katy kept her face pressed against Devin's neck as she spoke. "A couple of months ago, I went back to my place, and Poe was there. I don't know how he found me, but he did. We fought, and I was knocked out. I woke up here, bound in a cage. Poe was in the room with Doyle and Theodrick. Apparently, they kept me imprisoned so you wouldn't find out they had my piece of the talisman and... He—he..."

Devin hugged her tighter and rocked her. "Poe is gone, Katy, and he won't hurt you anymore. None of them are going to hurt you anymore."

"They'll be back. They always come back." The desperation in her voice broke Lula's heart.

"No, they won't," Michael assured her in a soft voice. "We destroyed Poe. Theodrick and Doyle ran off."

"You mean *Shea* destroyed him," Lula said, crossing her arms.

"I would love to know how I was able to do that too," Shea said with a low rumble.

Lula's brow furrowed. "I thought you'd killed a Death God before."

"Yeah, with a special knife. Not with my bare hands. Not like that."

"Like how?" Thomas asked.

"Wait, you ripped out Poe's soul?" Lula pushed.

"Yeah, and I have no idea how I was able to do it."

Thomas's eyes popped as he took Shea in. Lula wondered to herself how he could do such a thing. That was something only Death Gods and Pets like herself could do. Pets that were given special powers.

"He ripped out Poe's life energy," Michael corrected. "Death God's don't have souls. Enid didn't create them; Sephtis did, and all he could give them was energy."

Thomas never took his eyes off Shea. "What it is, is crazy. I'd expect Lula to pull something like that, but not Shea."

Lula glared at Thomas. "I guess I earned that."

"So shouldn't only a Death God or Sephtis be able to do that?" Shea asked.

Michael ignored the question, while Devin seemed to ignore the entire exchange. He continued to hover over Katy as they continued their own conversation.

"It's only a matter of time before we destroy them as well. The end is here, Katy. We have what we need. Sephtis will rise and rule once again," Devin said.

"You mean *everything*?" Her eyes swept over the group standing around her once more. "You found the Statera?"

"We did." Devin said.

Devin helped Katy to her feet. She stood about a head shorter than him, which put her eye to eye with Lula. He led her over to Lula, who brushed her skirt. She watched with wide eyes as Katy looked her over before breaking out into a bright smile.

"This is her?" she asked, offering her hand.

"Yes. Katy, this is Lula."

"It's so nice to finally meet you, Lula."

Lula took Katy's hand and squeezed. "Are you okay?"

Her smile became even brighter. "I'm wonderful now. I'm sure you've heard. We've been waiting a long time for you."

"They went over it a little with us," Shea answered for Lula. "We're all hoping that now that we've saved you, we can get more answers."

Katy turned to Shea and lit up like a Christmas tree. "Of course we will, my lord. We will tell you everything you need to know."

Shea's mouth dropped open, and his eyes widened. "I'm sorry?"

Devin moved in a flash, taking Katy by the arm. "Not now, Katy. Wait until we get to the cabin."

Lula frowned as she watched Michael join Devin in trying to get Katy out the door.

Thomas snorted out a laugh. "Did she just call you 'my lord'?"

"She did." Shea stepped in front of the retreating group, blocking their way. "Why did you call me that?"

Katy's eyes widened. "I have always addressed you that way."

"Always?" Shea clenched his fists and took a step forward. "This is the first time we've met."

The blood drained from her face. "Oh, dear. Devin, I thought you said that you had everything?"

Michael cursed under his breath. Thomas joined Shea as the four argued. Lula stepped back, not sure what to do.

"We do, Katy, but we haven't made it to the cabin to put the talisman completely back together."

Katy whirled back to Shea. "I'm so sorry. I spoke too soon."

"Too soon about what?" Shea took another step forward, getting right in Katy's face. "*Now*, what the hell aren't you telling us?"

The Death Gods explained why they needed to keep their secrets. They were nothing but the same lines they had given *ad nauseam* by now. Shea and Thomas couldn't get past the secrets and lies. They were supposed to be in this together. Why did Devin insist on keeping everyone, especially Shea, in the dark?

"It's just like you Death Gods to want to control everything." Thomas shoved his finger in Devin's and Michael's faces. "This is why we can't trust you."

"I'm inclined to agree," Shea said.

"Please, I promise. You'll be so proud of us once you learn the whole truth, Sephtis," Katy pleaded with her fingers laced together.

Silence fell over the room as the blood drained from Katy's face. Devin closed his eyes, and Michael slumped where he stood in defeat.

"What did you call me?" Shea asked, barely above a whisper.

Wringing her hands, Katy tripped over her words, trying to explain. "I, uh, called you by your name."

"Sephtis is the name of the God of Death."

"Dammit, Katy," Devin snapped.

"Don't yell at her, Devin. It's not her fault," Michael said.

Ignoring Michael, Devin turned to Shea. "Shea, listen to me. Everything is going to be fine."

"The fuck it is," Shea growled. "*I* am the God of Death? Is that what she's saying? Is that the big secret you wouldn't tell me?"

Devin approached Shea like he was a wild animal about to strike. "Shea, the best place to hide something is in plain sight."

"But I have memories," Shea said, backing up a step. "Memories of my entire life, of growing up. How can that be if I'm some deity?"

"They're memories of your mortal life, Shea. You have lived a mortal life over and over again."

"My m-mother?" Shea stammered. "I had a mother who died."

"Be careful, Devin," Michael warned.

"You never had a mother."

"No!" Shea screamed, grabbing his head. "I remember her. I remember when she died."

"Shea..." Devin's whole body sagged, looking defeated.

Micheal grabbed Shea's arm. "The best place to hide something is in plain sight, right? In order to keep you hidden from the Death Gods who wanted to see you destroyed, we came up with a plan that essentially turned you mortal. Then, we each took turns posing as your parent or another relative and moved you around while looking for the Statera. When we moved, we erased your memory and replaced it with a new one, all in the name of keeping up the facade until we were ready to move forward like we are now."

Lula glared daggers at Devin. "How could you keep something like that from him?"

"I had no choice."

Devin's words made her pause.

"You have to see that. He had to be kept in the dark. If he knew, do you think I would have been able to keep him safe all this time?"

"Why wouldn't you tell me when you told Lula who she was?"

Shea's question sounded fair. Of course that meant they would completely mess up the answer.

"We decided to wait until the cabin," Devin said.

"*Why?*"

Michael shrugged. "It sounded like a good idea at the time."

Lula watched the scene unfold before her in horror. The air stuck in her lungs, unable to breathe past the shock. She didn't know what to do. Everything was spinning out of control.

Shea's face darkened as he stiffened. "I've had enough." He turned and stomped out the front door, leaving everyone behind.

Lula seethed. "*This* is how you tell him?"

"In all fairness, we weren't trying to tell him yet." Devin said.

Lula moved to follow Shea. She didn't even try to hide how appalled she was as she stomped towards the door. "Whatever."

"Where are you going?" Devin asked.

"Where do you think?" Lula spat.

Shea needed help to sort this mess out, and that's what she would do.

Lula found Shea half a block away. His shoulders heaved, and he clenched his fists as he marched down the street.

"Shea!" she called out to him, but he didn't stop. "At least this explains a few things. The two of us are getting along so well. You killing Poe with your bare hands. Maybe it even explains the vision things we had?"

He met every word with silence. Shea continued marching down the street, fists at his side, not slowing for even a second.

Lula jogged so she could gain some ground and have a chance of catching up with him. "Shea, please wait! Talk to me." She grabbed his arm, and he finally turned to look at her. She gasped at the anger burning in his eyes.

"Leave me alone, Lula," he demanded, then pulled away from her.

"Not gonna happen." Lula kept pace with Shea.

"He lied to me. All of these years, he's lied to my face."

"I know, and he deserves to get his ass kicked over it. It's just..." She took a deep breath. "I kinda get what they were doing."

Shea glared daggers at Lula and her step faltered. "It's true that the best place to hide things is in plain sight. They did a really terrible job of letting you back into the loop, though."

"Terrible job? Lula, I don't know what to believe anymore or even *who* to believe."

"I know it's rough, but just remember I've got your back."

"Yeah, because you have been the pillar of honesty."

Lula jerked back, his words landing like a slap in the face. "What the hell is that supposed to mean?"

Shea halted and spun to face her. His long finger pointed right in her face as he aimed his hateful words at her. "You never told me you were in leagues with a Death God. You never told me about being connected to your ex-boyfriend. And worst of all, you never told me about how you took and absorbed Melissa's soul!"

Lula stumbled a step back, blinking rapidly. Heat spread like wildfire through her body as the world around her blurred. Several breaths later, she still couldn't trust herself to talk. Swallowing convulsively, Lula worked to get her voice back. "I'm going to give you grace because I know you're upset."

Shea scoffed, making a move to walk away again.

Part of Lula knew she should just leave him alone so he could work things out on his own. Another part, though, knew he needed someone to help him through this. What he'd learned today in rapid succession were no small things. No one could navigate that much whiplash on their own.

She grabbed his arm before he could take off on her again. "Please, Shea," she pleaded.

"I don't want to talk about this." He jerked his arm away again, but she held tight. "Why won't you just leave me alone?"

"For so many reasons. I want to be there for you the way you've been there for me. Because no one should have to go through something this huge alone. And because I love you," Lula blurted out.

Shea stopped struggling against her hold and gaped at her.

Watching his reaction, Lula wished more than ever she had kept her big mouth shut.

"What?" The voice cracked as he pushed out the word. His whole body trembled.

"I love you," she pushed the words past the lump in her throat.

Shea's eyes shone with tears that did not fall. He pulled away from her, shoving a knife right through her heart.

Lula let go of his arm and took a step back. "I mean, it makes sense we would love each other or that I love you. They said the Statera and Sephtis would at least get along."

When Shea continued to stare at her, unmoving, Lula panicked. Her heart raced as she attempted to fix her obvious blunder.

"I'm sorry, I shouldn't have said that. I just wanted you to know why I'm out here." She sniffed and rubbed at her eyes, which were now on fire.

"Lula..." His voice cracked. "How could you possibly love me?"

"How could I not? You make me happy. I feel safe and comfortable with you. You're the first person who's made me feel special in...ever. I could keep going, but it all adds up to the same conclusion. I love you more than I've ever loved anyone, including Max."

With Shea by her side, she was whole and more alive than in her entire life. How could she not love him?

"Lula, I..." He swallowed hard, backing away another step.

"It's okay, I understand," she assured him with a smile as her heart shattered into a thousand pieces. It would be too much to ask for him to love her back. She understood that. "Take your time. I'll be with the others and... Yeah, come back when you're ready. We'll put an end to this, and you can take your rightful place. Then the two of us will...whatever."

She spun on her heel and started walking as fast as she could back to the house. He called out to her, but she refused to look back.

No way would she let him see her heart shatter.

Chapter Thirty-Five

L ula burst through the front door of Poe's house. Devin, Michael, and Katy whipped around from where they sat to watch her.

Slamming the door, Lula made for the stairs.

"Where's Shea?" Devin demanded, using a parental tone that made Lula laugh.

"He's coming to terms with the fact that you three suck at your job."

She marched up the stairs and entered the first room she came to, slamming the door behind her. Lula's chest rose and fell as she sucked in thick gulps of air. Her eyes darted around the room, taking in the extravagant bed and porcelain figures displayed on the shelves. Gaudy figurines of animals, children, and various individuals were posed mid-task. This had to be Poe's room.

Her eyes settled on a couple, arms around one another, about to kiss. They sat on a dresser and were posed on a doily in front of a mirror. Lula's heart crumbled even more when she caught her reflection. A stream of tears raced down her cheeks, pouring out of red-rimmed eyes. Around her neck rested the two necklaces, one with the black opal stone, given to her by someone she couldn't remember, and next to it, the moonstone Shea had given her. The moment he slid it around her neck flashed through her mind and shattered her resolve.

The moment was a lie. The whole thing was a lie. Again.

Lula picked up the figurine of the couple and threw it at the mirror. A savage cry ripped out of her as porcelain met glass. The dam broke. Knickknacks of every kind flew across the room, exploding as they hit the wall, the floor, and the furniture. When there was nothing left to throw, she focused on the furniture itself. Tipping tables and smashing drawers, Lula didn't stop until her arms gave out, and she hit herself in the leg. A yelp leaped from her mouth, and she fell to the ground, landing in a poof of down feathers. She rubbed her throat, having screamed herself raw. With shaking fingers, she reached behind her neck and removed the moonstone necklace. Shea had made it clear where they stood. No sense in nurturing the dead.

A light tap came from the door. Lula looked to see Katy in the doorway.

"I would ask if you're okay, but that seems like a silly question," she said, taking in the destruction.

"What do you want?"

"I wanted to let you know we need to leave. If Shea isn't back in a few minutes, we're going after him. It's important we get to the cabin and heal the rest of the talisman."

"Why? He knows who he is."

"After we seal all four pieces together, his memory will return, along with all of his powers. Then he can release your powers. Only together will we be victorious."

Lula laughed without humor as she poured the necklace from one palm to another.

Katy kneeled before her, taking Lula's hands and squeezed. Lula glanced up to see Katy's bright green eyes sparkle as she smiled the saddest smile she had ever seen.

"Everything will work out, Lula, now that you're here."

"Because I'm the Statera." Lula kept her eyes on the necklace in her hand. "Whatever that's supposed to mean."

Katy's eyes twinkled as her smile grew even brighter than the morning sun. "You *are* the Statera. I can tell."

Lula sniffed, and the tears began to slow. "But how?"

"When Enid told of who we were to look for, who the Statera would be, she described someone who would bring life to Sephtis, and not just balance."

"Bring life to Death? That sounds strange."

"It does sound strange. I didn't know what she could possibly mean until I saw him with you. You light him up in a way we, his first deities, could never do."

Lula choked on a sob. The idea that she could bring such a thing to Shea's life was more than she could hope for. The scene from earlier played in her mind, and the sting of his rejection stabbed at her chest. The pain took her breath away. Of course, he didn't love her back. How could he when there was nothing good left of her to love?

"He doesn't want me. He told me."

She cupped Lula's face, forcing her to look into Katy's eyes. "He is simply finding himself once more. He knows he can't do that without you. Be patient."

Lula stared straight ahead, knowing what needed to be done. The only thing was, she didn't know if she could do it. Picturing all the Pets that deserved to be free of their tortured lives, Lula steeled her resolve. "Katy, what's going to happen to all the Pets once this war is over and Sephtis retakes the throne?"

"The only right thing there is to do. We shall offer them the opportunity to go through the Gate to the Realm of the Dead. They will be given the paradise they were robbed of."

She kept her eyes on the hand that clutched the necklace. "Does that include me?"

Katy's sharp gasp drew Lula's eyes up. Those beautiful green eyes shone with unshed tears as she bit into her lower lip.

A wave of guilt washed over Lula. Through sheer force of will, she pushed it down. She deserved at least the option to pass through the Gate.

"Is that what you wish?"

"My job is to help make sure Sephtis is successful. After we're done, I think it's fair you should give me the opportunity to choose. Don't you think?"

"It is fair. I ask, though, would you keep an open mind until then?"

Lula sighed and stood, leaving the necklace on the floor. She wouldn't need it anymore.

The two went downstairs to find Michael and Devin sitting on the couch, Devin clutched his head. Katy cleared her throat, and the two looked up almost desperately. Lula couldn't imagine what they were thinking.

"Is Shea back?" Katy asked.

"No, not yet." Michael said, monotone.

"Because he's pissed," Lula snapped.

Devin's face turned red. "We were doing our job, keeping him safe."

"Sure, you kept him safe, but did any of you think about a good way to bring him back into the fold? Or was shocking him your go-to plan?"

"I didn't mean to upset him, Lula," Devin said.

Lula scoffed. "You didn't upset him, Devin, you *destroyed* him. He has no idea what's going on, who he is, or who he should even trust. And you know what? I don't blame him. If I were him right now, I would be good just sitting back and letting the cards fall where they may."

"There are huge consequences to that decision."

"You think I don't know that? That *he* doesn't know that?" Lula thrust a finger towards the front door. "Out of all the ways you could have told him that he's actually the God of Death and destined to fight with me, of all people, this was the worst way you could have done it! You have to know that."

"It's my fault, Lula. I shouldn't have said anything." Katy placed her hand on Lula's shoulder.

"I don't understand why you guys took his memory in the first place," Thomas piped up. "I mean, I understand wanting to hide him, but couldn't you do that and *not* manipulate him at the same time?"

Devin didn't move from where he sat as he answered, talking more to the floor than anyone in the room. "Using the talisman to hide away his memories as well as his powers was the only way to truly hide him. The other Death Gods couldn't locate him once both were locked away."

"He has a tattoo that hides him," Thomas said.

"Yes." Devin peered up at him. "But it didn't work with only his powers locked up. Believe me, we already tried that. It's why *he* came up with hiding himself this way—no memories and no powers. That way, there was nothing for them to lock onto."

Thomas huffs out a laugh. "This whole thing was his idea? No wonder it sucks."

Devin launched off the couch and jabbed his finger toward Thomas. "You know, I'm about done with your smart ass. We've done the best we could over the centuries, risking everything—including our lives—while looking for the Statera. Now can we please get past this and get to Albert's?" His chest heaved as he scowled at Thomas.

The weight of everything they had been through settled over Lula.

Only after Katy reached up and took Devin's hand did his breathing slow, and his shoulders sagged.

"Who is Albert?"

The sound of Shea's voice drew everyone's attention. Standing at the front door, it looked like one light breeze would topple him over. His eyes narrowed as he took everyone in.

"He is the fourth of us, the final Death God loyal to you and your cause. He is good, Shea, I promise," Katy said.

"There sure are a lot of original Death Gods," Thomas murmured.

"I'll say. Was I that desperate for company?"

Katy stood and took a small step forward. She wrung her hands together and bit her lip. A shine formed in her eyes. "Seph—I mean,

Shea," she corrected when his eyes bugged at his old name. "I know this is hard. It has to be. I'm so sorry you feel deceived, but I promise you, everything was done not only for a reason but with your guidance. Once we heal the talisman, everything will be clear."

Shea took a deep breath, though it didn't help him look any calmer. "Then let's go." He barked out and marched back out the door.

Michael and Devin took off after him, with Thomas trailing behind.

Lula took a moment to gather herself. Closing her eyes, she took a calming breath of her own, bracing herself for the ride to the cabin.

A gentle hand squeezed her shoulder. Katy smiled at her. "I—"

Michael cleared his throat, cutting into the moment. Katy and Lula turned to see him standing at the door with his hands shoved into his pockets, shifting from one foot to the other. "Sorry, but we need to go."

Lula swiped at her eyes and followed Michael out of the house, holding Katy's hand. She paused at the door, giving a glance back. She was free of Doyle, yet the knowledge seemed unreal, like a farce with a twisted punchline where she woke up finding herself back in her room, and everything else was a dream. Her freedom remained some distant goal she would never reach. As relieved as Lula was knowing that her bond with Doyle truly was severed, a part of her mourned. Not being bound to Doyle was so unfamiliar. Strange as it was, there had been an uncomfortable comfort in the deal that had bound her for so long. Lula had to laugh at herself as she realized that, more than hating Doyle, she feared the unknown. Especially with Shea's rejection fresh in her mind.

As heavy as her heart felt, it somehow helped to lift up her lighter soul. Before her stretched a road to a new future. One of her own making.

Chapter Thirty-Six

The long ride to the cabin was filled with a faux sense of calm. As they raced down the road, the tires against the pavement were the only sound piercing the silence. The sun, so high in the sky when they left Poe's, dropped like a rock as they drove. Silhouettes of mountains loomed in the distance, a prelude to the monsters that lurked in the shadows, ready to overtake them.

Lula watched trees pass by in a blur, much like her thoughts racing. So much had happened, too much to process. Perhaps it was for the best. With the impending fight, she needed to shove those thoughts about Doyle, Max, and Shea far away. There would be plenty of time to dwell on them later. The most important thing to focus on now was the goal.

The mission.

Restore Shea to the throne.

Lula glanced at Shea in the front seat. He had reached out a hand and helped her get into the truck. A flicker of hope had flared, then died as he slammed the door shut and took the front seat. Shea wanted nothing to do with her. How could Katy insist that Lula was the Statera? She couldn't figure it out. Lula may have the added power, but she didn't bring Shea any peace or balance, or even strength.

About thirty minutes after exiting the freeway, Michael turned down a long gravel road. Lula breathed a sigh of relief when a small cabin appeared in the distance.

"This is Grandpa George's cabin," Shea said.

Devin kept his face forward. "It's actually your cabin."

"Mine?"

"You got the cabin back when settlers first moved into the area, back before you hid your memories."

"Hid. Don't you mean before I lost them?"

"No, Shea, I mean hid. All we have to do is put the talisman back together, and you'll know everything you knew before. Then maybe you'll cut the attitude and cut us some slack."

Shea sneered at Devin's assurance but didn't say another word as they drove up and parked behind the cabin.

Everyone piled out of the truck and walked around toward the front door. Devin retrieved the bag of books and the incomplete talisman from the back of the truck.

Michael broke off, heading down a small trail leading into the woods. "I'll hurry back with Albert," he called out, waving his hand.

Inside, the small cabin had few furnishings and an overabundance of cobwebs draped in the corners. A small table and chairs sat close to the wall next to a counter and sink.

Devin strolled over to the table and pulled it far to the right, revealing a door hidden in the floor. Without a word, he yanked it open and descended, bag in hand.

Lula made her way over to see a rickety staircase. Taking each creaking step with care, she watched Devin light candles in a fixture hung from a thick, black chain in the center of the room. Light swept over the tiny room, revealing a dirt floor and walls of stone. Shelves filled with books and trunks lined the walls, and in the center, below the hanging candelabra, stood a round pillar that came up to Lula's waist. Everything reminded her of the hidden room behind the shelf in the library.

Devin set the bag on the pillar. With Katy's help, they unloaded all the books, placing them with all the others. The last thing to come out of the bag was the talisman. Devin placed it on the pillar before looking around at everyone gathered.

"We just need to wait for Michael and Albert to show up with the final piece," Devin said.

Everyone stood where they were in awkward silence.

Katy gave a nervous laugh. "Hopefully, they won't be too long."

Thomas rolled his eyes, but Shea inspected the talisman.

"What will happen once this thing is put back together?"

"You will regain all of your memories, along with all of your powers. With Lula, the Statera, at your side, you will fight and take back the throne and restore balance," Katy said with a smile.

"I know that much." Shea yanked his fingers through his hair. "I just—"

"Don't worry, Shea," Devin said. "We'll help you out. The first thing after you get your powers back is you will have to fight and defeat

Theodrick. He's the one that poses the biggest threat. After that, we'll need to get rid of all the other Death Gods, starting with the ones loyal to him."

"Does getting rid of all the Death Gods include you?" Thomas raised an eyebrow at Devin.

Devin shrugged. "We'll see."

"What will happen to the rest of us...or them?" Shea glanced at Thomas.

Devin sighed, and Katy bit her lip, neither of them wanting to give an answer.

Lula relaxed and focused on the words Katy had spoken to her in Poe's room, the same words she spoke now.

"All the Pets will be free, no longer bound to this Realm. We shall offer what should have been given to them all along—passage through the Gate to the Realm of the Dead."

Lula brought her fingers to her mouth, trying to hide the smile playing at the edges of her lips. Her eyes fell closed as she soaked up the words once more. *Will be offered what should have been.*

Lula was so immersed in the moment that Shea's voice right beside her startled her. She opened her eyes to see Shea's wide eyes locked on her as he asked, "We will offer all the Pets the opportunity to pass through the Gate?"

The intensity of his stare caught Lula off-guard. His mouth hung open in horror as Katy answered the question. Of course they would offer Lula the chance. Why wouldn't they?

"Would you want that?" Shea rasped.

Lula swallowed hard. "I mean, why wouldn't I want the chance?"

His eyes traveled down to her neck. Pain sliced across his face, and Lula knew what he saw. His hand raised to touch the only necklace that hung around her throat now.

Upstairs, the front door to the cabin slammed, and footsteps made their way across the floor. The spell broken, everyone turned their attention to the stairs as Michael descended. A short man trailed right behind him.

"Found Albert. I also filled him in. So he's up to speed on current events." Michael said.

Albert stood no taller than Lula. He walked like a kid who could barely contain himself at the park. His wide smile made his round cheeks even rounder, and his bright eyes twinkled. His long, sandy hair was pulled back into a ponytail, showing off the large bald spot on top of his head. He walked straight up to Lula and Shea, grabbing their hands in his.

He squeezed as he spoke. "I can't believe this day is finally here. I'm so excited."

Albert released them and skipped over to a shelf. From inside a box, he pulled out a large piece of stone, the biggest one yet. With a steady hand, he placed the piece on the pillar. Light radiated off the talisman as the stone healed, and a burst of light filled the room before fading away.

Shea's gasp drew Lula's attention, and she watched as his body stiffened and his eyes took on an eerie glow. When he relaxed again, and the glow faded, Shea looked down, as he opened and closed his hands.

Everyone held their breath.

"Sephtis?" Katy asked, taking a tentative step closer to him.

Shea looked at Katy with wide eyes. He took a steadying breath and held out a hand. A clean, white, and silver glow with sporadic sparks of blue surrounded him in a brilliant aura. His soul, his beautiful soul, was now that of a god.

A warm smile graced Shea's face, and he reached out to take Katy's hand. "Thank you, Katy, thank you all for sticking by me." He shot a smirk in Devin's direction. "I apologize if I was difficult."

"You're fine," Michael said.

Devin lowered his head in guilt. "If you were difficult at all, it was my fault, Sephtis. Lula was right. I should have handled things better."

At Lula's name, Shea turned toward her, his entire face lighting up. Lula held herself tight so she didn't squirm. The look of adoration fell as he took her in, replaced with a sadness she didn't understand. He should be happy now. He had his memories and his powers back. They were one big fight away from restoring balance.

His hand trembled as he reached for her. "Lula. My Statera. I should have known."

Lula sniffed and backed a step away.

Shea dropped his hand and frowned. "I can't tell you how much I regret hurting you."

"It's fine. We just need to go fight this battle, right?"

"I need to finish unlocking your powers first."

"Okay."

Raising his hand once more, he didn't stop until it rested upon her head.

Heat flowed through Lula, tickling through her veins. Power, like she had experienced when she had taken Melissa's soul, only stronger, coursed through her. The world around her became clearer. Details she had never seen before popped into view. Colors shone brighter in the auras of all those around her. The rainbow of light overwhelmed her to the point that she couldn't catch her breath. Raising her arm, she now saw all the vibrant colors that made up her own aura. Lula choked back tears as she looked at the motley mix of gold, white, and silver. But no black. Her soul, despite everything she had gone through and everything she had done, was good.

Albert threw his head back and laughed. "I knew it was you. I told them all the way back then. Didn't I tell you?" his baritone voice filled the room. "I knew it in a glance."

"I don't remember you saying anything, Albert," Michael said.

"Ahh." Albert waved a dismissive hand in their direction. "That's because they never listen to wise old Albert."

Lula raised a curious brow at the man.

"You two. You were so in love. It broke my heart when you had to leave her." Albert blinked up at Shea.

Lula glanced at Shea, a million questions rolling around. He cupped her cheek, never taking his eyes off her as a new wave threatened to take her under. A fresh set of memories bombarded her. Lula, the young, carefree English girl, standing in a field with her love, her heart—Sephtis. He came to her every day, played for her, and talked to her. A thousand memories of them walking hand in hand washed over her, followed by more memories of stolen kisses and laughs. Shea, known as Sephtis to her then, spent endless days and nights with her until one day, he left. She cried as he said goodbye and assured her everything would be all right. Then he gave her the necklace to remember him by. Only the next morning, she remembered nothing.

Lula couldn't explain why her empty heart, or why this small piece of jewelry was the most important thing in the world to her.

"Because I had to take your memory," Shea answered her unasked question. "For your safety, as well as mine. Still, I had to leave you with something, a part of me."

Lula reached up to touch her beloved keepsake, only to brush her fingers against Shea's.

Someone cleared their throat.

"I hate to break this up. However, we have a fight we need to prepare for," Devin said.

"Right." Shea said, and everyone began making their way up the stairs.

Lula brought up the rear, trying to calm her racing heart. The well-laid path before her now seemed less certain.

Shea's hand found hers, and they ascended together.

"I don't know exactly how I'm supposed to help you bring balance back." She cleared her throat, trying to keep her voice from breaking again. "I'll do my best, though, to help."

Shea frowned. He opened his mouth to speak, but the door flew open and slammed into the wall.

"There will be no need for that, Lula. He won't be around to help."

Theodrick waltzed into the cabin, Doyle trailing behind him. A sinister grin pulled at his lips as he took in the scene before him. Doyle looked fixedly at her, seeming to avoid everyone else in the room. Power crackled in the air, raising the hairs on Lula's arms. This was it. This was the moment they had been building up to.

The battle, at long last, had begun.

Chapter Thirty-Seven

After a moment of stillness, fists clenched and feet spread as everyone assumed a defensive stance. Shea shifted his body in front of Lula's, trying to shield her. He couldn't do that, though. They had charged her with protecting him.

Grabbing Shea's arm, Lula stepped beside him. He shot her a disgruntled glance that she chose to ignore. Everyone waited on bated breath, trying to figure out who would dare act first.

Devin took the first bold step forward. "Forget it, Theodrick. You're too late. The throne belongs to Sephtis."

Theodrick's smile widened at Devin, showing off his white teeth and laughed. "And who is going to stop me? You or Katy? That little girl over there who thinks she's a Death God now herself? Or let me guess, the mighty Sephtis himself is going to take me on." He laughed even louder.

"You're damn right I am," Shea said, drawing everyone's attention.

Curses rang out from around the room. Doyle paled and shifted behind Theodrick, whose smile only seemed to grow.

"You?" Theodrick said, eyeing him and Lula. "Even with your precious Statera, you're no match for me."

Doyle's fingers flexed like he wanted to reach out and take her. "Lulabelle."

The motion didn't slip by Shea, and he stepped forward again, blocking her from Doyle's view.

Doyle's lip curled upwards and he growled. Lula jerked back at the sound.

"What is it, Doyle?" Theodrick asked. "Is it hard seeing your Pet with Sephtis?"

Doyle's expression contorted in rage. "She is mine."

"Not on your life," Shea declared.

Shea launched himself at Doyle, his war cry echoing off the walls. He slammed into Doyle, pinning him against the wall. Theodrick wasted no time raising his hand, revealing a long silver knife. He moved to plunge the blade into Shea's back. Lula cried out as she quickly released a blast of energy. Her aim connected perfectly as it threw Theodrick flying back out the door. Shea picked up Doyle by the throat and threw him outside.

No one hesitated to follow.

Waiting outside in the fading light of day, four more Death Gods Lula had never seen before stood around the truck.

"You see," Theodrick wagged a finger in their direction. "They have brought back the God of Death himself to destroy us all. Stand with me and stand with our right to exist as we please."

Chaos erupted.

Lula joined Katy, fighting tirelessly to keep two of the new Death Gods back while Devin pried Albert's attacker off him. Theodrick lunged at Shea, and the two traded blows. Only Doyle stood back, watching the events of the battle unfold.

Lula swung with all her might at one large Death God but wasn't sure the hits she landed would ever be enough. Out of the corner of her eye, she saw Katy rip out the life energy of one of the Death Gods, bringing him to the ground, never to move again. Nausea followed relief as Lula realized what she would have to do to beat them. This wouldn't end until they had ripped every one of their life energies from their bodies.

With a savage cry, she attacked the Death God before her. She only focused on what she was fighting for: restoring the balance and saving the innocents.

Blinking out from in front of the Death God at the last second, Lula reappeared behind him and reached in through his back. Finding the energy nestled right in the center of his chest, she latched on and pulled at the Death God's energy. He let out a deafening scream until Lula pulled her hand out, the amber flame filling her fist until it faded away like a candle being snuffed out. The Death God dropped to the ground like a stone.

She let out a long breath before looking around her. The truck sat by the cabin. Its door still stood open. The bodies of three dead Death Gods littered the ground. As the first sounds of the evening began to fill the air, Lula's pulse raced. Everyone had disappeared. She could hear only the faint sounds of fighting in the distance.

She had to find them. She had to help.

A massive blow hit Lula on her back, throwing her across the yard toward the trees. She pushed herself up on her hands and knees and turned to see Doyle making his way toward her.

"Lula!" Doyle burned with rage that mixed waves of black into his aura. "How could you? You betrayed me."

Lula panted as she focused all she had into a blast of energy that she released at Doyle's chest. He dodged in the nick of time.

"Lulabelle, we had a deal."

"You broke that deal when you destroyed Max." She released another blast of energy, only to have it miss and hit a tree.

"That was not my fault. He should have stayed out of the way."

"I'll rip your soul out!" A scream tore from her with yet another blast of energy. Another near miss. Lula struggled to stand.

"No." Doyle admitted. "I intend to eliminate your dear Sephtis before taking care of you, as well."

Terror gripped Lula, immediately followed by determination in its wake. She would die before Doyle got anywhere near Shea.

Lula released one last blast of energy, this time hitting Doyle right in the chest. The problem was, she'd used up so much energy. It knocked his shoulder back but did nothing to slow him down. Exhausted, Lula fell back to the ground.

Doyle reached down and scooped her up, forcing her to stand. "You belong to me, not some broken-hearted twit." He shook her as he spoke.

"No," Lula whimpered, trying to push away. "I'm the Statera. I'm made to be with him."

As she said the words, she knew in her heart it was true. Lula was made to be with Shea, and no amount of time or distance could keep them apart.

She grabbed onto Doyle's arms and focused. His eyes widened as the glow coming off her lit his face. She pulled energy from him like she had with Max, but much more aggressively. She didn't hold back, welcoming the flood of energy that poured into her and renewed her. His hold on her weakened. Lula slid a hand up to his chest. Releasing the largest blast of energy yet, she dropped to the ground as Doyle flew across the yard and into the side of the cabin.

Easing herself off the ground, Lula rubbed her neck as she let out a cough and walked over to where Doyle lay in the rubble. A small smile played at the edges of his lips, even as his chest heaved with every labored breath.

A body crashed into Lula's side, sending her skidding across the ground. Far-off footsteps pounded the ground, heading her way.

Theodrick marched up to her, both hands engulfed in dark energy. "I don't care what you are anymore. You will die."

Lula scurried out of the way, but not fast enough. The energy blast that hit her stole her breath. She attempted to get up and failed. Everything hurt, and all her energy had drained away. Pushing with all her might, Lula attempted to stand once more. Tears streamed down her face as she ran on nothing more than obstinate willpower.

Theodrick stopped right beside her and clicked his tongue like she'd disappointed him. "This could have gone differently, Pet. If you had stayed loyal to your master, you wouldn't be about to die." He let out a patronizing laugh. "No paradise for you."

Lula braced herself for the blow. There would be nothing left of her. Anger welled up, burning in her chest. She didn't have the strength to do anything about it.

This couldn't be happening. She hadn't fought this hard just to end up in this evil deity's clutches.

A blood-curdling scream ripped from her throat as a bright white light enveloped everything around her.

Somewhere in the distance, a cry sounded. A blazing white light flashed, and Lula buried her face in the ground to cover her eyes. When the light faded, she found Shea standing in front of her, facing Theodrick. An intense glow enveloped his entire frame.

"You can't get away from me," Shea's voice rang out with authority.

"You can't stop me. I'm too powerful," Theodrick declared, even as he swayed on his feet.

"How many souls did you absorb to become this powerful?" Shea demanded.

"More than enough."

"All those innocent souls, and you still won't beat me. I promise you that."

Shea threw a punch. Theodrick barely dodged it, throwing a punch of his own. He connected with Shea's side, and the two stumbled apart. Shea attacked again, this time connecting with Theodrick's midsection, sending them both to the ground. Theodrick rolled, coming to a stop beside Lula. His manic eyes darted between her and Shea.

Theodrick raised an open hand in her direction. "Surrender, or I'll kill your precious Statera."

Shea jumped to his feet and charged. "You won't lay a finger on her."

He swung his foot to kick Theodrick, but the Death God vanished, only to pop up behind Shea.

"Behind you!" Lula cried.

Shea grabbed the hold of Theodrick's arm and held it. Light illuminated his hand, and Theodrick jerked, trying to pull away. Unable to break free, he grabbed Shea's shoulder. His hand glowed in its own light. The two stood locked in each other's hold. The energy came off them in waves.

Someone touched Lula's shoulder, and she jumped.

Katy wrapped her arm around Lula. "It's okay."

The two watched as the light around Theodrick and Shea grew brighter. Both men let out a cry, and the light pulsed with energy.

"The throne is mine," Theodrick ground out.

"Never. This ends now!" Shea declared.

The energy that Shea released was like a bomb exploding. Everyone was thrown back by the blow. Theodrick lost his hold. Shea took the opening and shot his hand straight past Theodrick's futile attempts to stop him and buried it in the center of the Death God's chest. Theodrick let out a cry as Shea snatched the life energy out. Theodrick fell silent, never to move again.

Sephtis had won.

Lula watched the amber fire in Shea's fist fade. They were free, now and forever. No one would ever become a Pet ever again. With Shea back on the throne, peace and balance would reign.

Above her, the setting sun turned the sky into a beautiful mix of blues, grays, and oranges. It reminded her so much of the sky in the Realm of the Dead.

Lula's heart fluttered in her chest, making her weightless.

Far off, she heard Shea call her name.

Everything would be all right now, she longed to tell him. Instead, she slipped away.

Chapter Thirty-Eight

A soft hand touched Lula's cheek, pulling her further from the darkness that held her. Somewhere far away, someone called her name. She knew that voice, knew it so well. She struggled against the darkness, like rising through tar.

Her eyes fluttered open, and the world came into focus.

Her name was whispered in her ear like a prayer, "Lula."

Above her, the first stars of night sparkled in the sky. Cold, soft ground dampened dress. She took in a breath of fresh grass mixed with the scent of deep spice.

She reached a shaking hand up, her fingers finding their way into thick hair. At the touch, Shea's face jerked into view. "Shea." She took in his pained expression and frowned. "What's wrong?"

Shea's eyes glimmered as tears ran down his cheeks. He leaned into her after gracing her with a soft kiss to her brow. "Don't leave me, Lula. You can't."

But I'm right here.

His words made no sense at all. Surely, he knew she would never leave him, not after everything they had been through. Her earlier thoughts of crossing through the Gate drained away.

"I don't understand."

Devin and Albert caught her attention behind Shea. The two stood stiff as boards. Michael held Katy as she wept. Their eyes were locked on the scene before them.

Lula's brow furrowed. She didn't understand any of what she was seeing. Had they lost? Had Theodrick somehow taken the throne? That couldn't be. The last thing she had witnessed was Shea ripping out Theodrick's life energy.

Lula raised her hand to touch her head and froze.

Her brilliant aura now shone nothing but blue—the Mark of a soul ready to leave its body.

Her heart stuttered inside her chest.

Shea took her hand, bringing it to his lips.

"Shea," she breathed. "I'm so sorry."

"No," he said fiercely. "*I'm* sorry, Lula. I was supposed to protect you and failed."

"But you're back on the throne, right? We won. You won. All those souls are now free. You can bring balance back to the world."

"I can't do it without you."

Before Lula could utter a word, a sudden movement diverted everyone's attention. A wispy woman stepped out from the trees.

She walked on air as her long, raven hair swayed around her ankles. She knelt beside Shea and Lula, taking them in. Her ruby lips pulled up, accentuating her cherub cheeks and making her crystal-blue eyes sparkle.

"Enid," four voices spoke in unison.

Katy, Devin, Albert, and Michael all gave a sweeping bow. The woman took in the four Death Gods and let out a delicate laugh. Turning to Shea, she ran her fingers through his hair before settling on Lula.

"My goodness, brother. What trouble have you gotten yourself into now?"

"Enid, please, you have to help her," Shea pleaded.

Enid.

Goddess of Life.

Sister to Sephtis.

Her delicate brow furrowed. "Why would I need to assist her? She has you, Sephtis."

"She is Marked. I cannot save her, and I will not take her through the Gate. Please don't make me. I can't heal life, but—"

Enid's perfect mouth formed an O in realization. "Fear not, you shall not be parted." Enid crouched down beside Shea and laid her hand on Lula's chest.

Tingles danced over her skin, and a light breeze blew across her, breathing life into her lungs. Lula drew in a cleansing breath as her strength returned.

Enid pulled her hand away and smiled. Hope filled Shea's eyes while warmth filled Lula's cheeks. Gently, Lula sat up.

Shea sat up on his knees before her. "How are you feeling?" he asked.

Lula stretched her arms and rolled her head on her shoulders. A twinge of pain in her neck made her wince. Other than that, she felt as good as new, better even. Around her arms, her aura had returned to its previous hue of gold, silver, and white.

She grinned. "I'm fine."

Shea helped her to her feet and pulled her straight into a tight embrace. "Thank you, Enid. Thank you," he repeated over and over again.

Enid swayed where she stood with a smirk. "Of course."

Shea grabbed Lula's waist, refusing to let her go. He huffed out a rough laugh before meeting Lula's eyes. The way he looked at her through his lashes and bit into his lip had her complete attention. All the people standing around them disappeared until there was just Shea. He looked so vulnerable.

"Lula, I am so sorry for the way I acted. I feel awful about my horrible reaction," the words poured out of his mouth in a rush.

"I forgive you."

"I'm so glad because I love you, too, Lula, so much."

Lula's heart stopped before picking up speed. "You do?"

"Yes, I have since the first moment I saw you. This life and the last. You are the most beautiful person I've ever met, inside and out. I love your compassion and your strength. You make me laugh and push me to be better."

"There's a good reason you're his Statera," Enid added.

"Yes, sister, you made me my perfect match."

Enid's face scrunched in confusion. "Who said I made her?"

She laughed when both Lula and Shea turned, looks of confusion on their faces.

"Brother, I found our beautiful Lulabelle with you in England. I watched the two of you from afar. I saw the happiness you shared together and the sadness at being apart. There was no one else for you, Sephtis. I actually made her your Statera after the first time I witnessed you together in the field. That's why it baffled me when you left her."

Shea paled as he gaped at his sister. "I was such a fool."

"Lucky for you, I helped Fate lay a new path to reunite you."

Lula practically ogled the goddess and couldn't conjure a single thought. Enid had laid out her path, which had dictated her fate. So much of Lula wanted to be angry. Considering everything she had gone through, she would be justified. Looking up at Shea, she couldn't hold on to it. If Enid hadn't interfered, they wouldn't be together, and there was nothing she wouldn't do to be with Shea.

Shea appeared to be at a loss for words as well. His fingers reached up and brushed the necklace at Lula's throat. Her stomach sank when she reached up and found only one.

"Shea, I'm so sorry."

"It's fine, Lula. I understand."

"I got mad and took the other necklace off."

"You mean this necklace?" Katy said, stepping forward with the moonstone necklace dangling from her fingers.

Lula beamed at Katy. "You grabbed it?"

"I figured you'd want it back when you calmed down." Katy winked.

Seeing the necklace dangling from Katy's fingers, Lula wanted to cry. "Thank you. Thank you so much."

Shea took the necklace from Katy before removing the one around her neck. Holding them both in his hand, he closed his fist, and it began to glow. "One, I gave to you as Sephtis, the black opal. One, I gave to you as Shea, the moonstone. The reason for the stones that I chose is the same: I wanted to protect you and honor your pure spirit. Simplified, I love you, and I want nothing but joy for you."

Opening his hand, the two necklaces had become one. The moonstone and black opal encircled a small, round rose stone. The centerpiece sat flanked by two square-cut rubies on each side, all held together on a long silver chain. Shea slipped the new necklace around her neck.

Lula brought her hand to her mouth, trying to contain all the joy bubbling in her heart. "Thank you, Shea." Lula paused. "Or is it Sephtis now?" She wasn't sure what to call him anymore.

"I don't care, as long as you call me yours."

"Only fair, since you are mine."

Lula's heart raced in her chest, and as her lips met Shea's, she wouldn't have been surprised if she could fly.

Chapter Thirty-Nine

Y ou don't cozy up to death and not have it affect your soul.

Lula laid on the blanket she had spread over the grass. The rose bushes were showing signs of coming back to life, marking the beginning of spring. While the playground sat empty, the chatter of people enjoying a break from the rain surrounded her. Settling back into the park that meant so much to her was like slipping into her favorite dress. In so many ways, this park had changed her life. Bittersweet memories always found their way to the surface here. Memories of Shea. Memories of Max. Placing her earbuds in, she closed her eyes, losing herself to the music while soaking up the sun. Six months had passed since that night on the mountain.

Fresh air filled Lula's lungs with a sigh as her mind drifted over what had happened since that fateful night. They'd traveled the globe, searching for the remaining Death Gods and their Pets. Lula had helped guide countless grateful Pets through the Gate to the Realm of the Dead. Conversely, they hadn't hesitated to take out the Death

Gods they came across without mercy. There was part of it that didn't sit well with Lula. The alternative—letting them continue to exist unchecked—wasn't an option. Trepidation made Lula shiver. The one Death God that still eluded them was Doyle. Finding and destroying him would only be a matter of time. Devin, Michael, Katy, and Albert had helped to continue the fight to free Pets and help Shea take care of the rogue Death Gods.

Shea.

Lula reached up and brushed the necklace sitting at her throat. He had been devoted to the cause with overwhelming force. In the quiet moments, Lula could see the guilt weighing on him. She did her best to support him and help guide him to the promise of balance. Her lips pulled up in a full, warm smile. She thought about the biggest change since Shea had taken the throne.

Lula remembered her trip to the hospital earlier that day, not to take but to guide that sweet soul to the Realm of the Dead. She had stood at the end of the old woman's hospital bed and waited. Waited while the old woman's family gathered around her. Waited while they shook with grief, crying, clinging to a peaceful hand. She waited until the family had stepped out to talk to the doctor before she approached the woman.

Lula sat on the edge of the bed and used her powers to learn about this old woman. Mary had been happy and active in her church until, one day, she collapsed. Her family spent a fortune on doctor's visits and treatments, trying to find a cure for the illness that plagued their mother and grandmother. Mary did her best to put on a brave face for her family even as she grew weary of this life. She kept a diary, stories, and memories of her long life. She hoped they would read the words one day. She had filled it with messages of love and encouragement from a brave woman who had seen and done it all. Mary had made sure to fill every moment of her life with love and experience, determined never to waste a day.

Mary's eyes fluttered open when Lula took her hand. Her wrinkled brows pulled together as she looked up to see a visitor dressed in a short-sleeved blue dress with an empire waist and a long, billowing skirt.

Mary licked her dry lips. "Who are you?"

"I'm here to help you."

"Do you work for the hospital?"

"Not exactly." Lula took a deep breath before continuing. "Mary, you are very sick, and I'm afraid your body is just not strong enough to go on anymore."

The light in Mary's eyes dimmed. "I know."

"I'm here to take your soul to a place where you can live on in peace."

Mary's jaw went slack. "So you're an angel?"

Lula let out a nervous laugh and bit her lip as she thought about how best to respond.

"No, I'm more like the gatekeeper to the next realm. I don't know if that makes any sense."

Mary peered at Lula with a keen eye, taking her in. A slow smile warmed her face.

"You look like my grandmother," Mary mused

Lula grasped her cheeks as they burned. "Really?"

Mary beamed at Lula. "She was a suffragist. Went around town and raised some hell." The old woman chuckled.

"She sounds like she was quite the lady."

"No one ever accused her of being that."

Lula thought back over her years. Was it possible she'd taken this woman's grandmother through the Gate?

"Are you here to take me now?" Mary asked.

Lula's smile faded as she nodded. Mary sniffed before reaching up and rubbing at her eyes.

"It's about time," Mary chided. "Can I...can I ask a favor of you first?"

"Sure."

"My grandson is on his way here now. My daughter is bringing him from the airport. He lives across the country, and I haven't seen him in months. Can I say goodbye to him first?"

Lula's heart squeezed in her chest. "Of course you can. I'll be over in the corner waiting."

"Won't they see you?" Mary's voice squeaked.

A soft smile warmed Lula's face as she revealed another trick she had inherited when Shea unlocked her powers.

"Only those whom I want to reveal myself to can see me."

Lula didn't have to wait long before the door to Mary's room flew open, and a young man, who was around twenty, ran into the room. The two embraced and shared stories about their day. Mary's tone changed as she told her grandson goodbye without saying the word. She told him how much she loved him and how proud she was of him. She knew he would do wonderful things in life and how, even if he couldn't see her, she would always be there watching over him. The young man seemed to understand and accepted it all without hesitation. When Mary's children came in and joined them, everyone got caught up in the conversation. Mary took her daughter's hand. With a haunting grace, Lula called the old woman's soul, and the brilliant blue flame rose above the family, and Mary's hand went slack.

Lula escorted the soul through the Gate to the Realm of the Dead. Colors swirled above her as the sweet fragrance of flowers filled her nose. Like every other time she had been there before, an overwhelming sense of belonging filled Lula. However, as she released Mary's soul, Lula didn't feel the longing she had before. Because Lula was cherished and loved once again.

The soft breeze tussled Lula's hair, bringing her back to the park. She brushed the errant strands out of her face and behind her ear. Immense peace filled Lula. She could feel it deep in her heart. Another breeze blew, rustling her hair once again. Gentle fingers brushed them out of her face and back behind her ear.

Lula broke out in a huge smile. "What are you doing here?" she asked without opening her eyes.

"Admiring the view," Shea purred in her ear.

Lula opened her eyes to see Shea staring down at her. A bright smile lit his face as he continued to play with her hair.

"Admiring the view, huh?" She smiled up at him while basking in his warm gaze.

"It's the most beautiful view I've ever seen."

Lula burst out laughing. "God." She continued to giggle. "That had to be the cheesiest line I've ever heard you say."

Shea just shrugged, unrepentant. "Doesn't make it untrue."

All she could do was shake her head. "You're so lucky I love you as much as I do."

"Oh, don't I know it." He smiled. "With all my heart." Shea leaned down, capturing Lula's lips with his own.

She melted into the kiss, letting both joy and passion sweep over her until she was completely lost in the love enveloping her. Her arms came up and around his neck as she pulled him closer until their bodies were flush against each other.

"I love you too," Shea said against her lips. "In case you were wondering."

"Oh yes, I know," she stated with great fervor. "With all my heart."

Acknowledgements

I am so grateful to everyone who supported me throughout this journey. A huge thank you to my husband and son, who never stopped encouraging me to go for it. Thank you to all of my family and friends who have been incredible cheerleaders. This book wouldn't be what it is without the help of my dear friend and critique partner Becky. I also want to acknowledge the beta readers who took the time to give me incredible feedback: Katie, Karmen, Duckett, Rev, Cat, and Damon. I am continually touched by the people in my life. I don't know what I would do without you.

About the Author

Candice Beebe, a romance author from Portland Oregon, believes nothing beats a good happily ever after. *Death Defiant* is her debut novel. She's been scribbling stories in notebooks for as long as she can remember. Candice runs on caffeine and optimism. When not writing, you will find her either under her favorite blanket with a good book and coffee, or enjoying a night of board games with family and friends.

CANDICE BEEBE

Before You Go

Dear Friends,

Thank you so much for taking the time to read Death Defiant. Before you leave, I would like to invite you to hop over to my website candicebeebe.com to sign up for the monthly newsletter. You can keep up to date on upcoming releases, and even get special content, like seeing covers early and deleted scenes.

You can follow me on social media.
Instagram: @candicebwrites
Facebook: Candice Beebe
Goodreads: Candice Beebe

Finally, if you enjoyed Death Defiant, please leave a review.

Until next time, remember how awesome you are!